P9-CDC-061

Scot on the Rocks

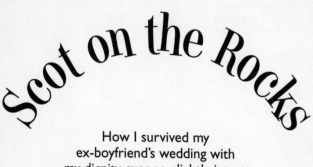

Scot on the Rocks

How I survived my
ex-boyfriend's wedding with
my dignity ever-so-slightly intact.

Brenda Janowitz

RED
DRESS
INK
TM

If you purchased this book without a cover you should be aware
that this book is stolen property. It was reported as "unsold and
destroyed" to the publisher, and neither the author nor the
publisher has received any payment for this "stripped book."

SCOT ON THE ROCKS

A Red Dress Ink novel

ISBN 13: 978-0-373-89528-1
ISBN 10:   0-373-89528-3

© 2007 by Brenda Janowitz

All rights reserved. The reproduction, transmission or utilization
of this work in whole or in part in any form by any electronic, mechanical
or other means, now known or hereafter invented, including xerography,
photocopying and recording, or in any information storage or retrieval
system, is forbidden without written permission. For permission please
contact Red Dress Ink, Editorial Office, 225 Duncan Mill Road,
Don Mills, Ontario, Canada M3B 3K9.

This is a work of fiction. Names, characters, places, and incidents are
either the product of the author's imagination or are used fictitiously,
and any resemblance to actual persons, living or dead, business
establishments, events, or locales is entirely coincidental.

® and TM are trademarks. Trademarks indicated with ® are registered in
the United States Patent and Trademark Office, the Canadian Trade Marks
Office and/or other countries.

www.RedDressInk.com

Printed in U.S.A.

ACKNOWLEDGMENTS

Thank you to Sherry and Bernard Janowitz, my parents. Without your love and support, I would be nothing. And to my brother, Sammy, and my sister-in-law, Stephanie, too. You are my family, but you are also my close friends. All four of you are always there to help me bounce ideas around, to brainstorm with me, and just generally make my life better. I appreciate you more than you can possibly know—thank you.

Thank you to Mollie Glick, my amazing agent. You were the first person who believed in my writing (besides my parents, that is. And my brother and sister-in-law, but the first person in publishing. You know what I meant. And, geez, learn to take a compliment, would you!?!). You helped me navigate the tricky waters of getting a first novel published, and I am so grateful for all of your advice and guidance along the way.

Thank you to Selina McLemore, my fabulous editor. When *Scot* came to you, it truly found its perfect home. Your comments and suggestions were always spot on—I always knew that I was in excellent hands every step of the process.

Thank you to Grandma D for being one of my earliest readers and for letting me borrow your maiden name.

Many thanks to Shawn Hecht, my best friend and first reader, for your support and encouragement. You may not be an objective reader of my writing, but you are an amazing friend, which is far more important.

Many thanks to JP Habib for your constant encouragement and willingness to read draft after draft. I can't wait to be thanked in your first novel.

Special thanks go to Aunt Myrna, Robin Kaplan, Lauren Lindstrom, Jessica Shevitz Rauch, Jennifer Rauch, Greer Gilson Schneider, Esther Rhee, Donna Gerson, Tami Stark and all of my great relatives, friends and wonderful readers of early drafts of this novel (it's totally different now, so even though you read it before, you should still buy it).

xoxo,
Brenda

To all of my ex-boyfriends.
Really.
You've given me endless amounts
of material about which to write.

Prologue

A recent *New York Times* article said that "new love can look like mental illness." Really. That's a quote. Actual real live neuroscientists studied brain scan images and found that falling in love prompts brain activity akin to a blend of mania, dementia and obsession. (And neuroscientists are, presumably, really, really smart people, so you can totally believe them.) These scientists found that the drive for romantic love in humans is similar to their drives for hunger, thirst or even a drug craving—a drive that is so strong, it can be stronger than even the will to live. That falling in love is the most irrational of all human behaviors.

So, in my pursuit of love, can I really be expected to behave rationally? I don't think so. I mean, it's a scientific fact!

1

As I walked back to my apartment that day, on my way home from work, I had a feeling that nothing could go wrong. You know that feeling you get when everything seems to be right with the world? When the planets seem to be in alignment? One of those days when you're actually running on time, your apartment is (relatively) clean, and you haven't gotten into an argument with your mother/best friend/boss/therapist in at least a week? That was exactly how I felt as I strolled home from work down Mercer Street to my apartment on 301 Prince Street.

I had left my office that evening at 8:30 p.m., which—at Gilson, Hecht and Trattner, the large Manhattan law firm where I work— is actually considered early, so I was feeling as if I had the whole night ahead of me. And I was going home to pick up my gorgeous Scottish boyfriend so that we could go out and meet friends for supper at some fabulous little downtown brasserie where everyone is European and the waiters only speak French, so I could hardly wait. I had the perfect New York City evening planned out.

Since I usually got out of work closer to 9:00 p.m. than 5:00 p.m., I considered myself lucky to have a boyfriend who liked to eat dinner late. I once dated a math teacher who left work at 4:00 p.m. and was in bed by ten. That relationship was destined to fail. Ditto for the guy who traded foreign something or others who started his day at 3:00 a.m. and ate his dinner before I even thought about getting lunch. My boyfriend, Douglas, on the other hand, thought that people who ate dinner before 8:00 p.m. were uncivilized.

I walked into the lobby of my apartment building—the poshest building in all of Soho—with a skip in my step. The Soho Triumphe, a building so fancy that, in addition to its staff of eight doormen, it boasts a twenty-four-hour concierge who can get you into any restaurant in Manhattan (not like Douglas ever needed any such help). It even has in-house dry cleaning, like at a hotel. I said hello to the evening doorman who, despite the fact that I had moved into Douglas's apartment a full two years ago, still couldn't quite remember my name.

"Um, 32G?" he asked with a pained expression that indicated to me that he was thinking, at least, very very hard about who I was. I nodded my head yes and pulled my hair out of the bun I usually wore at work while he checked his book for deliveries. Douglas loved my hair—dark brown with natural auburn highlights that was so long it fell down my back to just below my bra strap— so I always took it down right before I got up to our apartment.

The doorman handed me a mountain of dry cleaning—five custom-made Italian suits (Douglas's), five monogrammed shirts (Douglas's) and one skirt (mine). I checked the mail and took out four bills (Douglas's) and the Barneys New York Spring Look Book (mine)…or maybe it was Douglas's. You never could tell with European men.

Balancing it all in the crook of my arm, with my oversize work bag forcing my body to lean perilously to the right, I made it to the elevator just as the door was about to close. I kicked my foot out and stopped the door with my leg. Inside, I could see a tiny little man furiously pressing the "door close" button.

"You could lose a limb trying to get to your apartment," I said to the man with a laugh. Rather than being embarrassed for not holding the elevator for me, he looked annoyed that I had made it in.

"Or you could just wait for the next elevator," he replied under his breath. And they say that chivalry is dead.

With my free arm, I pressed the button for thirty-two. My work bag slid down my shoulder, catching my long hair underneath the strap. I tried to jump up to release my hair, turning my head quickly to the left as I did so. The dry cleaning began to slip from my grip and I begged it not to fall, whispering "We're almost there," to it as if talking to a small child. The man looked at me, his expression saying, "The economy must really be bad if our co-op board let *this* woman into the building."

But I didn't care. The night would still be perfect. No doubt I would get back to my apartment, and Douglas would be waiting for me with open arms. Seeing me with all of my packages, he would grab them from me, throw them on the couch and kiss me passionately. In his charming Scottish accent, he would say, "Darling, I missed you so much today I could barely stand it," or something as equally romantic and heartfelt and we would go meet our fabulous friends for a fabulous evening out. On our way to the restaurant, he would turn to me and say, "How is it that you look even *more* beautiful after working a full ten-hour day?"

I bet that that tiny little man in the elevator didn't have a gorgeous Scottish boyfriend to go home to. Or, actually, maybe he did. He was wearing really, really nice shoes.

But I did. I walked in the door to my apartment, starving to death (because, let's face it, I'm totally uncivilized), and before I even had a second to put down our dry cleaning, my gorgeous Scottish boyfriend broke up with me.

Normally, my life isn't this complicated. You see, I'm a simple girl with simple hopes. Up until two weeks ago, all I really wanted in life was for my boyfriend Douglas to buy an engagement ring. And he did! He just didn't give it to me. But I was fine. Even though the breakup was difficult, I remained very dignified.

Well, not so much dignified as a screaming crying mess. But it's not as if I embarrassed myself or anything. Unless you'd call throwing yourself at the tails of someone's suit jacket embarrassing. Which, luckily for me, I do not. We had a very mature conversation, really, if you think about it. I sweetly said, "Please don't go! Please don't leave me!" Okay, so maybe I was screaming it at the time, but you get where I was going with that one.

"I'm sorry, Brooke," Douglas said. "It's not you. It's *me. You* are an amazing girl. *You* have so much to offer. It's just that this doesn't feel right. It's just not the time for us."

Now isn't that mature? So, I answered him in kind.

"And it is the time for you and that—that—bimbo? What the hell is her name?"

"Beryl."

"That's not even a naaaame!" I bellowed.

"Brooke, let's not get hysterical," Douglas said. Hysterical? I was, like, so *not* hysterical. "Can't we make this friendly? Can't we try to still be friends?"

"Okay. You're right. Friends." See how mature I was being?

"Right then," he said, sounding very Scottish. How I loved that accent. "I'll be going."

This *may* have been the part where I lunged for the tails of his suit jacket and he then dragged me about twenty feet to the door.

"No!" I was screaming. "No, please, no!" Okay, yes, now that I'm telling you about this, I distinctly recall being dragged across the floor screaming, "Don't go!"

Oh, please. As if you never did that, too.

As a last ditch effort, I cried, "You can't do this! Please don't go! It isn't right!" In an instant, his expression changed. *I'm getting through to him,* I thought. I lightened my viselike grip on the tails of his suit jacket.

"You're right. I shouldn't go. It isn't right."

I shook my head in agreement and breathed a sigh of relief. As visions of wild, passionate makeup sex floated through my mind, he said, "After all, I own the apartment." And with that, he opened the door.

I should never have let go of the tails of his jacket.

2

Really, I blame the breakup on Trip's wedding. That's when everything started to go downhill between Douglas and me. And what's worse, everyone I know thought that I shouldn't have gone to the wedding in the first place. Somehow, everyone who knew me *just knew* that Trip's wedding would be the end of Douglas and me. (Except little old me, of course.) I really hate being a foregone conclusion.

When I told my mother that I was going to Trip's wedding, she said, "Trip's wedding? Trip who?" (As if Jewish girls from Long Island know that many men named Trip.) "Trip from law school Trip? What woman, in her right mind, would want to go to that?"

Vanessa, my best friend from law school, initially RSVP'd no to the wedding, since she assumed that I wouldn't want to attend. When she found out that I wanted to go, she later called Trip to tell him that her "big case" had settled and that she and her husband, Marcus, would be there—but not before asking me approximately 472 times if I "wanted to talk about it?"

And when I told the partner I worked for at my firm that I would be out of town for a four-day weekend to take my boyfriend to L.A. to go to Trip's wedding, even he asked me, "Why the hell would you want to do that?"

I could have sworn that I even saw my therapist look at me sideways when I told her that I was going to my ex-boyfriend's wedding.

Okay, so I understand that this isn't exactly your typical "girl goes to wedding" kind of situation. But, just because Trip is my ex-boyfriend from law school doesn't mean that I care more about this wedding or am more nervous about this wedding, or that this wedding is any different from any other wedding in any way at all! Because it's not. Trip's wedding is just another wedding. And Trip is just another friend of mine. Even if he is my ex-boyfriend.

What's an ex-boyfriend anyway? Everyone has an ex-boyfriend. Everyone. I mean, even some lesbians I know have them. Nothing special about them, right? I don't care any more or less about him just because he's my ex-boyfriend. He's just a person. And staying friends with your ex is a piece of cake. I barely ever think about him and how he may or may not have been my last chance at happiness in this cruel and unforgiving world.

Really. I have the satisfaction of having a great career and a great independent life filled with fabulous friends and, of course, even more fabulous shoes. I am such a woman of the new millennium that I can go work a full ten-hour day, keep in touch with friends through e-mail, do a few errands on the way to meet my friends for dinner, and then go meet cute guys over martinis at the bar after I eat. All in three-and-a-half-inch heels. I am such a woman of the millennium that I can do anything, even things that previous generations would have thought completely impossible—Betty Friedan be damned! I can even stay friends with an ex-boyfriend.

And it's not like Douglas was jealous or anything. Douglas wasn't really the type to ever get jealous. He was far too manly and European for such things.

When I told Jack, my best friend from Gilson Hecht, about Trip's wedding, he simply said, "You and Douglas are going to break up."

"What?" I practically screamed as I slammed the door to his office shut and sank into his visitor's chair. His computer screen was turned slightly off center and I could see in the reflection of his window that he was working on his fantasy football league.

"Ignore me. I don't even know what I'm saying," he said, one eye still on his computer screen as he flipped it back to the brief he was drafting. "I think it's great if you can go to your ex-boyfriend's wedding. In fact, if we had dated and then broke up, I would fully expect you to come to my wedding."

"We did date and break up," I reminded him, picking up the silver paperweight from his desk and turning it slowly in my hands. It was engraved *Congratulations on Your Graduation* and signed *With Love* from all three of his older sisters.

"One kiss does not constitute us dating and breaking up," he said, baby blues now burning into me, as he brushed his shaggy brown hair out of his eyes. This particular conversation always made Jack nervous for two reasons. The first was that he was the one who called things off, and being the gentleman that he was, he never liked to do anything that would make a woman unhappy. The second was that he hated the implication that he would ever act in such an unprofessional manner by running around kissing associates who were junior to him.

I love bringing this conversation up with him.

"You say potato…." I said as he snatched the paperweight from my hands. I moved my attention to the sterling-silver picture frame that housed a photo of Jack and his parents at the swearing-in ceremony to the New York State Bar. It always struck me as so odd that Jack's father was the only one smiling.

"I'm sorry I said that you would break up with Douglas. If you want, to make it up to you, I will tell you your fortune," he said, picking up the Magic 8-Ball that was at the end of his desk. He'd had that Magic 8-Ball since I first came to the firm. While most people would be satisfied to let it sit nostalgically on the edge of their desk, Jack actually used his. Since coming to the firm as a first-year associate, Jack and I had been staffed together on nearly every case I worked on—me the junior associate and he the senior for five years running—and we would often consult the Magic 8-Ball for our most pressing decisions:

"Magic 8-Ball, should we order in Chinese for dinner tonight?"

"Magic 8-Ball, are we going to have to work this weekend?"

"Magic 8-Ball, should we include a cause of action for nuisance in this complaint?"

Sometimes, if a case was particularly difficult, we would cross-reference the Magic 8-Ball with our horoscopes for that day (mine: Cancer, Jack's: Scorpio). I can only assume that the head of the litigation department, who affectionately referred to Jack and me as his "Brain Trust," did not know this little fact. Or maybe he didn't really care, as long as we billed our Miss Cleo time to the appropriate client.

"Magic 8-Ball, will Brooke have a happy life?" he asked and then studied the ball carefully. Looking up at me, he said, "You can be certain."

"Good," I said.

"See, I told you this thing is good," he said to me. "Magic 8-Ball, will Brooke have four children and move out to the suburbs?"

"That thing had better say no," I said. "Why would you ask it that?"

"Not likely," he reported. I breathed a sigh of relief and ran my hand theatrically across my forehead as if to say *phew.* Like how Bette Davis would have done it. If Bette Davis ever worked in a large Manhattan law firm and played with Magic 8-Balls, that is.

"Thank goodness," I said.

"Will Brooke…"

"Get to the part about the wedding, Nostradamus," I interrupted.

"Magic 8-Ball, will Brooke have fun at Trip's wedding?" he asked and gave the ball a vigorous shake. I pulled my hair out of its bun and twirled a strand of hair with my finger. He looked at the answer, and after a dramatic pause, triumphantly told me: "Signs point to yes."

"You didn't ask it the important question," I said, grabbing the Magic 8-Ball from his hands. "Will I break up with Douglas?" I gave the ball a little shake and slowly, carefully turned it over. I remembered how I would actually get nervous when we would ask the Magic 8-Ball if we would be working over the weekend, somehow thinking that whatever the ball told us would be gospel. I felt my stomach tighten.

"What does it say?" Jack asked me.

"Yes."

"It doesn't say yes," Jack told me. "The Magic 8-Ball doesn't talk like that. Let me see." I slowly showed it to him, careful not to let the insides move. "Yes," he repeated.

"Oh, my God, I'm going to break up with Douglas?" I asked him.

"Don't be ridiculous, Brooke," Jack said. "These things are stupid." Whenever the Magic 8-Ball told us we'd be working over the weekend, Jack would always say that the Magic 8-Ball was stupid. Nine times out of ten, the Magic 8-Ball called it.

"Do it again," he told me. "Best two out of three."

"Magic 8-Ball," I said quickly, "will I break up with Douglas?" I shook it twice and turned it over.

"What's it say?" he asked, leaning out of his seat to try to steal a look.

"Yes—definitely," I told him, and quickly put the Magic 8-Ball back onto the edge of his desk as if the mere act of holding it would make its fortune come true.

"Well, it doesn't make any sense," I said. "How will I have fun at Trip's wedding if I break up with Douglas?"

"Let me try," he said, picking the ball back up.

"Magic 8-Ball, now I am being very serious. This is an important matter we are discussing here, so don't screw with us." He looked up to me and I shook my head to show my support of his chastising the Magic 8-Ball. "So, Magic 8-Ball, tell us now—are Brooke and Douglas going to break up?" He shook the ball over his head and closed his eyes. He drew the ball down and looked inside.

"What?" I asked him, barely able to wait, like a defendant getting her sentence. He didn't respond at first, just kept staring at the answer.

"Jack," I said. "What does it say?"

"You may rely on it."

"You may rely on it?" I parroted back. "What's that supposed to mean?"

"I don't know, Brooke," he said. "I only read the fortunes."

I didn't necessarily blame the Magic 8-Ball for the breakup with Douglas. Not entirely, anyway. But I did blame it on Trip's wedding.

Six weeks before the wedding, Douglas and I had been in total domestic bliss, living together in Douglas's apartment—a space that I had single-handedly transformed from a spare-looking, modern bachelor pad into a warm, inviting home. Okay, fine, so he wouldn't really let me change anything, from the mammoth sixty-inch TV down to the leather-and-chrome couches, but I did bring in fresh flowers every week. Well, maybe not every week, but whenever I could think of it. Or could find flowers that Douglas wouldn't accuse of being too "girlie" (which is not easy, I assure you). Okay, okay, so I didn't even really ever do the flower thing, but I thought about it. And furthermore, I already told you that I am a big-time lawyer at Gilson Hecht, so get off my back. It's not exactly as if I have that kind of time on my hands. And anyway, that sort of thing isn't billable.

We were getting ready for work one morning. I was in the bedroom getting dressed while Douglas was in the bathroom shaving. Like I said, total domestic bliss.

"Very funny," I said.

"What's very funny?" he asked, calling from the bathroom.

"It's very cute. It's funny," I said, walking into the bathroom.

"For fuck's sake, would you please tell me what you find so goddamn amusing?" he asked, still shaving. Douglas used to shave with a straight blade, like at a barber's shop. How sexy is that?

"What you just said," I explained, looking over his shoulder as he shaved. "That you're taking your kilt to the dry cleaners to be ready for Trip's wedding."

"Ah," he said, understanding me. "Well, you need to give

them a couple of weeks. It's a very special cleaning they have to do. That's a two-thousand-dollar kilt that I've got."

Suddenly, I was not laughing anymore.

"Oh, my God, you were serious."

"Well, of course I was serious, girl. What did you think I was going to wear to a black-tie wedding?" he asked. This conversation was not going anywhere good.

"Here's a crazy idea—a tuxedo?"

"Well, fuck me! Why the hell would I want to do that?" he asked, laughing as if I'd just asked him to go to the wedding naked or something. Actually, maybe that wouldn't have been such a bad idea. Douglas had an amazing body…but, I digress.

"Because it's a black-tie affair…" I explained.

"Right," he said, sounding very Scottish.

"Right," I said, sounding very confused.

"Right."

"Wait, are we being serious or are we joking?" I asked.

And with that, Douglas stormed into the bedroom, leaving the towel and razor he had been using in his wake, with me following closely behind on his heels. I hated when his face got that menacing look to it. In fact, I lived most of the two years we'd spent together doing anything I could just so that his face would not get that menacing look to it.

He tore the stepladder from its hiding place and brought it over to the closet. Slamming the stepladder down, he then stepped up and pulled down a large box. He gently placed it on the bed and took off the cover, revealing a jacket. I smiled. He was joking all along. Those crazy Scots! As I put my arms around his neck, my hands inching up to his wavy black locks, he picked up the jacket, only to reveal a kilt.

"Oh, my God," I cried, my arms falling from his neck. This was no time to mince words.

"Beautiful, isn't it?" he asked, oblivious to the look of horror now crossing my face. "This tartan's been in the family for over two hundred years."

"Oh, my God."

"Go on, take a proper look, would you?" But I didn't want to touch it. I didn't want to do anything that might suggest that I approved of my boyfriend wearing a skirt to my ex-boyfriend's wedding. Don't panic, I thought. Be cool. Use your super litigator skills to make this man realize that he does not, in fact, want to wear this skirt. He wants to wear pants. But, be so smart as to make him *think* that he came to this conclusion himself. The sort of Jedi mind trick young single women everywhere are forced to use on their boyfriends every day.

"You can't wear that," I instead blurted out. Yoda would not have approved.

"What do you mean, I can't wear it?"

"I told you, ex-boyfriend's wedding, trying to be low profile…"

"But I'm Scottish," he told me. Did he think that I didn't notice that or something? Did he think that American men excessively used the expression *Fuck me,* or that American men obsessively watched World Cup soccer or that American men had such thick accents that I could barely understand what they were saying half of the time? Were people on the street accusing this man of being American and this was why he was explaining that he was, in fact, Scottish to me? Anyway, that's not really the point. The point is that no matter what nationality you are, in America, we encourage men to wear pants. Especially at our ex-boyfriend's weddings.

"I know, honey, but we're trying to go low profile. Remember, the whole low-profile thing...."

"Well, we can still be low profile," he said.

"Don't want to stand out...."

"Are you ashamed of me?"

"Honey, no! God, no! It's just that I was going for the whole 'quiet-complacent-ex-girlfriend' thing, not the whole 'loud-flashy-ex-girlfriend-with-the-hottie-in-a-skirt' thing." At this point, I felt it prudent not to even mention the fact that his wearing of said skirt would totally, completely screw up my outfit selection for the night. How does one even try to find a dress that will not clash with her boyfriend's skirt? I thought that I would have to consult the Scottish embassy on that one.

"It's a kilt," he said, interrupting my thoughts.

"I know that, I'm looking right at it."

"You called it a skirt."

"Whatever it is, you can't wear it."

Putting his shirt on quickly and grabbing his jacket, he asked, "Oh, and you are going to decide that, are you?"

"Well, it's *my* ex-boyfriend's wedding that we're talking about, so, yes, I'm going to decide it!" I yelled at him.

"Why don't you want me to be proud of where I came from?"

"I'm not saying that you shouldn't be proud of where you came from, I'm just asking you to wear some goddamn pants!"

Already down the corridor, he yelled, "Why are you so ashamed of my culture?"

Still in the bedroom, I screamed, "Why do you hate America?"

Yes, I asked him why he hated America. I couldn't help myself. I'm really very patriotic.

3

Now, you may be asking yourself how a brilliant big-time lawyer like myself managed to get herself into such a predicament. Funny you should ask that. I've been asking myself that very same thing, too. So has my mother. So has my best friend. So has my therapist. But I digress.

It all started with an innocent little phone call. From my exboyfriend. Now, some people would think that that's an oxymoron. I mean, how many women can honestly say that they've stayed friends with their ex? But it was a no-fault breakup: we were graduating from law school, he asked me to move with him to California, and I said no. I stayed in New York to begin the glamorous job at the large big-time law firm that he wanted but didn't have the grades to get, and he went off to California to settle for the not-so-glamorous job that he didn't want but my father's connections helped him to get.

When the phone rang, I was sitting in my big-time lawyer office. I was feeling kind of good about myself, what with being practically engaged and on the verge of making partner at my firm. I mean, after all, I'd been living with Douglas for almost a year, so it was just a matter of time until he popped the big question. Mere minutes, really. And I hadn't cried because of a partner yelling at me in well over a week. That alone qualified me to make partner myself.

"Hi, is Mrs. Palsgraf there?" a voice queried. I smiled. Trip and I were always making really stupid law jokes with each other. It was sort of the foundation of our entire relationship. You see, there was this huge case in first-year torts class involving a woman named Mrs. Palsgraf. We spent about three weeks on the case, that's how important it was. For the entire first semester of the first year of law school, just mentioning the name Palsgraf was enough to throw our study group into fits of laughter. If you went to law school, you would have appreciated that one. Or thought that Trip and I were major dorks. One of the two. Either way, I told you so. Stupid law jokes. It remained the dynamic of our relationship up until the very end of it.

"Your father's connection panned out," he said with a boyish smile as we lined up at our law-school graduation. "I'm going to L.A. I should be representing famous movie stars in no time." We still had our graduation caps on our heads. Mine was standing at full attention, tilting upward, while Trip's was sliding down off his dirty-blond head, as if the mere act of staying on his head for the whole of the ceremony had simply been too much for it to bear.

"I don't doubt that you will," I said back, looking straight at him. And I didn't doubt it, actually. Trip could be really hard-working when he wanted to be. And also kind of sleazy. He may or may not have been still dating his girlfriend from college when we first started up in law school.

"Is this a change of residence or domicile?" I asked. Stupid law joke. You see, residence is where you are living right now, whereas domicile is your permanent residence.

"Domicile," he said, looking down.

I didn't even cry about it. (Which for me, as you may have picked up by now, is a major feat.)

I suppose it was because I somehow knew we weren't going to end up together. Throughout the entire three years of law school that we dated, I just knew. There were little hints everywhere. Like the fact that when I was with his family, I felt as if I were on an audition. (Them: "So, Brooke, where does *your* family summer?" Me: "Summer? You mean like in the summer? Where do they summer in the summer? Uh, in their backyards?" Them: "Backyard... Ah, yes, is that off the coast of Maine?" Me: "Yes.") Or the fact that it was like hanging out with the Kennedys. Seriously. They actually played flag football in their backyard and stuff. And his father was the president of their country club. And his uncle was always looking at me in a kind of inappropriate Ted-esque way. Okay, wait, if they had actually *been* the Kennedys, that would have been kind of cool. Or even the Shrivers. Or, say, the Rockefellers. Now that I think about it, I heard a rumor a year or so back that there were still some Rockefellers running around Manhattan. Single ones, too. Now, why didn't I ever date a Rockefeller? Life can be so unfair sometimes.

During the summer after we'd completed our first year of law school, the week before Trip and I were to start our jobs—mine for a very prestigious Second Circuit judge, Trip for a family friend of my uncle's—we went to stay with his parents out at their summer home on Martha's Vineyard. It was a wonderful weekend. You would have loved it. Well, unless you are the type who would let the little things get to you, like the fact that Trip's mother couldn't deign to remember my name and instead referred to me only as "that Jewish girl." Which, luckily for me, I do not.

After I met his family, things really fell into place. I'd always assumed that the little competitive thing that Trip and I had going on was just his cute little precursor to sex ("Oh, I'll habeas your corpus"), but it turned out that he was actually serious all along. Trip and his siblings were constantly trying to best one another, from how many eggs each one could eat in the morning to where their undergraduate schools ranked on the *U.S. News & World Report* list. (Trip's ranked last.) In the pool, they tried to see who could hold his breath for the longest, and at the end of the day, they held up their arms to see who had the fiercest tan. To be fair, I really put Trip at a disadvantage in this regard, what with my slathering SPF 30 all over his body every chance that I could get.

What? You really need to be careful in the sun!

Meeting his family also really explained that look on his face when, at the end of the summer, I made Law Review and he did not.

And it definitely explains this little exchange we had one day after pulling one too many all-nighters with our study group:

"Okay, Brooke, you're up. What is a writ of habeas corpus?"

"Oh, I'll habeas your corpus!" What, you thought that I *didn't* really say that?

"Actually, babe, habeas corpus is an unlawful detention, so you really mean to say, 'I'll habeas corpus you.' Did you even bother to do the reading for Con Law?"

"Just take off my goddamn bra!"

See what I mean?

But when I got that innocent little phone call, it all faded away. At the sound of his voice, all of the fun times came rushing back to me. I smiled the smile of a cat that has just swallowed a goldfish.

"No, I'm sorry," I said, "she's out with Pennoyer and Neff." Another stupid law joke. You see, there is this civil procedure case that you read the first week you are in law school. No one really understands it and… You know what, forget it. Even *I* think that it's dorky at this point.

"How are you, B?" I had forgotten how much I loved it when he called me that.

"Great. How are you?"

"Great. I've got news," he said. My God, I thought, the guy's still in love with me. After all these years, still in love. How sweet! He's probably on a plane to New York as we speak, ready to whisk me away to California to be his. When he sees Douglas, no doubt a fight will break out. A fight for my honor. With Douglas being Scottish and all, it will probably be more like a duel. Yes, Trip will challenge Douglas to a duel. I wonder if Douglas knows how to fence? Fencing is hot.

I'll have to let him down gently, I thought. I'm really very sensitive, you know.

"News?" I asked. Gently.

"I'm getting married."

"Great!" I said back, a little too quickly. He kept on speaking, but I don't think that I heard a word. I was still registering the fact that my ex-boyfriend was getting married before I was. Shouldn't there be some law against that?

"So, who's the lucky girl?" I asked, grabbing for the little stress ball that was on my desk.

"Ava Huang," he replied. *Ava Huang? The movie star? No way* in hell did he just say Ava Huang. No way in hell is my ex-boyfriend is marrying a movie star. Even if he did say Ava Huang, he must mean some other Ava Huang. Why, there must be about a million other Ava Huangs running around L.A. right at this very minute! Now, be cool, be subtle, act like you don't even care.

"The movie star?" I asked. Way to be subtle, Brooke.

"The very one. I represent her. It's so refreshing to talk to someone on the East Coast about it, though. Everyone here has been freaking out about it. It's not like you guys even care about movie stars out there." Trip is so right. We *so* do not care about movie stars here on the East Coast. For example, when I told Jack that my ex-boyfriend was engaged to Ava Huang, he managed to rattle off her entire filmography, complete with analysis as to which films she "looked her best" in (read: took her clothes off in).

"You're so right, Trip. We totally don't," I said, clutching my little stress ball even harder. "In fact, just the other night, I saw Leonardo DiCaprio and I, like, didn't even care about it. Didn't even think twice."

"DiCaprio's back in New York this week?"

"I don't know. You see, that's how little we care about movie stars in New York. It's, like, I didn't even check to see if it really was Leonardo DiCaprio. And neither did anyone else. We're, like, far too busy reading books and stuff."

"Gosh, Brooke, you're taking this really well. You know, I was kind of nervous to call you. I thought that you might get upset or something."

"Upset? Me? I never get upset! Why on earth would *I* get upset?"

"You know, Brooke," he said, "we always did have that little competitive thing going on back in law school."

"We did?" I said. "I hadn't noticed. I must have been too busy making Law Review."

"I made Moot Court," he said. I could practically see him pouting through the phone wires.

"I didn't want Moot Court," I said, tossing my little stress ball into the air and catching it.

"That's because you couldn't argue your way out of a paper bag," he said, his faux "I'm just kidding!" laughter rising an octave.

"You're right," I said, "I was far too concerned with my writing. I guess that's why I got my Student Note published."

"I guess that's why I won the National Moot Court Competition," he retorted.

"Because I got my Note published? How very interesting," I said with a smile. Dead silence on the line. And he says I can't argue?

"Well, I'm just glad that you're not upset."

"Not in the least," I said.

"What was that noise?" Trip asked. Hmmm. That noise *may* have been the sound of me throwing that little stress ball against the back of my office door. Okay, yes, now that I'm telling you about this, I distinctly recall slamming that cute little stress ball against the back of my door, just before I cleverly said:

"You know, Trip, life is so funny sometimes. You see, I'm engaged myself!"

"You are?" he asked. I am?

"Why yes!" I said, suddenly sounding like Barbra Streisand at the very end of *The Way We Were,* "Don't sound so surprised!"

"I'm not surprised at all. I just didn't hear about it, is all. And I was just e-mailing with Vanessa all last week," he said. "Any guy would be crazy not to nab you. Who's the lucky guy?"

"His name is Douglas. He's fabulous. He's Scottish."

"I forgot how much you love Euro-trash," he responded. He was probably smiling his Cheshire-Cat smile when he said that little gem to me.

"He most certainly is not Euro-trash. He is a very class act. In fact, speaking of movie stars, he *looks* like a movie star, but he's far too intelligent for Hollywood."

"And probably has no time for Hollywood what with reading all of those books."

"No offense," I said.

"None taken," he said.

"I'm sure Ava can read, too."

"Yes, she can," he assured me. "Well, then, I can't wait to meet him."

Okay, so it was a little white lie. But, as I already told you, I believed myself to be *practically* engaged at that point in time, so I figured that by Trip's wedding, I would surely be engaged. Who knew, depending on timing, I could even be married *before* Trip was!

4

Yes, married! It wasn't so far off to think. You see, Douglas and I had a real whirlwind romance. The night we met, he swept me off my feet, and I fell head over heels in love with him without even thinking twice about it.

It was a perfectly magical evening at the charity party the Guggenheim Museum threw each year on Halloween. The Guggenheim has long been my favorite New York museum, as the museum itself is a work of art, with its sweeping lines and interior painted a pristine white. The artwork adorning its walls seems the perfect accessory to the main attraction—the architecture. The Met, to me, was always too immense and imposing, and the MOMA was simply too complicated.

For their annual masquerade ball, orange spotlights wash over the museum's milky walls and floors, giving the space an intense and entirely unfamiliar glow. A string quartet plays quietly in a corner, reminding you that you are at the most exclusive charity ball of the season, rubbing elbows with the best and brightest New

York has to offer. Waiters surround you, enticing you with the sweet smells of hors d'oeuvres too fancy to even identify. Follow the clickety clank of wine and champagne glasses, and you will find that the bar is off to the side, leaving a large space in the middle of the entranceway, which will later be used for dancing, once the guests have paired off.

"Act like we're together," Douglas whispered, as he slunk over to me seemingly out of nowhere with eyes shifting all over the room. He was dressed as a rugby player and I was dressed as a French maid.

Oh, please. As if you never used Halloween as an excuse to dress like a slut.

"Excuse me?" I said in my most righteous voice. Granted, he really had me with the accent, but what exactly did he take me for? Okay, don't answer that one.

"Please," he begged with enormous brown puppy-dog eyes, "this girl has been following me around all evening long. If you pretend to be my girlfriend, I will treat you to a dinner at any restaurant in the city that you want."

Without waiting for an answer, he pressed his lips against mine.

My knees got weak. I actually felt my knees get weak. He later told me that he "had" to do that, since said girl-stalker was quickly approaching us. I never saw her, though.

"So, do you want to get out of here?" he asked me with sexy bedroom eyes. I didn't really know who he was or where he was going, but when he looked at me with those eyes and leaned into me the way he did, there was no place else I'd rather have been.

"Yes," I replied breathlessly. And with that, this man that I had just met grabbed my hand and we were off into the cold New York City night. Although it was only the end of October, it already smelled like winter. He introduced me to his friend, Franc, and Franc's girlfriend, Allie, a couple of Parisian transplants. Neither had come dressed up to the party. They were both young and attractive, but somehow, they didn't look as if they fit one another. We all hopped into a taxicab together and Franc gave the cabbie directions to a loft party in Tribeca. Now, I probably would have followed Douglas to a pizza place in Queens to play tabletop Pac-Man if he'd asked me to, but I was nonetheless delighted to be going somewhere as hip and fabulous as a loft party that was probably even more exclusive than the party we'd just left. I immediately looked down at my French maid getup and quietly removed the little doily that was on my head.

I was between Allie and Douglas in the back, with Franc in the front. Douglas's left leg pressed against my right and I smiled to myself. *This is one of those perfect New York City nights when you live for the moment and don't think about tomorrow,* I thought. I turned my head toward Douglas and caught him looking at me. We locked eyes and I began to think wicked thoughts.

"I don't want to go to another party!" Allie screamed to the front, interrupting my thoughts, "I want to go home!" Franc looked back at her and laughed and shut the plastic divider that separated the front of the cab from the back of the cab and told the cabbie to keep driving. The cabbie had to stay toward the middle of the road to avoid the massive potholes that were lined up like a collision course along Broadway.

"I am getting out right now!" Allie yelled again, opening the divider as she yelled. When Franc didn't turn around, Allie pretended to open her car door, with the cab still moving, for effect. *How very French,* I remember thinking to myself. The cabbie began to yell something in a foreign language while Franc tried to calm him down. I looked at Douglas and he rolled his eyes. I smiled a quiet smile back as he mouthed the words *drama queen* to me. I giggled a silent giggle that only Douglas could see and he put his hand on my leg. I giggled out loud.

"I am getting out of this cab right now!" Allie screamed, and the cabbie pulled over to the right-hand side of the street to a chorus of assuring "She is not getting out!" coming from Franc. Allie, on the left side of the cab, swung the door open wide into traffic just as we stopped on the right-hand side of the street. As quickly as she opened the door, another cab came whizzing by and knocked Allie's cab door right off its hinges.

Everything was silent for a moment. The cabbie turned around, and upon seeing that Allie was all right, began to yell at Franc very fast in a foreign language. Franc began to yell back in French and Allie sank deep down into her cab seat. Douglas got out to referee and I stayed in the cab with Allie. I was surprised that she didn't feel sorry for what she had done, rather, she somehow thought that it was the cab driver's fault, or Franc's fault, or just anyone's fault but her own. I heard Franc outside talking, now in English, to the cabbie about what he should do and how he could fix things. When it seemed that Franc had squared things with the cabbie, Douglas opened the right-hand door of the cab, where I was sitting, and put out his hand for me to take.

"Shall we?" he asked.

"Is everything okay?" I asked.

"Everything will be fine. Let's go to that party now."

I agreed, but suggested that we walk instead of taking another cab. Douglas laughed and we began to walk. I told Douglas that I somehow felt like a fugitive leaving the scene of a crime or something and asked him if he thought that Franc and Allie would really stay and do right by the cabbie.

"Allie? No. Franc? Yes," he replied. I agreed, but told him that I still felt as if we were fugitives. He told me that he did, too.

It was cold, so we soon began running, holding hands and laughing. We were running in the middle of the streets; it was so late at night there weren't any cars on the tiny downtown side streets. I was scared that I would fall, but I somehow knew that Douglas would catch me if I did. We reached Varick Street, where the next party was still going strong. You could hear the pounding bass of the music coming out of the windows and see the empty cups lining its sills.

"I don't really feel like going to another party, do you?" Douglas asked with those bedroom eyes. It was so cold out that I could see his breath as he spoke. I shook my head no.

In an alleyway somewhere off Varick Street, still feeling like fugitives, we kissed again.

One heavenly month later, Douglas begged me to move in with him. Seriously. It was, like, embarrassing. I really couldn't say no. I mean, the guy was deeply, madly, passionately in love with me! You would have done the same thing. But, don't worry about me, because I did it all very much by the rules. Literally. I was reading that book called *The Rules* at the time. It's all about snagging a man and then getting said man to marry you. Quickly. Okay, so even on its truncated deadlines, that book didn't suggest even having sex with a man within the first month of dating, much less moving in with him, but those girls never met Douglas. And if my grandmother asks you, we may have been living together, but we most certainly were not having sex. You know what, if my grandmother asks you, don't even tell her that we were living together. That's just easier. And anyway, I don't think that Grandma even realized it at the time. Even when Douglas picked up the telephone, he had such a thick accent that she usually hung up thinking it was the wrong number. But I digress.

The whole thing seemed to be in the bag. By the time I got Trip's wedding invite, I'd be blissfully engaged (or even married!) to my handsome Scottish boyfriend. Piece of cake, right?

5

No! That's not right! It was definitely *not* a piece of cake! By the time Trip's wedding came around, not only was I *so not* engaged, but Douglas and I had also broken up, leaving me both boyfriend-less and homeless! And he proposed to another woman! Who, as you might have caught earlier, had a stupid, stupid name!

Aren't you even paying attention?!

Luckily for me, my best friend Vanessa *was* paying attention. Post-breakup, she was my rock. She was even kind enough to let me stay with her and her husband Marcus. After I showed up on her doorstep crying hysterically, begging to come in, that is.

Even in my time of need, though, I was really a pleasure to be around. In fact, I think that in their heart of hearts, they actually enjoyed having me there. Marcus was always working late and was never at home, so I kept Vanessa company on the nights that we, ourselves, didn't have to work late.

I was also very helpful in the kitchen. I even made dinner once or twice. Well, not so much made dinner as stood in front of the fridge staring blankly into its vast coldness. But it's really the thought that counts with those things.

"Did the governor call?" Vanessa asked me on one such evening, as she walked into the apartment. She took off her three-inch stiletto heels, which she wore every day despite the fact that she was five foot eight.

"No," I told her, marveling at the fact that I have such impressive friends, they were actually sitting around waiting for the governor to call. Yes, my friends were out waiting for heads of state to call, while I was standing in front of the refrigerator in my bathrobe, eating raw cookie dough straight from the package as if it were a hot dog, or some other food product that might be acceptable to eat while clutching said food product in one's fist.

Oh, please. As if you never did that, too.

I guess that's the way life is when you are the sole offspring of glamorous parents like Vanessa's—her father, originally from the West Indies, is a world-renowned heart surgeon, and her mother, a former model, now owns a gallery in Tribeca that specializes in African-American art. She grew up in a palatial house in New Jersey that was in the same cul-de-sac as a hip-hop mogul and his child bride. The only famous person in my family is my mother's cousin Ernie, who once placed second in the Ben's Kosher Deli matzo-ball eating competition.

"Do you want to talk about it?" she asked, sliding her long legs under her body as she sat down at the kitchen counter.

"Me? No. I'm absolutely fine. Why on earth would I want to talk about it?" I asked.

"When I come home to find my best friend eating like she's going to the electric chair, I figure she needs to talk about it," she explained. Electric chair? Governor calling… Clever.

I suppose to some people, that sort of behavior screams "cry for help." To me, it screams "typical Monday night at home."

"No, Vanessa. I'm okay," I said, slowly backing away from the refrigerator. The truth is that I *did* want to talk about it. It was the only thing that I wanted to talk about, but it seemed as if all I did all day was talk about it, so at night, I would be better off doing more productive things with my time. Like standing in front of the refrigerator in my bathrobe eating raw cookie dough from the tube.

You see, Vanessa never had to worry about the things that I worry about on a daily basis. Will I ever find someone? Will I ever get married? Will I ever have children? Or am I destined to end up like Old Mrs. White, the lady who lived next door to me growing up? I used to pass by her house every day on my walk home from elementary school. She always seemed like such a kind woman, tending to her garden and waving hello to every neighbor who passed by. There was always the faint smell of vanilla on her hands, as if she had been baking cookies all day. Some days, she would even bring out chocolate chip cookies to the neighbor- hood kids when she saw us playing kickball out on the street (store bought—go figure). One day, she told me that she recently became a grandmother and wanted to show me pictures. I was delighted! After all, what eight-year-old girl doesn't love babies? She pulled out the photos, and I was so excited to see them that I could barely get my hands around the pictures fast enough. Holding the photos by their edges, ever so carefully, I took a peek. To my horror, they were photos of kittens. Kittens! As in: baby cats. Basically, her kittens had been more successful at finding a mate and reproducing than she had. I was scarred for life. I went home that very night and threw out all of my Hello Kitty stickers. The sight of a cat still makes me cringe.

Vanessa, on the other hand, met her husband Marcus on her very first day at Howard University. How's that for luck? He spotted her attempting to pull her suitcase up a flight of stairs, and, ever the gentleman, offered to help. The rest is history. They got married exactly one year after graduation. Isn't that so cute you could die? I think that the story of the day they met also involved him inviting her to a fraternity party that same evening, and then making out with her shamelessly at said party, but that part of the story usually gets edited out in polite company. There's a rumor among people who have known her from her Howard days that one groomsman alluded to the alleged make-out incident at Vanessa and Marcus's rehearsal dinner. As the story goes, that man never made it down the aisle.

The first man that I met on my first day of college asked me who the "hot blonde" helping me move in was. It was my mother. I told him so. He asked if she was single. When I told him that she was not single, and in fact, was very much married, he asked, "Happily?"

And he didn't even offer to help me with my bags.

I met Vanessa at a law school event being cosponsored by the Black Law Students Association and the Jewish Law Students Association. We gravitated toward each other, seemingly the only two people there solely for the free pizza and beer. We spent most of our free time from then on out together, studying and just generally trying to make it through law school as a team. Marcus was rarely at home, since he was first in medical school and then starting out his residency in surgery. Trip, who became the third in our study group after we met him at a Student Bar Association happy hour, used to accuse Vanessa of making up Marcus entirely so that no one would ask her out, thus leaving her more time to study (logic that completely escapes me).

Vanessa and I made Law Review together and then went to the same law firm for our second-year summer. We're both litigators, which means that our offices are mere footsteps away from each other on the eleventh floor.

Which worked out perfectly for me the day after my breakup with Douglas, since I couldn't get out of bed and needed someone to go to my office and turn on the lights and computer to make it look as if I were actually there.

I lay in bed in Vanessa and Marcus's guest bedroom for most of the morning, simply unable to move. Everything around me reminded me of Douglas. The picture of Vanessa and Marcus on my bedside table—a happy couple; the earrings that I had forgotten to take out of my ears the night before—a present from Douglas; the red silk drapes covering the windows—his favorite color for me to wear.

How could this be happening to me? Why is this happening to me? What have I done to deserve this? Why didn't I deserve to be a happy couple, like Vanessa and Marcus?

My eyes opened at around noon, when the telephone began to ring. I listening to it ring, over and over, and threw the covers over my head in an effort to make it stop. The answering machine picked up, far and away out in the living room, and I heard Vanessa's voice calling out to me.

"Brooke?" she said. "Brooke, if you're there, pick up. Pick up! Pick up, pick up, pick up…."

My cell phone rang next. I pulled the covers back and threw my arm out to the bedside table to pick it up.

"Didn't you hear the phone?" Vanessa asked.

"No," I lied, eyes still shut.

"Okay," Vanessa said, "well, nothing's really going on here. I checked your voice mails and your e-mails and I told your secretary you were in court on some *pro bono* case."

"Thanks, Vanessa," I said.

"Are you still in bed?" she asked tentatively.

"Yes," I said.

"Well, you should get up and eat something," she said, "it'll make you feel better."

Vanessa was right. You should always listen to doctor's orders. Or doctor's wife's orders, as the case may be. I rolled out of bed and padded into the kitchen.

"What else is going on over there?" I asked, taking the half-eaten roll of cookie dough out of the fridge and plopping myself down on the couch.

"Quiet day," she said. "What are you going to do about your stuff?"

"Stuff?" I asked, flipping the television on.

"Your stuff, your things," she said. "As in, what are you going to wear to work tomorrow?"

"My stuff," I said. Right.

"You can borrow mine until you get back downtown to pick up yours," she said. That would have been a great idea if I could actually fit into any of Vanessa's things.

Vanessa was right. I should pick myself up, dust myself off, and go down to Douglas's apartment and collect my things. That would be the mature, responsible thing to do. I should just go down there, pack my bags, and go about moving on with the rest of my life.

Two hours later, I'd hit the makeup counters at Saks, bought a new pair of black pumps and was headed up to the fifth floor to get some new outfits when my cell phone rang. I could see Jack's work number pop up on my caller ID and I answered it.

"How's it going?" Jack said.

"Fine," I said, hoping he couldn't hear the music playing on the fifth floor of Saks. It was kind of loud.

"Did you win?" Jack asked.

"Win what?"

"Vanessa said you had a hearing on one of your *pro bono* cases?" Jack said.

"Oh, yes," I said, "that. Of course I won. It went great. Great! Great, great, great…"

"Excuse me, miss," a salesperson asked, "would you like me to start a fitting room for you?" I smiled and nodded, and quietly handed her the clothing I was holding.

"Brooke, are you shopping?" Jack asked.

"Well, you can't expect me to sit at home eating raw cookie dough all day," I said. "Saks can be very therapeutic."

"No," Jack said, "I expect you to come to work. Where you belong." Clearly, I was talking to a man. A woman would understand that I belonged at Saks.

"Douglas and I are having some problems," I said, brushing my hand against a row of spring dresses. "So, I just need a day to get back to myself."

"Vanessa said he kicked you out of the apartment," Jack said.

"Well, yeah," I said, "that's sort of, like, the problem."

"What are you doing in Saks?" he said. "Come to the office and I'll take you out for lunch."

"I don't want lunch, I just want Douglas," I said. I hoped he understood that I was saying that I wanted Douglas back, for things to be the way they used to be, and not that I was actually suggesting that I wanted to *eat* Douglas for lunch. Although I was not opposed to the occasional afternoon rendezvous….

"Well, it's over, so why don't you let me take you for lunch," he said.

"Can you even *pretend* to be supportive?" I asked.

"You want me to support your going to Saks?" he asked.

"I don't have any clothes or makeup," I said. "I didn't get a chance to pack anything on my way out."

Jack didn't respond. I could tell that he was brushing his hand through his hair as he thought.

"Well, then," he said, clearing his throat as he did, "I'll pick you up at Saks right now and take you to the apartment to pack a bag. It's the middle of the day so he won't be home." I could tell that he was deliberately refraining from saying Douglas's name, sort of the way Harry Potter only calls Voldemort "he who shall not be named."

"Thanks, Jack," I said, "but I'm fine."

An hour and a half later, I walked out of Saks with three enormous shopping bags, two garment bags and a tiny shopping bag that held all of my cosmetics. It was amazing that you could spend that much money at the cosmetics counter and the sum total of your purchases could fit into a tiny bag that would barely hold a pair of shoes.

As I pushed open the door to the Fifth Avenue exit, there stood Vanessa in front of a town car holding a sign that said "Brooke Miller."

"What on earth are you doing here?" I said, my eyes almost brimming up with tears at the sight of her.

"Jack said that you were here, so I thought I'd take you downtown to get your stuff." She grabbed a shopping bag and garment bag from me and signaled for the driver to pop open the trunk. "We'll do it quick and painless, like ripping off a Band-Aid."

"Thank you," I said, a tear escaping from my eye.

"Breakups suck," she said, putting her arm around me.

As the car sailed down Fifth Avenue, Vanessa and I sorted through my shopping bags, deciding which items I would have to return and which she would be borrowing.

We arrived in front of the Soho Triumphe and Vanessa got out of the car with me. I told her that I thought I should do this part alone.

"Hi," I said to the doorman as he stopped me on the way in, "I'm Brooke Miller, I live in 32G. Well, lived," I said, unsure of my new status. I finally settled on saying: "I'm in 32G."

I got up to the apartment and opened the door. Even though it had only been mere hours since I'd left, it already felt as if I didn't recognize the place. Everything somehow looked colder, more antiseptic, and I didn't see a trace of myself in it. I walked over to the windowsill and saw a picture of Douglas and me, taken when we were down in the islands for Christmas the previous year, nestled among the other *objets d'art* he had lined up on the sill like little soldiers.

It's not over, I thought. If it were over, that would have been the first thing I'd have thrown out. My first step in moving on. (I probably would have hurled it right out the window, but let's not get technical.)

Walking into the bedroom, I took a deep breath. It smelled just like Douglas. Woodsy and manly and dark. The bed was unmade and I smiled, thinking about how Douglas and I never had the time to make it during the week. I picked up his pillow and inhaled.

Then, remembering Vanessa waiting downstairs in a car for me, I quickly took out the step stool and grabbed a suitcase from the top shelf of the closet. I didn't need too many things. I would be back.

I went through the closet and heard a key in the door. A smile crept onto my lips. That unmade bed was about to come in very handy....

I flipped the suitcase shut and headed toward the bedroom door as I heard a voice on a cell phone. A woman's voice.

"I'm at your apartment, baby," she said as I stood frozen in my tracks. I couldn't believe that Beryl had the nerve to be there. The day after Douglas threw me out. A thousand thoughts flooded my brain—should I hide in the closet? Under the bed? What should I do? Even if I hid myself, the suitcase was still there in plain sight. With all of my things in it. And anyway, who was I—Lucy Ricardo?

There was nowhere to go. It was just like that scene in *No Way Out* where Kevin Costner's photo is coming up on the computer screen and he's about to be revealed as the bad guy, but really, he's not the real bad guy, someone else is the real bad guy, but he's totally stuck inside the Pentagon with nowhere to go.

"Pastis?" I heard Beryl say. "I'd absolutely love to!"

The room began to spin. He was taking Beryl to Pastis, a fabulous ultra-trendy French bistro downtown in the Meatpacking District. A favorite of local celebs and the New York Euro scene, Douglas used to call it "our place" since we had spent so much time there over the years.

I sat down on the unmade bed and laughed at myself. I couldn't believe that up until a few weeks ago, I used to indulge this pathetic little fantasy that Douglas would propose to me there. Actually drop down to his knees in the middle of the restaurant and proclaim his undying love to me in front of his friends and our waiter and the other diners and any celebrities who happened to be there that night. I would giggle like a schoolgirl and jump down to the ground to throw my arms around him, all the while kissing him and screaming, "Yes, yes, yes! I will marry you!" Of course, the crowd would applaud and the waiter would bring a bottle of champagne to our table. We would laugh and drink champagne and I would blind the other diners with the sheer size and brilliance of my new diamond ring. As my relationship with Douglas crept up to the two-year mark, my outfits on the nights we were going to Pastis got more and more "special" as I deluded myself further and further into thinking that my fantasy could become reality.

I used to tell myself that it was okay to have harmless little fantasies like that. Who were they hurting, anyway? And who *wouldn't* have such fantasies? But Douglas wouldn't be taking me to Pastis or anywhere else anymore. He was taking Beryl.

I heard the apartment door slam shut and I hurriedly threw more clothing and assorted pairs of shoes into my suitcase. I was packing so fast that I had no idea what I was putting inside the case. Somehow, I remembered to grab my jewelry, which I threw on top, zipped the suitcase shut and wheeled it out of the bedroom. When I walked into the living room, I saw an enormous crystal vase filled with three majestic calla lilies, arranged neatly. *That was what she came here to do,* I thought. *She brought in fresh flowers.* I looked to the windowsill and saw that the picture of Douglas and me was gone.

I rushed back to the car, threw myself into Vanessa's arms, and cried the whole way back uptown.

6

From: "Brooke Miller" <bmiller@gilsonhecht.com>
To: "Douglas MacGregor" <douglas.macgregor@waldmansecurities.com>
Subject: I miss you

Do you miss me, too?

Brooke Miller
Gilson, Hecht and Trattner
425 Park Avenue
11th Floor
New York, New York 10022

*****CONFIDENTIALITY NOTICE*****
The information contained in this e-mail message is confidential and is intended only for the use of the individual or entity named above. If you are not the intended recipient, we would request you delete this communication without reading it or any

attachment, not forward or otherwise distribute it, and kindly advise Gilson, Hecht and Trattner by return e-mail to the sender or a telephone call to 1 (800) GILSON. Thank you in advance.

Delete.

It was the fourteenth e-mail message that I'd drafted and then deleted so far. But it wasn't as if I could concentrate on work two days after Douglas threw me out of our apartment. My assignment for the day—talk to Douglas and clear this whole mess up.

From: "Brooke Miller" <bmiller@gilsonhecht.com>
To: "Douglas MacGregor" <douglas.macgregor@waldmansecurities.com>
Subject: hey

We need to talk.

Brooke Miller
Gilson, Hecht and Trattner
425 Park Avenue
11th Floor
New York, New York 10022

*****CONFIDENTIALITY NOTICE*****
The information contained in this e-mail message is confidential and is intended only for the use of the individual or entity named above. If you are not the intended recipient, we would request you delete this communication without reading it or any attachment, not forward or otherwise distribute it, and kindly advise Gilson, Hecht and Trattner by return e-mail to the sender or a telephone call to 1 (800) GILSON. Thank you in advance.

Too angry and defensive. Men hate angry and defensive.

From: "Brooke Miller" <bmiller@gilsonhecht.com>
To: "Douglas MacGregor" <douglas.macgregor@
waldmansecurities.com>
Subject: hi

Can we talk?

Brooke Miller
Gilson, Hecht and Trattner
425 Park Avenue
11th Floor
New York, New York 10022

*****CONFIDENTIALITY NOTICE*****
The information contained in this e-mail message is confidential and is intended only for the use of the individual or entity
named above. If you are not the intended recipient, we would
request you delete this communication without reading it or any
attachment, not forward or otherwise distribute it, and kindly
advise Gilson, Hecht and Trattner by return e-mail to the sender
or a telephone call to 1 (800) GILSON. Thank you in advance.

Send. A screen popped up asking, "Are you sure you want to
send this message?" Normally, I just click *Yes* as a matter of fact,
but this time it gave me pause. Did I really want to send this
message? It was as good of a question as any, I supposed. My life
had changed in an instant and my computer wanted to know if I
wanted to take a step in making it back the way it was.

I clicked *Yes* and walked down the hall to Vanessa's office to
discuss the breakup.

"Do you think that we'll get back together in time for Trip's wedding?" I asked.

"You asked the man why he hates America," Vanessa said, barely looking up from the document she was typing.

"Mistakes were made," I said.

"You think?" Vanessa asked me, still typing away furiously on her computer.

"I can't believe that I have no boyfriend," I said. I eyed the photograph of Vanessa and Marcus at their college graduation that was on her bulletin board. They were holding on to each other for dear life, cheeks pressed together, smiling like two little kids. It was the day Marcus proposed to her.

"And apparently," Vanessa kindly pointed out, "you may be a racist, or a nationalist. Or some sort of Scotsman-hater in general."

"I just wanted the man to wear pants. Who knew that once you found a man in Manhattan who was straight and single, you then had to worry about whether or not he wanted to wear pants?"

"The things we take for granted." Vanessa sighed.

"Are we still talking about Douglas?" Jack asked, walking into Vanessa's office, balancing three coffee cups in his hands. I picked a paper clip up off of her desk and began to unravel it. Vanessa's desk was always neat and ordered with everything in its proper spot. The paper clips had their own tiny tray right next to her stapler and tape dispenser. She kept her pens and highlighters in a Howard University mug, right next to her Rolodex, right next to her *In* and *Out* boxes. I always marveled at how she could keep herself so organized since my own office always looked as if it had been recently hit by a tornado. I hadn't even *seen* my own Rolodex since I was a first-year associate.

"It's not like I'm obsessed with him, or anything," I explained. I didn't want Jack to worry about me. Or see how pathetic I was being. Jack had broken off an engagement six months prior and he never became completely unhinged about it the way I was over Douglas. In fact, six months later, he seemed totally fine about it. Well, I mean, I'm sure he was upset at the time—I'm not meaning to say he's cold or some sort of monster or anything. It's just that he didn't seem to have to discuss it constantly with his friends in the ensuing days. Although maybe that's what they did at all of those firm intramural basketball games. Jack was the captain of our firm's team, so maybe that's what they did while reviewing the playbook, lament past relationships and cry over it the way we women would, quoting Oprah and trying to figure out where it all went wrong. In between shooting hoops, I mean.

Or maybe Jack was able to recover so quickly because he had been engaged to his fiancée for three and a half years without ever having set a wedding date. I always thought that it was totally ironic that in Jack's junior year, he played the Nathan Detroit role in his high school's production of *Guys and Dolls.* I was sure his fiancée didn't find that fun fact quite as charming.

"I'm not obsessed with Douglas," I said. "I can move on…. To obsessing about Trip's wedding instead. Totally different."

"Totally more healthy," Vanessa said, with her hands in her desk drawers, getting out sugars and various other fake sweeteners for us to put in our coffees.

"If you want to be healthy," Jack said in his best game-show announcer voice, "drink coffee from Healthy Foods. Wholesome, delicious, and also," he continued, segueing into his normal speaking voice, "our firm's biggest new client."

"And the bane of Jack's existence," Vanessa said. Healthy Foods was, in fact, the firm's biggest new client, having just been sued in a sixty-million dollar false advertising class action lawsuit claiming that Healthy Foods coffee was not, in fact, healthy, as the name might suggest. The firm now stocked Healthy Foods brand coffee in all of its kitchens and, of course, in the twelfth-floor cafeteria. Jack, up for partner in six months, was put on the case, since the powers-that-be knew that he would do anything for the firm in a year that the firm was voting on his partnership. As per our usual assignment, I was the junior associate on the matter. I didn't know if Healthy Foods coffee was healthy or not, but it was pretty darn good either way. Especially when someone hand delivered it right into my hot little hands. Then it was tasty *and* convenient.

Jack was always doing sweet things like that. Last June, Jack and I were supposed to take summer associates out to lunch to our favorite midtown restaurant. With my feet practically out the door, I was called into a meeting and was unable to attend the lunch. I sat in my meeting pouting for upward of two hours, all the while fantasizing about the delicious time Jack and the summers were having without me. When I got back to my office, as if on cue, Jack swept in with a doggy bag—my favorite chocolate dessert from said favorite restaurant. We could barely see each other across my desk because the files on it were piled up so high, but even through the haze of discovery documents, Jack could see me smiling from ear to ear.

It's hard to believe that I only met Jack when I came to the firm as a summer associate myself a few years ago. I feel as if I've known him forever. There I was, the summer after my second year of law school: one of the elite few walking the halls of Gilson,

Hecht and Trattner, one of New York City's largest and most prestigious law firms. Okay, so it wasn't really an elite *few* since the firm boasts over four hundred attorneys in its New York City office alone, over six hundred worldwide, but you get the general point I'm trying to make. I was one of the elite four hundred some odd people walking those halls.

With a twenty-four-hour command center including a word-processing center, mailroom, cafeteria and supply room (not supply closet, mind you, an actual room dedicated solely to the mission of ordering and giving associates whatever supplies their hearts desired), the twelfth floor should have its own postal code. It even has a cash machine. There is a staff of eight whose sole responsibility is to send and receive faxes (all of which makes it even more shocking when your faxes are actually not sent or lost entirely). When you're a summer associate, you think that these facts are very cool and glamorous. You don't seem to realize that if the firm has the capacity to run twenty-four hours a day, that the associates, likewise, are expected to have the capacity to run those same twenty-four hours a day.

Which, incidentally, explains why I didn't know that my ex-boyfriend was dating one of the most famous movie stars in the world. I've been doing a motion for summary judgment for the last six months. I won't bore you with the details of what a motion for summary judgment entails—suffice it to say, a motion for summary judgment means fourteen- to sixteen-hour days, six to seven days a week. Sleep is a luxury that even on our six-figure big-time lawyer salaries, we cannot afford. Wow, didn't that sound, like, totally dramatic?

Can that also be my excuse for why I didn't realize that my boyfriend was cheating on me? Okay, yes, that's good. Remind me to tell my mother/best friend/boss/therapist that later. And since you're so chummy with my grandmother, would you be a dear and tell her that very thing, too?

When I interview unsuspecting law students interested in coming to Gilson Hecht for the summer after their second year of law school, the question I am most often asked is "What is your favorite thing about Gilson Hecht?" I love being asked that question because it is the one point in the interview where I can just be myself and not deliver the firm's party line about the training (so-so), the mentoring program (my partner-mentor got drunk the first time he took me for lunch), and the amount of experience junior associates get early on in their careers (is that what they call the fourteen- to sixteen-hour days?). Sometimes I fantasize about just telling them the truth—that the associates at Gilson Hecht seem to want to kill themselves ever-so-slightly less than the associates at most other major New York City law firms. And that's saying a lot. But saying that sort of thing is very much discouraged in interviews.

The reason why the "favorite thing about Gilson Hecht" question is so easy for me to answer is that the best part of working at Gilson Hecht is, by far, the friends I have made here.

Jack was already a first-year associate at the firm when I started. I was in the self-serve photocopy room up on the eighth floor, having a total *Nine to Five* moment—paper flying every which way—clueless as to what I should do to make the copy machine behave and stop simultaneously spewing out and chewing up paper, when Jack swept in and saved the day. And saved the memo I had been photocopying at the time.

"Consider me your knight in shining armor. Or khakis, as the case may be," he said, introducing himself, baby-blue eyes gleaming. He's been saving me ever since.

"You can stop obsessing about your ex-boyfriend's wedding," Jack declared. "Your problem is solved. *I'll* go with you to the wedding."

"Thanks, but I already told Trip about Douglas," I explained, putting my head down into my coffee.

"And warned him that he'd be wearing a kilt," Vanessa explained, finishing my thought for me.

"Yes, and told him that my date would be in a skirt," I agreed.

"Kilt, Brooke, it's a kilt," Jack said. "Not a skirt. I'm beginning to see why Douglas broke up with you."

"Et tu, Brute?" I said, looking up from my coffee. "Anyway, I mentioned the *kilt* thing to Trip last time I spoke to him because I just didn't want him to be all surprised about it at the wedding. I didn't want to make a whole scene on his big day."

"Because," Vanessa explained, "we all know that Trip's wedding is really all about you."

"Thank you for that very sensitive commentary. You just don't understand. You've been married since you were twelve."

"And exactly what does that have to do with it?" she demanded.

"Should boys leave for this part of the conversation?" Jack asked, smoothing his shaggy brown hair from his eyes.

"You've just never been in my shoes," I explained, the coffee suddenly too hot for my hands. I set it down on Vanessa's desk. "You don't know how hard it all is. You've never been thirty years old and recently dumped by the man you thought you were going to marry. You've never been invited to an ex-boyfriend's wedding. You've never made plans to go to an ex-boyfriend's wedding only to have your whole world fall apart two weeks before you were set to go. Look, I told Trip that I was coming to his wedding with my gorgeous Scottish fiancé, and that is what I'm doing. I will just have to get Douglas back in time for the wedding."

"Boys should definitely leave," Jack said, making a hasty exit without even grabbing his coffee.

"It has to work. At this point," I explained, "it's either bring Douglas or bust."

"Well," Vanessa said, stirring her coffee, "then, I guess you're busted."

7

Having only two weeks to go before the wedding in which to win Douglas back, I got to work immediately the following morning. Douglas hadn't e-mailed me back yet from the other day, but that didn't matter. First order of business—call him at work, tell him I forgive him and I am ready to move on. A phone call would be much better than sending an e-mail I wouldn't even know if he ever received. For all I know, that last e-mail could be lost somewhere in cyberspace.

I picked up the phone and, as it began to ring, a smile came to my face. This was easy. Now, why hadn't I thought of this sooner? It felt good to be proactive. Peace and order would be restored to the universe, at this pace, by lunchtime—1:00 p.m., the latest. God, I'm good.

"This is Brooke calling," I said to Douglas's secretary. Dead silence on the line. "Brooke Miller," I explained, "his *girl*friend." Close enough, right? "What's that?" I asked. "He's in a meeting?

All right then. When do you expect him to be back?… Oh, you're not sure…. Okay."

So, he was in a meeting. A minor glitch. That was all right, though, Rome wasn't built in a day. And it most certainly wasn't built in two hours. I could wait.

When I hadn't heard back by eleven, I decided to give him a call again. After all, how long could his meeting really take? In the course of the two years that I'd been with Douglas, I never really figured out precisely what it was that he did for a living. I just knew that it was something financial that entailed the wearing of expensive custom-made Italian suits.

"Oh, he'll be back at one?" I said, tapping my pen on the tip of my desk. "I'll call him then."

Back at one? That was okay. It would be a good opportunity to get some work done. What with the stress of the whole breakup and all, my billables really had been quite low. Time for the big-time lawyer to earn her big-time salary. First order of business, some computer research for the Healthy Foods case. I was such a woman of the millennium—multitasking at its best. I would get back my man *and* get some quality billable hours in. All in one morning. God, I'm good.

Two hours later, I hadn't done an ounce of billable work, but I did manage to pick up some killer boots on sale at Saks. What? If I was going to get back my man, I'd have to look good!

"Oh, he's out to lunch now?" I said to Douglas's secretary at 1:00 p.m. "Got it. And, when do you expect him back exactly?" Tap, tap, tap.

"What has that pen ever done to you?" Jack asked, appearing in my doorway just as I slammed the phone down. "Let's go pick up something for lunch."

"Okay," I said, "but only if it's quick. I have a lot of work to do. Which you should know, since you assigned it to me."

"And who do we bill shopping at Saks to these days?" he asked. Note to self: must seriously consider moving computer screen so that it is out of the eyeshot of office visitors. Have been meaning to do so ever since a partner caught me reading a forwarded e-mail entitled: *Ladies, Learn to Love Your Fat Rolls,* but I forgot. Now, moving the computer screen was definitely in order.

"I wasn't shopping at Saks," I informed Jack, minimizing the screen as I did. "I was at Saks *dot com*. Big difference. In fact, sometimes there is entirely different merchandise on the Web site. You really need to be more precise if you want to be a good litigator, you know."

"Duly noted," he said as he motioned for me to come with him with a flick of his wrist.

"And anyway," I said, grabbing my pocketbook from underneath my desk, "I suppose that it would be the same billing code that you and your friends use for your fantasy football league." (Because I already *was* a good litigator.)

"Clever," Jack said, opening the door to my office for me and following me out. "But the relationships I foster with my colleagues will pay off later tenfold. A fantasy football league is the equivalent of playing golf with your business contacts. You see, all of those lawyers at various large firms throughout the city will someday be CEOs, CFOs and in-house counsel to some of the country's largest and most important corporations. And when the time comes, I won't even need to go out looking for business—the business will simply come to me. All because of my fantasy football league. So, I should really be billing that to client development."

"Wow," I said as Jack stuck his arm out to hold the elevator door open for me.

"You see, Brooke, I already am an *excellent* litigator," he said, and pressed the button for the lobby. Touché. "So, what do you feel like eating?"

"I'll have whatever you want," I replied. "I'm easy."

"I was going to get a chicken parm sub at the pub around the corner. You feel like a sub?"

"How about sushi?" I asked.

We walked into the sushi place around the corner and I promptly informed Jack that I did not have time to eat there— we would have to get our orders to go—because I had so much work to do. That he had assigned me. (Read: go back to the office and call Douglas again.) But then Jack pointed out that sushi really is best when it's fresh. Which is totally true. So, we got a table near the window and sat down to eat. But I ate very, very quickly because, as I told Jack, I really, truly, deeply wanted to get back to the office to get my work done. That he had assigned me. Because really, I can be very conscientious when I want to be.

After a much-needed lunch break with Jack (What? Getting back your man can be hard work!), I got back to my desk at 2:00 p.m., and Douglas's secretary's story had not changed. I was perplexed. If Douglas had so many meetings, how did the man find the time to meet another woman, start dating said other woman, fall in love and get engaged? That guy really knew how to manage his time.

As I plotted out my next move, the phone rang. I checked the caller ID and it came up as Anonymous. I normally don't pick up the telephone at work unless I recognize the number, preferring instead to let my secretary pick it up and announce the caller, but Douglas's calls usually came in as Anonymous, so I dove for the phone.

"Brooke Miller," I said, trying to sound sweet and professional, like the kind of woman a man would most definitely want to get back together with and take to her ex-boyfriend's wedding.

"Hi, is this Brooke Miller?" a voice asked. I didn't recognize it. I couldn't believe I'd wasted a good "Brooke Miller" on a voice I didn't recognize.

"Yes," I said, already flipping my computer screen back on and checking my e-mail.

"My name is Jessica Shevitz Rauch and I do attorney placement. Do you have some time now to talk?"

It's such a funny question to ask a litigator when she's at work. Time to talk. A litigator *never* has time to talk unless it's billable. Granted, I hadn't done any billable work all day, but the point was that I did not, in fact, have time to talk to this woman. My nonbillable time today was being spent on plotting ways to get back my man and shopping online for outfits that would assist me in getting back said man.

And I love the term *attorney placement.* It's as if they think that even though you're smart enough to graduate law school, pass the New York bar and become an attorney, you won't get the fact that they're headhunters. Headhunters start calling attorneys at big firms the minute you walk in the door, offering promises of smaller firms with better hours and perfect in-house counsel positions at prestigious corporations. It's good to know there are options, but more often than not the headhunters just want to move you to some other big firm and take their thirty-percent cut of your vastly overblown salary.

"Sorry, I don't have the time," I said, picking up a nail file from my desk and fixing a crack in my thumbnail.

"Maybe some other time?" she asked. "Let me ask you, are you still happy at Gilson Hecht?"

"Yes," I said, "for now I am. But, I suppose you can always hold on to my number. Thanks for calling."

I hung up the phone and realized that I filed my thumbnail into a strange hexagonal shape. Figuring that I had the rest of the evening to get some really good billable work done/get back my man, I dashed out to the nail place around the corner from my office.

Five o'clock—one manicure, pedicure and ten-minute mini-massage later—and Douglas's secretary was still standing firm. I should never have encouraged him to get her such an expensive Christmas gift last year. If I'd let him give her the $10 Godiva truffles he wanted to give instead of insisting on the $100 facial gift certificate at Elizabeth Arden, I'd be talking to Douglas right now.

Tap, tap, tap.

Tap, tap, tap, splat! All over my best going out/getting back your man pants. Ugh. No wonder my dry cleaner wears a fur coat in the winter. It's not what you're thinking, though. It was one of those fancy desk pens. I think that they are, by their very nature, much more delicate than those regular pens.

Six o'clock and at last, I got a different story from the gate-keeper. Douglas was (finally!) not in another meeting. He had left for the day. I threw a Bic across my office, hitting the door. (It didn't break. I told you so.)

One more nonbillable hour later, at 7:00 p.m., I decided to call him at home. That was it! I would leave him a sweet, sexy message saying that I forgave him, and suggest that to celebrate, we should go to California for Trip's wedding. Perfect. I shut the door to my office and practiced what I would say to the answering machine.

I dialed the number—my old phone number—and waited for the answering machine to pick up. I knew that he wouldn't be home since he usually met up with clients for drinks after work. He didn't have a cell phone that I could call because he didn't own one. Douglas considered using cell phones rude. Now, I can't help but laugh—apparently for Douglas, speaking on a cell phone in public is rude, but sleeping with another woman when you're living with someone else is, on the other hand, perfectly acceptable in polite society.

"Hello?" a female voice answered. Who the hell was picking up our telephone? Someone had broken into our apartment. I had to call the police! "Police, a cat burglar has broken into my old apartment, and is answering the phone!"

"Gilson Hecht?" the cat burglar asked into the phone. How did she know where I was calling from? My goodness, the burglar was psychic! "Police, a *psychic* cat burglar has broken into my old apartment!"

Using my superlitigator powers of deduction, I soon realized that the firm's name and number must have come up on caller ID. I quickly hung up the phone as Beryl was still saying "Hello? Hello?" (Yes, my super litigator skills told me that, too.)

Beryl. Is that woman using my phone? The very phone I bought for Douglas? Well, didn't exactly buy for him, but the phone I totally used when I lived there! Has she moved in already? God, that man moves fast! He and I at least waited a month!

By 7:30 p.m., I had plan B in effect: I would reconvene a special court session at our local watering hole to discuss the matter further and figure out a plan C. Yes, plan B consisted solely of gathering the troops—Vanessa and Jack—but give me a break! I was under a lot of stress here!

After picking Vanessa up at her office, we sneaked down the back stairwell so as to avoid any partners who might catch us leaving before we had actually collapsed from exhaustion. We got to the gym at Public School 142 just in time to slip in for the last few minutes of the firm intramural basketball game against the lawyers from Arby Schweitzer.

The bleachers were completely empty, so Vanessa and I took front-row seats. The gym floor was scattered with briefcases and Redwelds full of documents with a row of BlackBerries lined up perfectly on the front-row bench. Jack's BlackBerry stood out in the crowd since one of his nieces had decorated it with Strawberry Shortcake stickers so that he would never lose it.

Vanessa sat down on the bleachers quietly and tucked her bag underneath her legs. I, on the other hand, sat down and knocked over the entire row of BlackBerries, which fell tumbling to the gymnasium floor like a set of very expensive dominoes. None of the Gilson Hecht associates seemed to care, since our firm pays for its unfettered 24/7 access to its associates, but judging from the looks on the Arby Schweitzer team's faces, I got the feeling that their firm did not. As I crawled on the floor picking them up as subtly as I could, I saw Jack give me a tiny smile and a slight wave. He was wearing a Gilson Hecht T-shirt with a long sleeve T-shirt underneath and had the sleeves pushed all the way up to his elbows. Jack had a million freckles covering his arms, but barely any on his face.

The score was tied and there were just a few minutes left on the clock. I puzzled over Jack's choice of crunch-time lineup: rounding out his usual starters (the two other attorneys in our department who were over six feet tall), he had Billie Cooper, a fourth-year corporate associate and Bob Frohman, a second-year tax associate, on the court.

While Billie Cooper was the tallest girl in the entire corporate department standing at five foot nine, I knew that she frequented the nail place around the corner from our office almost as often as I did. Now, I'm no basketball player, but I'm pretty sure that you need to use your hands to do it. Although I did meet Michael Jordan once and he had lovely hands. But, I digress.

Bob Frohman from tax was so timid, I could swear that I'd never actually heard him speak. And I had a sneaking suspicion that half of the tax department hadn't, either. At five foot four, even Billie was taller than him. When I would pass him in the hallways at work, he always looked as if he was terrified of his own shadow. At a large law firm, that sort of thing could be considered normal what with how stressful the work is, but Bob looked that way all the time. I once saw him at another tax associate's birthday party and there he stood, in a corner all night, looking downright scared, speaking to no one the entire time. I imagined that if you ever did speak to him, no sound would come out of his mouth. Or, if it did, he would have nothing else to discuss but the Internal Revenue Code. I could not, for the life of me, figure out why Jack had put him in the game at such a crucial moment.

The ball was in play, and I sat forward on my seat, anxious for a Gilson Hecht victory.

Two minutes left on the clock.

I called out, "Defense," and Vanessa shot me a dirty look. (Even though everyone knows that when you have courtside seats, you simply *have* to yell out "defense.") Billie was holding her own on the court—paired against an Arby Scheweitzer attorney who towered over her, she managed to block a few shots. Even Vanessa was moved to lean over and quietly tell me how well she thought Billie was playing. (Vanessa never really did get into the spirit of courtside seats.) The clock was down to a minute and Billie stole the ball from the player she was defending and passed it to Jack. He practically flew up the court toward the Gilson Hecht basket, leaving the Arby Schweitzer attorneys in his wake.

Vanessa and I sat forward in our seats, ready for Jack's big slam dunk. He got all the way down the court and paused for a moment. The breath was caught in my chest as I puzzled over just what Jack was doing. He dribbled and then passed the ball. Passed the ball to Bob Frohman. To Bob Frohman? What on earth was he doing? Was he losing the game on purpose? Was he trying to lose a bet?

Thirty seconds left on the clock.

Bob looked just as confused as everyone else as he caught the ball (barely).

"You got it, Bob," Jack said with a nod, as he looked on and threw his long arms out to block an opposing player.

Bob bounced the ball down once and then went for it. He threw it up toward the basket and everyone whipped their heads around to see if it would go in or not. The ball circled the rim, slowly, taking its time, like the tiny silver ball on a roulette wheel. The clock buzzer rang, signifying the end of the game, and everyone looked on, watching the ball go round and round. Everyone was frozen, heads tilted up, waiting for the final verdict.

The room stayed silent until, finally, the ball fell through the hoop with a tiny whoosh and the Gilson Hecht team erupted into a chorus of screams and yells. Everyone was screaming, jumping (myself included, and even Vanessa)—everyone except Bob. He stood frozen, still looking at the basket, not registering that it had actually gone in. The team dove into a huge group hug, and Jack grabbed Bob to get him in on it. At first tentative, Bob quickly fell into it, smiling and laughing. Jack directed the team to all put their hands into the center of the circle as he counted down from three.

"Three, two, one," he called out as the team joined him in screaming, "Gilson Hecht!"

Jack led the team in shaking the hands of the Arby Schweitzer players and then off the court. Bob looked like a kid in a candy store as he lined up to shake the other players' hands.

Vanessa and I rushed up to congratulate Jack.

"How did you know he would make it?" I asked Jack as he threw a towel onto his head.

"I didn't," he said, as he disappeared into the men's locker room. Ten minutes later, he reemerged with a wet head and we were off to our local watering hole.

This being New York, our local watering hole was actually the bar of a fabulously trendy new midtown hotel. It boasted views of the Empire State Building and Central Park, but New Yorkers are far too cool to act as if they care about such things. After all, someone might—gasp!—mistake you for a tourist.

For a mere eighteen dollars, you can have a martini so fancy, it even comes with a little orchid floating on top. Unless you order the apple martini. That one comes with an apple slice. Or a chocolate martini. That one comes with a Hershey's Kiss on top. But you get what I mean.

Only open for two weeks, already, the place was generating a huge buzz over the waitresses walking around clad only in slips. I was unsure if the fuss was about the women being nearly nude, or if it was offensive merely because slip dresses are totally out of fashion.

"Beryl moved in already," I told them once we had secured a prime table near the window, overlooking the Empire State.

"So what?" Vanessa said. "You were too good for that piece of trash anyway. Let him have someone on his own level." She set her enormous black Louis Vuitton work bag on the extra chair at the table.

"I agree," Jack said, setting his Redweld full of discovery requests down on the extra chair next to Vanessa's bag and putting his navy sports jacket on the back of his own. "Good riddance to bad garbage."

"Yeah," Vanessa continued, "Beryl isn't even a name!"

"I don't really think that we should be making judgments based on the poor girl's name, though," Jack said.

"No matter what her name is," Vanessa explained, "we automatically hate her. We love Brooke, we hate Beryl. That's just the way it is."

The waitress came to our table. Vanessa ordered an apple martini and I ordered a French martini. Truth be told, I didn't very much care for the taste of it, but it came adorned with that little flower, which I loved. Jack opted for a beer. A very fancy and expensive beer, but a beer nonetheless. Jack always told us that guys who went to college in the Midwest order beer as a matter of course—as if it were some sort of religious thing or a condition of keeping your diploma from the University of Michigan in good standing. Jack offered up his credit card to begin a tab, which he also always assured us was another throwback to good old-fashioned Midwestern values. Even though he, himself, grew up in the suburbs of Philadelphia.

"Why were you even calling him?" Jack asked. "Hasn't he done enough damage already?"

"I thought I'd try to get him back so that we could go to Trip's wedding together and I could keep my dignity ever-so-slightly intact and things could be perfect again."

"But, Brooke, they weren't perfect before," Jack said. I turned to him to find him looking me dead in the eye. I had to turn away from his gaze.

"And, anyway," Vanessa said, "what is he? Cattle? Get him? How very cavewoman of you, Brooke." She adjusted her bateau-neck cashmere sweater as the waitress set our eighteen-dollar martinis down on the table.

"Get back *my man,*" I explained, pulling my hair out of its bun and pushing it behind my ears.

"How very country-western of you," Jack said, taking a sip of his beer.

"Look, it's not like there is some law saying that you have to go to your ex-boyfriend's wedding or something," Vanessa tried to reason. "In fact, there should be a law against it. Save yourself the pain. I won't go, either, if you want. Do you really think that his ice-queen bride even wants you there?"

"Actually, I've heard that she's really very nice," I said, removing the flower from my drink and setting it on the napkin.

"Yes, if I was a stunning Academy Award–nominated actress with noble blood, I'm quite certain that I would be, what did you call her, nice, as well." Way to help out my ego, there, Vanessa. "She does have a title, doesn't she?"

"I forget," I said, my eyes floating over to the view.

"She's a countess," Jack chimed in, sipping his beer. "Or an empress. Some 'ess.' I'm not sure exactly what."

"Not helping," I said under my breath. I fingered the cocktail napkin that was under my drink.

"I saw this whole special on her on *Entertainment Tonight* when she was nominated for that Oscar last year," Jack explained.

"Still not helping," I said a little louder. I ripped my cocktail napkin in two pieces. And then in four.

"Oh, my God, I totally saw that, too!" Vanessa exclaimed.

"Yeah, she's part of the royal family of some obscure Asian country," Jack continued. Jiaolong, to be exact. A tiny island-nation nestled between China and Taiwan, population just under fifty thousand; native language: Mandarin Chinese; main export: fish. Not like I Googled her or her country or anything. Who doesn't know Jiaolong?

"Can we get back to me, please!" I said, my napkin now in eight pieces. "What am I going to do about this wedding? I RSVP'd yes and it's in two weekends. It is, like, totally rude to cancel now. They probably already have their count in." I took a big swig of my martini for effect.

"Well," Vanessa said, sipping hers, "it's not like Trip isn't rich enough to pay for one extra person who doesn't come."

I guess she was right. I could just go to the wedding by myself. I mean, who needs to have a man on your arm when you are a woman of the new millennium? In many ways, having the right pair of shoes is much more important for an ex-boyfriend's wedding than having a man on your arm. I mean, can having a man on your arm make your feet look so cute you could die? I don't think so. Can having a man on your arm make you look three and a half inches taller, thus making you look like a svelte five-foot-eight supermodel as opposed to the five-foot-four-and-a-half little shrimp you truly are? No. Can having a man on your arm make your butt and thighs look ten pounds thinner? I think not! So, I ask you: Who needs to have a man on her arm?

Okay, I didn't even convince myself on that one.

"Two," I pointed out, placing the sixteen pieces of my cocktail napkin back on the table. A slip-dress-clad waitress skimmed by our table, knocking my napkin bits to the floor like pieces of confetti. I grabbed for them, but they slipped through my fingers.

"Two extra people," Vanessa continued, without missing a beat. "He's only, like, one of the biggest agents in Hollywood."

"Exactly," Jack agreed, "and it's not like his fiancée Ava, the empress or countess or whatever she is, is hurting for cash."

"Still not helping!" I said, lifting Jack's beer to make a play for his cocktail napkin. "I get it. My ex is fabulously successful and wealthy and is marrying a woman who is fabulously successful and wealthy."

"And hot," Jack said. Hot? I suppose she was okay-looking if you consider that whole petite-dancer's-body-with-flawless-alabaster-skin-long-flowing-black-hair-and-face-of-an-angel thing attractive.

"And has a title," Vanessa said.

"Not! Helping!"

"And here you are with no boyfriend, no ring, and no Oscar nomination," Vanessa said, patting my head as if I were a child who had just lost her school's spelling bee.

"That pretty much sums it up," I agreed. "Can we get some more cocktail napkins here?" I asked the scantily clad waitress who was now delivering round two.

"Come on!" Jack said. "You are a brilliant attorney at one of the largest and most prestigious firms in New York City. You have a wonderful family, and, if I do say so myself, wonderful friends. In your spare time you volunteer at a nursing home. *That's* our Brooke. *That* pretty much sums it up."

Jack was right. I was a big-time lawyer at a big-time law firm.

I had a wonderful family and friends. And I volunteered at a nursing home, to boot! Sometimes I forgot how wonderful I truly was. Although, I hadn't really had time to volunteer much, what with my caseload and all. And that sort of thing isn't billable. But I really think that it's the thought that counts with those things.

"Wait!" Vanessa cried, putting both hands on the table as if she was about to yell out *Eureka!* or *Bingo!* or something equally as thrilling. "That's perfect. You can tell Trip that you can't go because of your volunteering duties at the nursing home!"

"Oh, yes," I said. "Hi, Trip, I can't make it to your wedding because I have to play Yahtzee with the elderly."

Vanessa removed her hands from the table and admired the view.

"Just don't go," she said, head still turned out to the Empire State.

"That is not an option."

"People get sick, don't they?" she asked, head still turned. "Just pretend you're sick."

"Yes," Jack said, "she can say that she caught something fierce spending all that time at the nursing home."

"Okay, then," Vanessa said, turning her head back to the table, "you should totally pay some hot escort dude to go and pretend to be Douglas. It would be hysterical. We could totally pretend that Douglas has a title, too! The wedding's out in California, so it's not like anyone would know! He does have an accent, after all."

"Just because you have an accent, you think that people assume that you're royalty?" I asked.

"Douglas certainly acted as if he thought he was royalty," Jack said.

"No," Vanessa explained, "an accent just makes it less of a stretch."

"Yes," Jack said, "and with all of those Hollywood egomaniacs there, it's not like anyone would really notice you, anyway. You could just be the stunning, mysterious lawyer with the international man of mystery on your arm."

"In a skirt," I pointed out.

"In a skirt," Vanessa said, lifting her arms to the table again.

"But with a title," Jack said.

"With a title," Vanessa sang.

"This could actually work, you know," I said, gulping down the contents of martini number two. I think I may have gulped the flower, too, in my haste.

"Yeah," Vanessa laughed, finishing her martini, too, "except for the fact that I was totally kidding!"

"No, really," I said, "this could totally work. This is the solution," I said, motioning for our waitress to come over.

"No more martinis for you," Jack said.

"He's right. No more martinis for me," I said to the waitress. "Three shots of Southern Comfort, please."

"And exactly where do you think you will be able to find this hot escort dude on such short notice?" Vanessa asked.

"And, more importantly," Jack asked, "did we learn nothing from *Risky Business?*"

"Well, then, I won't use a hot escort dude," I explained.

"You won't do it at all because it is totally insane!" Vanessa laughed.

I looked at Jack.

"Oh, I know that look," he said. "Don't even think about it."

But I kept looking at him. With that look. You know that look. That look of seduction. That look that you use to get what you want, when you want it. The type of look you'd use at the post office when you really, really, really need to get your package out that day and they tell you that you filled out the wrong form and you have to go back and get it and you do, only, you really, really, really don't want to wait on the line again, so you sort of smile that smile and pray that the man will take pity on you/want to sleep with you/think you'll like him if he'll be nice to you. That look.

"That's the look she gives word processing when she wants her job to get done before everyone else's," Jack said.

"That's the look she gives at Bergdorf's when she wants the salesman to pull out every size nine that's on sale," Vanessa said.

"What?" he asked.

"Oh, just look at her feet, man. Run while you have the chance!"

"You *are* a frustrated actor, Jackie…." I explained, hanging a little too long on the pronunciation of each word. The sweet talk is a quintessential part of the look. Although I wouldn't recommend using that part at the post office. For the post office, the mere look itself usually suffices.

But it was true. Jack was one of those lawyers who started out thinking that it was a day job (never mind those silly people who actually dream of becoming a lawyer). Jack made a deal with himself (and his father) after graduating college with a joint degree in drama and English—he would give his childhood dream of acting two years. If he wasn't a success (read: couldn't pay the rent on his fifth-floor walk-up studio apartment), he would go to law school and become a lawyer like his father, the federal judge for the Eastern District of Pennsylvania, wanted him to be. Even though he spent his two years after graduation waiting tables and going on countless auditions, he never made it big, getting only enough jobs to give him hope, but not enough to actually pay his bills. To his father's delight, Jack reluctantly made good on his end of the deal and went to law school once his two years were up.

Jack enrolled in his father's alma mater and didn't look back, throwing himself into the law as vehemently as he did everything else in his life. I always thought that he had to throw himself in with as much vigor as he could in order to make himself forget that it wasn't what he truly wanted to do. He made Law Review, Moot Court, got his Student Note published, and was the president of the Student Bar Association. And he somehow still managed to be in the top ten percent of his class. Vanessa and I made Law Review at our law school, too, but it was only because we didn't do anything else besides study. And shop for shoes, but back then, such trips were considerably less intense than they are nowadays, what with our student budgets. What? You need to release your law-school stress *somehow*.

But Jack still was—and I guess probably always would be, beneath the navy sports jacket—an actor at heart. In going to law school, he discovered that the natural place for any frustrated actor is in the courtroom. He became a litigator in the vain hope that someday he would be in a courtroom where he could dramatically yell: "I'm out of order? You're out of order! This whole courtroom is out of order!" (When in reality, we litigators know that it's much more likely that you'd exclaim: "You want the truth? You can't handle the truth!")

"Let me get this straight," Jack said. "I told you that I would save the day and go with you to this wedding."

"Yes," I said.

"And you said no," he said.

"Well, if you want to be technical about it," I said. I couldn't believe he was being so difficult. Didn't he feel bad about the whole kissing-a-junior-associate thing? How quickly they forget. Men can be so insensitive sometimes.

"But now you want to go to this wedding with me, pretending to be Douglas?"

"Did we not explain the power of an accent to you? Anyway, Trip is expecting me and my skirt-wearing boyfriend, not me and some other guy."

"No way in hell," he said, turning away. He grabbed his shot of Southern Comfort and downed it.

"Come on! It would be a great role for you. Great practice."

"Brooke, you have officially lost your mind," Vanessa offered.

"And offended me," Jack offered, but neither of us was really listening to him.

"Pleeeeease?"

"Luckily for me, I don't act anymore," Jack said, brushing his shaggy hair out of his eyes. Was that his strongest argument? He was going to have to try harder than that.

"Pretty pleeeeease?"

"And even if I did, I certainly would never condescend to play Douglas of all people," he said.

"Pretty pleeeeease with sugar on top?"

"That fact, coupled with the fact that I also hate L.A., makes it highly unlikely that you will be able, within the course of the next two weeks, to convince me to go with you to L.A. and perpetrate a fraud on the entire Scottish community."

"So your answer is no?" I asked, eyelashes batting. For the record, I never had this much trouble at the post office.

"No," he said, turning away from me and leaving the table for effect.

Famous last words.

8

"So, how long have you two been married?" a very old man with a neon-blue mohawk asked us. I think he was the owner of the shop.

"We're not," I said, looking at Jack and laughing. He smiled back at me, tugging at the kilt he had just tried on.

"If we're not," Jack whispered a little too close to my ear, "then how'd you manage to get me out of my pants?"

"Like it was difficult," I said back, pushing him away from me, still looking at him in the mirror. I was trying not to stare too hard at his bare legs.

Stop staring at Jack's legs.

I instead focused upon the fact that the firm "frowns upon" (read: fires) associates who date one another. Ever since those two summer associates got caught in a compromising position in the cafeteria late one night and that lovely rumor made its way into the *New York Law Journal* (*Gilson Hecht Summer Associates Make the Most of Their Summer Associate Experience,* the headline read), the firm has been hypersensitive about associates dating and the reputation the firm might derive therefrom. Since then, any time the firm got the slightest hint of impropriety among associates, Danielle Lewis, the head of the corporate department and all-around terrifying partner, would take you out for lunch and scare you straight. If lunch with Danielle Lewis didn't do the trick, word on the street was that the next time Ms. Lewis visited your office, she would be accompanied by a Gilson Hecht security guard and your last paycheck.

And this is the year Jack is up for partner. Must try not to get Jack fired in the year he is up for partner.

Stop staring at Jack's legs.

Must remember that Jack is totally on the rebound. Thus, even if you started dating Jack and got yourself fired from the firm, it would still never last. It never lasts when you're the rebound girl.

Although rebound sex is hot. Yum. Stop thinking about sex! Must remember that even if you had totally hot rebound sex and ended up dating Jack and getting fired, you would find yourself three and a half years later without a wedding date set. You'd have your heart broken again, but with the added bonus of also collecting unemployment.

As I puzzled over how much one could reasonably expect to make on unemployment, I watched Jack pull the kilt down over and over in a vain attempt to make it longer. Try as he might, and my goodness, he was trying, the kilt did not get any longer.

Stop staring at Jack's legs!

Remember you are trying to get back together with Douglas. This task will be infinitely more difficult if you start dating Jack. Especially since Douglas knows all about your history with Jack.

"It's crap," Jack said, touching the kilt's fabric as he looked at himself in the mirror.

"But it looks great," I said, smoothing it out.

"Why are we doing this again?" he asked me for the fortieth time in forty-eight hours.

"You are doing this because it will be the role of your lifetime and any good actor worth his salt knows how to do accents. I'm doing it because I'm trying to keep my dignity ever-so-slightly intact."

"And are you doing that?" he asked.

"Anyway," I said, ever so deftly changing the conversation, "it'll be like a big real-life acting workshop for you, with art totally imitating life, to boot."

"Did you answer my question?"

"I also think that you really need to spend some quality time with Marcus. I mean, Vanessa is one of your best friends and you barely know her husband."

"*Vanessa* barely gets to spend any quality time with Marcus. It's a miracle that *she* even knows him."

"Are you two finding everything all right?" the man with the mohawk asked us.

"Everything's fine," Jack assured him.

"You two really make a delightful couple," he said. Even with the fluorescent mohawk, he still looked like every other old man I've met. He was beginning to remind me of Mr. Rosenblatt, my grandmother's "friend." Though I was twenty-five years old at the time, my mother was afraid to tell me that my grandmother had found someone new after my grandfather died, so she called old Irving Rosenblatt my grandmother's "friend." Or maybe it was just because she just didn't want me to feel bad that my grandmother had found a single man faster than I had.

"When are you popping the question?" Mr. Mohawk whispered to Jack a little too loudly.

"Just as soon as I think she'll say yes," Jack said, eyes on me. He wasn't smiling, but I'm sure he was joking. He had just broken off an engagement six months ago, and since then, he's always had a million girls hanging around him. He's even more of a cad than Douglas! Well, maybe that's unfair—Jack had never been living with one woman and engaged to another at the same time. As far as I know.

I don't know why I ever even told Douglas the story about what happened between Jack and me; it only served to fuel the superiority complex Douglas had over Jack—he had succeeded in winning me over where Jack had failed—but I think that at the time, I was trying to best Douglas's "wildest place you ever had sex" story. Douglas's was in the bathroom at a wedding at the Rainbow Room with a bridesmaid he had just met. I now realize that for him, a black-tie affair means easy access.

Since Jack and I never slept together, my story was a bit anticlimactic, but it was a lame attempt to show Douglas that I, too, had had my share of wild spontaneous moments.

Jack and I were on our way back from depositions in South Carolina, racing to the airport in a rental car that smelled like cheap cologne and cigarettes. I had the windows down and was breathing in as much fresh suburban air as I could before getting onto the plane. We had just had an amazing day—Jack had gotten all of the testimony he needed from the witness and some he didn't even expect the witness to give up. At lunch, we had called the partner in charge of the case, who was elated, telling Jack that his performance would get the firm's membership talking about his partnership prospects.

It was after six o'clock, and we were rushing to catch the last flight of the evening out of Columbia, South Carolina. Columbia, from what I had seen in the twenty-four hours prior, was not exactly the type of place you wanted to stay any longer than you had to. When we'd checked into our hotel the night before, the receptionist said to Jack and me "I've never met a Jew before," as easily as if she'd said, "I've never met an alien before," or, even closer still, "I've never met the devil before." When you live in New York, you don't realize that for other parts of the country, that can be a perfectly acceptable topic of conversation.

The traffic was behaving for quite some time on the express-way and it felt like nothing could bring us down. Nothing, that is, until we hit the approach to the airport. About three miles from the airport, the traffic came to a standstill. An absolute dead halt. We tried to keep our cool for a while, him—trying to convince me that the traffic would break any second and that we would make our flight, me—playing with the radio, trying to find "happy" music that would make us forget the traffic altogether. We talked about taking shortcuts, experimenting with the service road, and that seemed to give us hope for a while. Except for the fact that we had no idea where we were and couldn't afford to waste any time getting lost.

I finally found a classic rock station that was playing one Doors song after the other. I let it play. The people in the car next to ours yelled over to us to find out what station we were listening to. I told them and they tuned into the Doors also. They got out of their car and started dancing along to "Hello, I Love You." I turned to look at Jack but he was unamused. He was on his cell phone trying to get through to the airline. Jack hated to work a second longer than he had to and was dead set on getting us home that night. I myself had already given up on any thoughts of getting home that night, consoling myself with the fact that I would be billing the client for all of my time. Other cars were listening to traffic radio and screaming reports out their windows ("Jackknifed tractor-trailer one mile up—sounds like we'll be here awhile—anyone got a Snickers?")

"L.A. Woman" came on the radio and I started to dance in my seat. All of the cars around us had emptied out and their owners were milling about the expressway, meeting other drivers and sitting on each other's hoods. It was already dark. The cars were all in park, and some were even starting to turn their headlights off.

"I'm getting out," I said to Jack and hopped on the hood of our rental car. It was the end of March and one of those first nights that promise the coming of spring with a little kiss of warm weather. I took a deep breath and enjoyed the fresh air.

"What are you doing?" Jack called to me from the inside of the car.

"Billing Janobuilder Corp. for my time. Only it's more fun to do it out here, watching the stars." I heard Jack's car door open. I took off my suit jacket and threw it into my window as Jack joined me on the hood, taking his jacket off, too, and loosening his tie.

"It's beautiful out here," he said and I nodded in agreement. "But what do we do if we're still out here when the traffic starts back up?"

"I don't think we're going to have to worry about that," I said, looking at my watch. According to my count, we'd been outside waiting for twenty minutes already. A gentle drizzle started to drop and the crowd cheered as if Jim Morrison himself had descended from the heavens and brought the rain with him. I put my hands out to feel the drops while Jack tried to cover his head. Jack, seeing that his fight with the drizzle was futile, finally gave in to the night and started to show me some constellations. Somewhere between the Big Dipper and my zodiac sign, we saw our plane leave for New York City without us.

We got back to the hotel around 9:00 p.m. and the only place still serving food was the piano bar in the lobby. The singer was dripping from the piano, dressed from head to toe in red satin and black lace like a modern day Mae West, with the cleavage to really back it up. From the looks of things, it seemed as if she and her piano player had a thing going on. Jack and I sat at the bar and ate burgers and drank beers and started to sing along as best we could with Mae's showtunes. Only Jack didn't really know any of the words, so I had to quickly tell him each line of the song—from *Cats* to *Pippin*—before it played. He kept leaning in real close, way too many beers on his breath, and I would whisper the lyric, way too loud, into his ear. The piano player moved on to *West Side Story* and Jack's face lit up—announcing to anyone at the bar who would listen that he played Tony in high school. He and Mae did a daring rendition of "America" before Mae took "A Boy Like That" as a solo. Then it was Jack's turn to shine. Mae sat down on the piano bench while the piano player cued up Jack's big number. Jack sang "Maria" to me in perfect pitch, except on the parts where he should have said "Maria," he instead inserted "Brooke Miller."

"Brooke Miller, I just met a girl named Brooke Miller. And suddenly that name will never be the same to me!"

He came over to the bar and grabbed me to dance. He held me close to his chest, my hand in his.

"Brooke Miller, I've just kissed a girl named Brooke Miller, and suddenly I found how wonderful a sound can be." He twirled me around and then sat me back on my bar stool.

"Brooke Miller, say it loud and there's music playing," he sang to me, "say it soft and it's almost like praying. Brooke Miller," he sang, leaning in tight for his big finish, "I'll never stop saying Brooke Miller, Brooke Miller, Brooke Miller. The most beautiful sound I ever heard, Brooke Miller!"

Is it any wonder that we ended up kissing by the time the bar closed? Truth be told, I'd secretly wanted to do that all day. There was something very sexy about Jack doing his job all day. Doing his job *so well* all day. Who knew he was so smart?

The following Monday morning, Jack came into my office looking dead serious.

"Are you quitting or am I?" he asked me. I laughed and he didn't laugh back.

"No one's quitting anything," I said. "Don't be ridiculous!"

"I'm talking about…" he said, brushing the shaggy hair from his baby blues.

"The kiss," I said, cutting him off. "I know."

"Shhh!" he said, jumping up and slamming my office door shut. "Someone will hear you!" I couldn't help but laugh at how cute he was when he was trying to be serious. I had the sudden impulse to kiss him again.

"No one's going to hear me," I said, jumping on the desk and crossing my legs, trying to look seductive, like Heather Locklear in *Melrose Place*.

"One of us has to quit," he said, and as he got closer to me I wrapped my legs around him. "Are you listening to me?" I pulled him to me and tried to kiss him. He pulled away.

"No one has to quit," I said, still perched on the edge of my desk, legs now dangling over the side like a little girl whose chair is too high for her.

"You know the firm's policy," he said.

"I guess I don't care about it that much."

"Well, I do. We work on every case together. I don't want to get fired. My father would kill me," he said. "So, then, maybe you should quit."

"Me, quit?" I asked. "I just got here seven months ago! I'm not going anywhere! Maybe *you* should quit!"

"Okay, then. I'll quit."

"Oh, my God! You can't quit! Not because of me, anyway. Are you insane?"

"Well, what then?" he asked and I didn't know what to say.

I was still puzzling over it that day at lunch. As I sat at my usual table in the Gilson Hecht cafeteria with Vanessa and seven of our closest friends from the first-year associate class, all I could think about was Jack. Vanessa and one of our other friends were engaging in a lively debate about whether or not the fat-free balsamic vinaigrette the firm stocked at the salad bar was, in fact, fat free.

"Which is why," Vanessa summed up her case, "there is no possible way that the vinaigrette is fat free."

"Bet I know what you're thinking about," our friend Sandy whispered to me from across the table. I smiled and tried not to react, instead feigning interest in the Great Fat-Free Balsamic Dressing Debate. Sandy could be such a troublemaker when her billables were low and she didn't have a lot of work to do. "*Who* you're thinking about, I should say."

"I have no idea what you're talking about," I whispered back and put my head down into my salad. I took a bite and determined that Vanessa was right—there was no possible way that the dressing could actually be fat free.

"Jack," Sandy said out loud and the entire table turned to look at us. Everyone except for Vanessa.

"What about Jack?" I said, tearing my whole wheat roll in half. I dipped it into my dressing and took a bite.

"It's too late, Brooke," Sandy said, "everyone's talking about it."

"Talking about what?" I asked, looking her dead in the eye. When the vicious Denise Rosen turned her sights on me in the first grade, my father told me that the best way to get a bully to back down was to stare her dead in the eye and fight back.

"You and Jack," Sandy said simply, not backing down one iota. I then realized that it would take more than a firm stare to get a first-year litigator to back down as opposed to an insecure first grader. "Keith in the file room told Ilene in corporate that you guys were totally making eyes at each other when you brought your documents back from South Carolina on Saturday afternoon. And then Ben Harper's secretary saw you having a lover's quarrel in your office this morning."

"A what?" I said. "That's ridiculous." I couldn't believe how fast the gossip was circulating around the firm. At this rate, people in our San Diego office would know the news by 4:00 p.m., their time. Who else knew and how were people finding out so fast? Was this information up on the firm's Web site under the "What's New at the Firm" section or something?

"You know what?" Vanessa asked from the other side of the table. "We should have the dressing sent out to a lab for testing so that we can figure it out for once and for all. Then we could bring it up as a topic at the next associate's meeting." I looked at

Vanessa and for a second, actually deluded myself into thinking that the conversation could turn back to condiments.

"I can't believe you told Vanessa and you didn't tell us!" one of the girls yelled out. I can't remember who it was. The entire table turned toward Vanessa like an angry mob.

"Well, there isn't anything to tell right now," I said.

"Don't listen to them," Renee said from two seats down from me. "I think it's great. Who cares if this stupid firm has a policy or whatever? It's your life." Renee had recently told me that, despite the fact that we had only been at the firm for seven months, she was two months pregnant and planned to leave the firm entirely after she had her baby.

"That would be so embarrassing to be fired," another girl said.

"No one's getting fired," Vanessa said.

"Or, worse yet, you could end up like Cheryl in tax," Sandy said. I looked up and she was smiling slyly, like an arsonist about to light a match. Someone has *got* to get that girl some billable work. "When she broke up with Henry Kaplan in litigation, she had to see him every day. And now he's married with two kids and she's still single. And she still has to see him every day."

"She's not going to end up like Cheryl in tax!" Vanessa said. "Honey," she said, turning to me, "you're not going to end up like Cheryl in tax."

"Well, I, for one, think it's a bad idea," Lori said. "Remember when we went to that women's luncheon? All of the female partners said that you have to work very hard to be taken seriously when you're a woman."

"Only two people said that," a voice from the other side of the table said.

"That's because there are only four female partners at the firm," another voice replied. Everyone was speaking so quickly, I could barely tell who was saying what.

"You really should try to keep things secret with him for a while, though," another voice offered.

"But you can tell us, of course," another voice said. "We won't tell anyone."

The whole table kept talking, giving their opinions, until they all turned into a blur. "I think you should." "I think you shouldn't." "Who cares what you think!" They all spoke over each other, louder and louder, all the voices melting into one. The room began to spin.

"Everyone, stop it!" I said. The table became silent. It was just like in a movie. I spoke and everyone listened. It felt good to take charge of the situation. I would just tell everyone to calm down and to keep things quiet, and no one else would know a thing as I figured it all out for myself. I could make a clear, well thought out decision without the interference of any outside opinions.

As a smile crept onto my lips, I felt a presence behind me. Everyone at the table was staring, fake smiles frozen on their faces. I turned around to find Danielle Lewis, the head of the corporate department, standing behind my chair.

"Brooke," she asked, "are you free for lunch tomorrow? We should go for lunch."

And just as easily as it had begun, it was over. Five months later, Jack was engaged to a girl he met at a Knicks game the week after our trip to South Carolina.

Jack and Mr. Mohawk were still quietly whispering. Mr. Mohawk winked at Jack as he walked away from us.

"How come no one ever mistook Douglas and I for married when we were together?" I asked Jack. "We were together for two years."

"Maybe that's because you two never really made a very good couple."

"But tell me, Jack, how do you really feel?"

"They're all crap. I'm taking this one off," Jack said, turning on his heel.

"No!" I protested.

"Yes!" he said. "None of these are any good. Why are we shopping for this at a costume shop?" he asked.

"You know why," I said, making sure I was speaking softly enough that I would not offend Mr. Mohawk. "The kilts in the tuxedo rental place cost a fortune. This way is so much cheaper."

"Well, it certainly feels cheaper," he said, pulling the kilt off, revealing his boxers. They were faded blue chambray and they reminded me of a guy that I'd had a crush on in college. I felt as if I were staring, so I fixed my eyes on the various angel costumes hanging on the wall.

"Who cares what it feels like?" I said, pretending to be interested in a marabou halo. "It looks fine, and that's all that matters. Let's just pick a color."

"Maybe you should focus on what things really are and not just what they look like."

"What did you just say?" I asked, turning around to face him.

"Nothing. I'm putting on the navy one again," he said, disappearing into the fitting room. I walked past the angel costumes into the "Corner of Terror" and looked at the various instruments of torture.

"How's this one?" Jack asked. As I turned around, he struck his best Marilyn Monroe *Seven Year Itch* pose. A fan that had been put on the floor to blow air into a ghost's sails provided the gust of air he needed to make the kilt pop up as he held it down with his hands. I laughed.

"I think I like the red. Would you mind throwing that one on again?"

"Your wish is my command," Jack said. Hmmm. Maybe *that's* why he always has so many girlfriends. I mean, Jack isn't exactly the best-looking man in Manhattan, yet women always flock to him. He does have a good job, though, and anyone who can read can find out how much he makes since they print the salaries big firms pay every year in the *Law Journal*. Okay, I mean, he's not *bad* looking. I'm not saying he's bad looking. He has the kind of looks that grow on you. He's tall, so that's good, but it's not like he's movie star handsome or anything.

Douglas was movie star handsome. Not was, is. I mean, it's not as if he's dead or something. I only wished he were dead. When I wasn't wishing he'd get back together with me, that is.

I walked over to a lightsaber from the *Star Wars* display and picked it up.

"That's a Jedi lightsaber," a woman with a shaved head and a massive tattoo creeping up her neck said to me. "Leia never carried a Jedi lightsaber." She was wearing combat boots, a black wife beater and a camouflage skirt. The fishnet stockings and bloodred lipstick completed the look. Her name tag said Jennie.

As I turned to her, ready to give her my best "Luke, I am your father," Jack walked out of the dressing room with the red kilt on. And a gorilla mask on his head—one of those big ones that cover your head and neck completely. I practically fell over I was laughing so hard. Jack grabbed me and threw me over his left shoulder, making gorilla noises all the while. Jennie laughed like a schoolgirl. She must've heard the whole "your wish is my command" thing.

Jack's cell phone began to ring, and he rushed to pick it up with me still over his shoulder. Putting me and the gorilla head down, he answered the phone while I began to talk to Mr. Mohawk about price.

"Healthy Foods," Jack said, coming out of the dressing room fully dressed and throwing the navy kilt onto the counter with a half smile. "I've gotta get back to the office."

"Do I have to get back to the office, too?" I asked, praying that he would say no.

He hesitated. Never a good sign.

"But it's Saturday," I whined.

"A lawyer's work is never done," Jack said.

"You're a lawyer?" Jennie asked Jack. She had put a hot-pink boa around her shoulders and was working it for all it was worth.

"Tell you what," Jack said to me, "to make up for having to go to work, let me buy you a present. After all, we've forgotten the most important part of the costume." He reached over to a display of "Fun Rings" and started to sift through them. He first pulled out a ring that looked like a skeleton's head, shook his head *no* and continued to sift. Finding what he wanted, he handed it to Mr. Mohawk.

"On me," Jack said as he looked at me and handed the ring over to Mr. Mohawk. It was a silver ring with a round faux diamond. It even had tiny fake baguettes. Putting it on my finger, he said, "Consider yourself engaged."

"That's so romantic," Jennie swooned. Truth be told, I kind of swooned, too.

9

"This newfound stalking obsession of yours is going to get very costly," Vanessa said, putting a piece of grilled salmon in her mouth.

Vanessa and I were in the Grill Room at the Four Seasons, the fabulously fancy midtown institution where I knew Douglas took a lot of business contacts for lunch. I had called the restaurant earlier that morning, under the guise of being Douglas's secretary, to "confirm" his reservation, and then took the liberty of making a reservation for Vanessa and myself for thirty minutes before his reservation so that I could pretend that we *just so happened* to be there and bump into him. A dramatic reconciliation would then surely ensue.

"He's going to walk in any second. Try to act normal," I said, "and anyway, I'm paying, so what do you care?"

"You wouldn't let me order an appetizer," she said, as I tried to remember how that expression about a gift horse went.

"That's forty-three-dollar salmon you're eating," I said.

"I know," she said. "Try it, it's divine."

"Divine?" I said as she stuck a forkful into my mouth. "Who says *divine?*"

I took a moment to savor Vanessa's dish. The mustard crust gave just the perfect amount of spicy kick to the fish, which remained moist, even though it was cooked through completely.

It was divine. As was my braised beef, which I ate carefully, so as not to get any in my teeth. Vanessa was devouring her salmon, barely even bothering to look up at me as we spoke.

"What?" she said, as I gave her a not-so-subtle look. "I'm training for the marathon. I need my protein."

"The marathon's in November," I said.

"So?"

"It's April."

I was straining my neck to get a glimpse of everyone who walked in. I had flirted shamelessly with the maître d' to get a table angled just so, all the better with which to get a great view of the doorway. I'd then appealed to the girliness of our hostess to try to get her to tell me when Douglas's party walked in, goading her with details of his gorgeousness and how we were about to get back together and dramatically reconcile that very day.

I took another ladylike bite of my beef just as two fake blondes walked in. They were total throwbacks to the 1980s—big hair, long red acrylic nails and both simultaneously chewing and cracking their gum. They looked as if they could be extras in a Whitesnake video. I could hear their nasal voices from where I sat.

They were both wearing jeans, which was totally inappropriate for the Grill Room, where everyone else was in a suit. Granted, they were wearing $250 True Religion jeans, but it was still inappropriate. The older of the two, who wore her bangs low around the sides of her eyes so as to cover her crow's-feet, was wearing the pair with the rhinestones all over the backside, while the younger of the two, who wore an excessive amount of makeup that created a dark tan line around her ghastly white jawline, was wearing the pair that were ripped to shreds. I'd tried them on at Saks (for Saturday nights out at clubs, not to wear to the Four Seasons) and couldn't get my legs inside because my feet keep coming out of the ripped knee holes. I took that as a sign that I should not be wearing such jeans.

The hostess rushed over to our table to announce that the Mac-Gregor party had arrived.

Of course they had. That was Beryl and her mother. As upset as I was that I wouldn't be seeing Douglas, all I could think was: *He never sent my mother and me to the Four Seasons!*

"While I respect your lifestyle choice," the hostess said to me in a whisper, "I don't think that they're Scottish."

"That's not him," I said, crouching down into my seat. Vanessa continued making love to her salmon, completely oblivious to the carnage that was about to unfold before her.

I crouched farther down in my seat as the maître d' walked by with Beryl and her mother.

"We have to get the check," I whispered to Vanessa as I tried to subtly cover my face with my napkin.

"Why?" Vanessa said, still looking at her salmon.

"Beryl and her mother just walked in," I said, leaning into her. "They took Douglas's reservation. We've got to get out of here."

"I'm not done with my salmon yet," Vanessa said, looking up at me for the first time since her food had arrived. "And, anyway, how would she know what you even look like?"

"Oh, I don't know," I said, "perhaps it's because she threw out the picture of me and Douglas that was on his windowsill a week ago?" I vowed right then and there that if Vanessa dared to say, "Well, maybe she didn't look at it," I would spit right onto her beloved salmon.

"We'll get the check." Vanessa looked around for our waiter and made the international symbol for "get me my check, stat" to any waitstaff that walked by. Within minutes, our check had arrived, I'd paid it and we were ready to go.

Keeping my head down as I quietly got up from my seat, our waiter swept in and gave us pretty little boxes that contained the desserts we'd forgotten that we'd ordered. I whispered thanks to our waiter and in one fell swoop, grabbed my bag, my dessert and my jacket and swung my body around toward the door. I planned to skulk out quietly and completely undetected, head down even as I walked so that if anyone did happen to look my way, I couldn't be seen. What I didn't anticipate was that another waiter would be walking right behind me at that exact moment in time with a tray filled with dirty dishes.

Crash! Leftover salmon, chicken and beef were strewn across the floor. Their sauces had splashed all over the place and had even gotten the pant leg of the man sitting at the table next to ours.

"Oh, my goodness, I'm so sorry," I whispered, crouching down to help the waiter with his dishes. I was partially down on the ground in an effort to help, but I must admit that a teensy-tiny bit of me wanted to get down on the floor so that when the crowd of people eating in the Grill Room (read: Beryl and her mother) turned around to see who had caused all the ruckus, I would be out of sight.

"We're so sorry!" Vanessa said as five busboys rushed to the scene of the crime.

"Please, miss, let me help you," one of them said to me as he helped me to my feet. I couldn't figure out a classy way to say, "No, really, I'll just crawl out of the restaurant on my hands and knees," so I let him help me up.

Vanessa grabbed me by the arm and led me out. Out of the corner of my eye, I could see Beryl talking to her mother and pointing at me.

"So, how did the stalking go?" Jack asked me as he stood in my doorway after Vanessa and I got back to the office from lunch.

"Stalking?" I said. "Whatever do you mean?"

"The Four Seasons, Brooke?" Jack said. "You normally would only go to the Four Seasons when the summer associates are here and the firm is paying." True.

"Not very well," I said, "but I brought you my dessert." I handed him the fancy box filled with carrot cake, his favorite.

"Thanks," he said, sitting down in my visitor's chair. I opened my desk drawer and took out a plastic fork for him. "Now, that's what I call service. So, what are you working on?"

"Nothing," I said, turning my computer screen, as quickly as a thief who was about to be caught, "absolutely nothing."

"How are those discovery requests going?" he asked in between forkfuls.

"Well," I said, "I haven't exactly gotten to them yet. But I did find tons of awesome information about Scotland."

"Scotland?" he asked as I reached for the Redweld folder where I'd put all my work.

"Research, silly," I said, "for the wedding."

"What about research, silly," Jack said, "for our case?"

"Did you know that Scotland is composed of over 790 islands?"

"No," Jack said, "I did not know that."

"Well, it is," I said. "I put some of the info I found on index cards for you. They're color coded based on category—history, arts and culture, food and drink, places of interest and geography."

"Thanks," Jack said, leafing through the cards, "but maybe we should do the discovery requests before we research Scotland."

"And here's an outline of some info you'll need to know," I said, handing him a fifteen-page outline on all things Scotland, with the little Post-it flags I used to use on my casebooks in law school placed strategically on each section in the same palette as the index cards.

"I can't believe how much time you've wasted on this," he said, grabbing the outline and putting it in his lap, but not flipping through it.

"It's not a waste of time," I said. And I didn't think that it was. I was quite certain that in my quest to get back Douglas, random facts about his homeland would be helpful. I bet that Beryl didn't know the first thing about Scotland. "And anyway, this information will make you a more informed New Yorker."

"I'm informed enough," he said, putting his fork down to leaf through the pages upon pages of research. "I'd like to be a New Yorker with all of his discovery requests drafted."

"Did you know that April 6 is National Tartan Day?" I asked, as Jack turned to the section of the outline dedicated to history.

"No," he said, "I did not. Do you think that someone's going to quiz me on that at the wedding next week?"

"Perhaps," I said. "The Scottish Declaration of Independence was signed that day. The Declaration of Arbroath. Remember that."

"No one's going to ask stuff like that. They'll ask me about where I'm from and things like that," he said, grabbing the map

I'd printed out from www.visitscotland.com that I'd clipped to the front of the outline. "What city should I pick?"

"Douglas is from Perth," I said, "So, let's stick with that. The less lies, the better."

"Perth?" he asked. "Isn't there a Perth in Australia? Hey, it's located right near Dundee! Check that out!"

"Keep your eye on the ball, Jackie," I said. "We're only trying to master one country here."

"G'day mate!" he said, smiling like a little boy who had just told a little girl that her epidermis was showing.

"Don't say that at the wedding."

"What is this about the St. Andrews Society?" he asked, his finger on the Arts and Culture tab.

"Oh!" I said, excited that Jack had found the pièce de résistance. "It's a Scottish society, right here in New York!"

"I'm not joining a Scottish society," Jack said. "First of all, I'm not Scottish. I'm Jewish."

"Scots can be Jews. Anyway, you're not going to join," I said with a laugh. "We're going to go to their Cocktail Reception. Every year they have a reception just before the parade for Tartan Day."

"What?" Jack said. "Are you actually serious?" I could have sworn I saw him looking around my office for a hidden camera.

"Well, I really wanted to go to the Kirkin O'Tartan Ball, but there's no time. The St. Andrew's thing is tonight!"

"We have to work late tonight," Jack said.

"We'll stop by this thing, we'll meet a few people. You can totally learn about Scotland and brush up on your Scottish accent. Think of all the Scottish people who will be there!"

"You can tell me about it," Jack said. "I'm going to be drafting those discovery requests you neglected all week."

Oh, please. Was he trying to give *me* guilt? Was that his plan to get out of this? Rookie mistake.

A few hours later, Jack and I, against Jack's better judgment, were walking into the St. Andrews Society Cocktail Reception. Or, crashing, I should say, but no one seemed to mind. Vanessa was running late because she went home first to change. Even though I'd run to the cheap hair place around the corner from the firm to have my hair blown out straight on the off chance we'd run into Douglas, I was still back at the firm in time to walk over to the St. Andrews Society with Jack.

The Society was housed in an old prewar building with original marble and various Scottish artifacts encased in impressive-looking glass armoires everywhere you looked. The ceilings seemed to be three stories high, and various flags and tartans hung from sconces all along the walls. Douglas had never taken me to Scotland, but I presumed that the whole place was very Scottish.

"Gaelic name for Scotland?" I asked Jack as we grabbed two glasses of wine from a passing waiter.

"Alba," Jack said.

"Where is the stone of destiny?" I asked.

"Edinburgh Castle," he said. "What time did Vanessa say she'd be here?"

"Are you *not* enjoying my company?" I asked.

"No, I love being quizzed when I'm out at night," he said. "Did you bring the index cards, too?"

I knew he was making fun of me, so I said *no* even though I had stuffed them into my pocketbook before we left the firm.

"What Scottish sport is similar to the sport we know here in the States as hockey?" I asked.

"In the States?" Jack said.

"I'm very international," I said. "Do you know the answer?"

"Shinty," Jack said. "Here comes Vanessa."

Vanessa walked in, making an entrance as she did. Jack and I had, in the short time we were at the reception, realized that there were no actual Scotsmen at the St. Andrew's Society, rather, it was a society comprised entirely of Scottish Americans. So much for our evening of research. Vanessa was clearly as unaware of this fact as Jack and I were: heads turned as Vanessa walked in wearing an immense Vivienne Westwood skirt—layers upon layers of bright red tartan with strands of gold—with black platform Jimmy Choos that had a long satin ribbon that tied around her ankles.

"I'll have a water of life," Vanessa said to a passing waiter. Then, to us she whispered with a smile, "That's what the Scots call whiskey."

"Are *you* trying to pass yourself off as Scottish or something?" I asked.

"I'm just trying to embrace the culture, Brooke!" she said. "Are you getting good research on your accent, Jack?"

"Everyone here's American," he said.

"Well, that's unfortunate," Vanessa said.

"Look, guys," I said, "let's just have a drink, have a quick bite to eat, and then we can go home."

"So, Douglas isn't here?" Vanessa said.

"Try to look Scottish American," I said, ignoring her and taking a spin toward the buffet.

"Hi, I'm Duncan," a man said to me in line at the buffet as I tried to remember from my outline what haggis was made from.

"Brooke," I said and smiled. He smiled back, followed by an uncomfortable silence. We both reached for plates. I never did well with the whole uncomfortable silence thing. I'm not the type of girl who can just let the silence lie and be quiet. It always seemed to make me talk more, whether or not I actually had anything to say. "You know, Aberdeen is where Paris ought to be," I said, quoting Robert Louis Stevenson. He nodded without smiling and then muttered something about having to tend to his girlfriend.

"Do you want me to throw pearls like that into conversation at Trip's wedding?" Jack asked me over my shoulder.

"Robert Louis Stevenson said that," I said.

"Ah," he said.

"He wrote *Dr. Jekyll and Mr. Hyde,*" I said, defending myself with Stevenson's literary pedigree.

"And *Treasure Island,*" Jack replied. "I know. I read your outline while you were getting your hair done. I also know that the thistle is the symbol of all things Scottish. Actually a weed, the thistle is both a legend and a symbol—"

"Alexander Graham Bell invented the telephone," Vanessa said, coming from the opposite end of the buffet, "and Alexander Fleming invented penicillin. Both Scottish born."

"What?" I said.

"Oh," she replied. "I thought we were just quoting random bits of information from your outline." I sighed as we took our plates of food and found a little place to stand around and eat.

I hate when people at parties stay clustered together with only the people they came to the party with, but really, what are you supposed to do when you don't know anyone but your two friends? Vanessa, Jack and I wound up standing in a corner, balancing our plates filled with various Scottish delicacies (and also some cocktail franks) and glasses of wine in the other hand.

"We have to make it more natural at the wedding," I instructed Jack and Vanessa.

"Spouting out random bits of information on Scotland is never going to sound natural," Vanessa said.

"Yeah," Jack said, "let's only use the information defensively. Only if someone asks."

"Agreed," I said, leaning back toward the wall.

All of the sudden, the lights went out. It wasn't entirely dark, since the room was filled with candles all over, but the crowd began to murmur.

"What was that?" Jack said, looking around.

"I have no idea," I said. "Maybe it's some sort of Scottish tradition! And you two thought we wouldn't learn anything here. I guess it's something where halfway through the party, they turn out the lights. I wonder what happens when the lights go out?"

I was thrilled. Even though the place was crawling with Scottish Americans and not actual, real live Scots, we would *still* get some quality research done. See, this was exactly the sort of thing we would need to know for the wedding that you can't learn from Internet research alone!

"Um, Brooke," Vanessa said. "What's that behind your elbow?" I looked behind me and lo and behold, what was behind my elbow was a light switch.

"Oh, my God," I whispered, "I just turned off the lights!"

"Turn them back on," Jack said through clenched teeth.

"I can't!" I said. "I'm too embarrassed!" The murmur of the crowd began to get louder. Everyone seemed totally disoriented, and I saw some of the party planners scurrying about, trying to fix the lighting situation.

"Just do it," Vanessa said. "Standing here in the dark is worse. Eventually, someone's going to tell everyone where the light switch is."

As swiftly as I'd accidentally turned them off, I lifted my elbow, quickly hit the light switch while still balancing my plate and my glass and the lights came back on. Only, the light switch must have been a dimmer switch, because it got very, very bright. Uncomfortably bright.

"Turn them down," Jack said, teeth still slightly clenched. The murmur of the crowd got louder, still. Everyone continued to look around and just generally act confused.

"I can't," I said. "Then everyone will know it was me!"

"I think they know already," Vanessa said and she was right. The entire crowd began staring at me, waiting for me to re-arrange the lights.

"Sorry!" I said, as I turned around and readjusted the dimmer.

"So much for learning about Scotland," Vanessa said, looking for a place to put down her plate and glass.

"Yes," I said, "our work here is done." I then made a hasty exit toward the door, without making eye contact with any of the other party guests, with Jack and Vanessa following closely in my wake.

10

"I don't think that anyone is going to see your bikini line," Vanessa called in to me as the hair was being ripped from my flesh at the nail place around the corner from our office.

"You never know," I called back in between rips. I was raised to believe that a woman must always be ready for battle, no matter what. Manicures and haircuts even when you don't have any plans and pedicures and bikini waxes in the winter because you just "never knew" when some dashing gentleman caller might come around and whisk you off to an exotic weekend in Rio. Okay, granted, that has never happened to me or anyone that I've ever met, but isn't that the point of the whole "you never know" thing?

"I don't even want to know who you think is going to see your bikini line," Vanessa said to me as we walked over to the pedicure chairs.

"Well, now," I assured Vanessa, "anyone who wants to." Vanessa sighed.

The tubs beneath the pedicure chairs had already been filled with hot water and honey-lemon-scented bubbles. I took off my shoes, pulled my hair out of its bun, put my feet in and closed my eyes. The hot water felt like a warm blanket and I melted into the pedicure chair. I took a deep breath and tried to relax for the first time in two weeks. Who knew that perpetrating a fraud on the entire Scottish community would be so stressful? With my eyes shut, I tried to forget about everything—about work, about Douglas, about…

"I brought you some of my old research on likelihood of con-fusion," I heard someone say. I was pretty sure it was not the nail technician who was removing the polish from my toes. I opened one eye to find Vanessa thrusting hundreds of pages of case law into my hands. "I thought it might be a good jumping-off point for you," she said. She took out her own work—piles and piles of documents she was reviewing on another case to get ready for a round of depositions, all color coded to indicate whether they would help or hurt her client.

"So tall, so thin," Vanessa's nail technician commented as she massaged Vanessa's long lean legs—the product of two New York City Marathons and six-mile runs through Central Park each day.

"Thanks," Vanessa said back, brushing a nonexistent hair behind her ear. Her hand brushed her drop earrings, making a tiny sound like a set of elegant wind chimes. Vanessa wore her hair incredibly short, like Halle Berry circa 2002, and always wore long drop earrings to fill in the space between her ears and shoulders.

"Beautiful shoes," the nail technician said to Vanessa as she picked up one of Vanessa's tan Chanel ballet slippers. "So pretty." Vanessa smoothed her hair again as she smiled, careful not to hit her earrings again and draw even more attention to herself.

"Can you just tell me what these cases say?" I asked Vanessa.

"I took notes in the margins," Vanessa said, "and I put the

holding of each case on the top so that you can quickly tell what proposition of law each case stands for."

I put the cases in my lap while I took my BlackBerry out of my pants pocket. I'd taken to carrying my BlackBerry everywhere I went (even attaching it to my pajama bottoms as I lounged around at night) in case Douglas called or e-mailed me. I checked for missed calls or e-mails from Douglas, but he still hadn't tried to contact me.

I sent an e-mail to Jack:

From: "Brooke Miller" <bmiller@gilsonhecht.com>
To: "Jack Solomon" <jsolomon@gilsonhecht.com>
Subject: pop quiz

when are the highland games played each year?

Brooke Miller
Sent from my wireless handheld

A moment later, he e-mailed back:

From: "Jack Solomon" <jsolomon@gilsonhecht.com>
To: "Brooke Miller" <bmiller@gilsonhecht.com>
Subject: Re: pop quiz

Does Douglas even know this stuff?

Jack Solomon
Gilson, Hecht and Trattner
425 Park Avenue
11th Floor
New York, New York 10022

*****CONFIDENTIALITY NOTICE*****
The information contained in this e-mail message is confidential and is intended only for the use of the individual or entity named above. If you are not the intended recipient, we would request you delete this communication without reading it or any attachment, not forward or otherwise distribute it, and kindly advise Gilson, Hecht and Trattner by return e-mail to the sender or a telephone call to 1 (800) GILSON. Thank you in advance.

A smile came to my lips.

I began to shuffle through the cases Vanessa had given to me and marveled at the detail of her work. I looked up to tell her what a great job she had done, and in so doing, let half of the cases slide off my lap and fall into the pedicure tub. My nail technician and I gasped simultaneously and began frantically fishing for the papers, as Vanessa looked up from her own work, balanced perfectly in her lap.

"Gee, your cases smell terrific," she said.

"I think that this is a sign from God that I shouldn't be doing work right now. Is it really ethical to bill at the nail salon, anyway?"

"Of course it is," Vanessa said, looking down at her work and pursing her lips for emphasis.

"Men have it so easy, don't they," I said. "They just wash and go. If you're lucky, you get them to shave." Vanessa nodded her head as if she was listening, so I kept going. "Just to go to this stupid wedding, I have to get waxed, manicured, pedicured, visit the skin doctor, and take over an hour doing my hair and makeup."

"I'm very interested to see how your dress will reveal your freshly waxed bikini line," Vanessa said.

"I hope that Marcus appreciates all that you have to do just to get gorgeous."

"I seriously doubt that he does," she said, head still buried in her work.

"Well, then I hope that he appreciates all that *I* have to do just to get gorgeous," I said, lifting the foot that the nail technician was not filing to show Vanessa just how hard I was working.

"I'm sure he will."

"I still can't believe that Trip has never met Marcus," I said. Vanessa had missed her own law-school graduation because Marcus had been asked to scrub in on his first major surgery that day and Vanessa had gone to watch.

"Such is the life of a surgical resident," she said, as she continued to review her documents. "Now, can we try to get some work done? It's only ethical to bill at the nail salon if you actually do work." I nodded, making a mental note to myself to bill Healthy Foods for the six-tenths of an hour that I actually attempted to read the cases that Vanessa had given me. Even if I did spill half of them into a pedicure tub, I still thought I should get the credit.

"So far you haven't done anything that you can bill for," Vanessa said. I haven't done anything that I could bill for? Didn't she see me concentrating, like, totally hard, on those cases for a solid six-tenths of an hour? Jeez.

"Wouldn't it be great, though, if you could just bill for primping?" I asked her. The next best thing to billing actual clients was talking about billing them. In fact, you should be able to bill for that, too. "Just bill the client for your hair and manicures and stuff? It should really be write-off-able, if you think about it. You have to look good for court, don't you?" Vanessa kept reading her documents, although I could swear that I saw the sides of her mouth pull a bit as she tried to keep a straight face. "And, now that I'm thinking about it, you should be able to write off your makeup, too. I mean, could you imagine if you showed up for a meeting with a client without any makeup on? That would be, like, totally unprofessional."

"Work, Brooke!" Vanessa said with a laugh.

Seeing as Vanessa was not in the mood to discuss the issues plaguing women in today's modern world, I picked up my wet cases and began to blow on them. They were still drenched through and through, and just the mere act of holding them up was making some of them begin to rip in half. I considered putting them under the nail dryers, but thought better of it. I began to leaf through the cases I hadn't dropped into the pedicure tub. I looked over to Vanessa and tried to balance my cases on my own lap the way she had done herself.

The nail technician began to massage my legs. I closed my eyes and sank into it. I mean, a girl can't reasonably be expected to read cases and bill her client during a massage, can she?

"You know, I don't even know if Marcus is going to be able to make it to the wedding this weekend," Vanessa said, not even bothering to look up from her work.

"What?" I asked, turning to her. As I twisted my body to look at her, the dry cases slid off my lap and fell into the pedicure tub. The nail technician, having already run this drill, slowly began to peel each case out of the water and fan the papers out next to her stool.

"I think he's going to have to work," she said, head still buried in her documents, documents still balanced perfectly on her lap.

"Work?" I asked.

"Yes, work, Brooke," she said, picking her head up. "What you're not doing right now. Work."

"What color?" our nail technicians sang out in unison. I knew which color Vanessa would choose. Vanessa always wore the same color on both her hands and feet—Hitchcock Blonde—a barely-there nude color with a dash of pink that was only two shades away from clear topcoat. It was the sort of thing you would imagine Grace Kelly in her Princess Grace years wearing.

I usually changed it up each week, never matching my hands to my feet, a move that Vanessa considered completely déclassé and was never too shy to tell me. I knew for a fact that she obeyed the same rule about matching with respect to her bras and panties.

"I don't know," I thought aloud. "What color do you think?" I asked Vanessa.

"Have you tried Hitchcock Blonde?" she asked.

"Maybe a red on my toes since my dress for the wedding is nude with a black overlay?" I asked. Vanessa rolled her eyes as if to say, "Why even bother to ask when you ignore my sage advice?" and my nail technician ran off to the wall of nail polish to pick out a few reds.

"Are you going to wear red on your hands, too?" Vanessa asked me with a look of disdain that indicated that if I answered yes, our friendship may very well be over, or, at the very least, she would be unable to be seen in public with me.

"I was thinking something beigy for my hands?" I said it like a question.

"Okay," Vanessa approved. "Hitchcock Blonde?"

"Leather and Lace?" the nail technician called over to me.

"That sounds like something Beryl would wear," I said and she nodded, even though she had no idea who Beryl was. Presumably.

"Fresh Strawberries?" she asked and I shook my head no. Too Pollyanna. We were going to Los Angeles, for God's sake.

"Ah!" she said, seemingly having hit gold. "Weekend in Rio." Weekend in Rio—how perfect! This weekend was going to shape up quite nicely. This was a sign. I could tell.

"That sounds like it would match my bikini wax perfectly!" I cried out and she nodded as if I had just said something that made sense.

"That sounds a little whore-ish," Vanessa said. I thought she was working? Was she billing the client for coming up with little wingdingers like that?

"Totally whore-ish or just a little whore-ish?" I asked. Vanessa stopped to think for a second. Grabbing the bottle from my nail technician, she studied it carefully.

"A little whore-ish," was her final determination.

"But would it look good with nude with black overlay?" I asked. "And don't call my dress whore-ish," I quickly added.

"Not even whore-ish," she qualified. "Just a bit slutty."

"I'll take it," I said to my nail technician and she began to paint. "Are you upset?" I asked Vanessa.

"You can pick any color you want," she said.

"Not about my toenails, Vanessa," I said. "I meant about your husband."

"You've been living with us for two weeks, Brooke. Haven't you noticed that Marcus works a lot?"

"You're right, Vanessa, I know," I said. "I've only seen him once in the entire two weeks."

"I told you to use the guest bathroom off the kitchen if you were going to go in the middle of the night," she said.

"That *was* rather embarrassing, wasn't it?" I said.

"Only for you," she sang with a smile.

"Well, I hope that it all works out," I said, looking at her.

"So do I, Brooke," she said, turning to look out the window. "So do I."

11

"What does it all mean?" a young guy with dreadlocks flowing down his back asked me in a thick English accent. He was wearing a chocolate-brown bandanna in his hair, the way I did when I went to the gym, to keep it out of his face. On him, it somehow looked elegant.

"I have no idea," I said, trailing off and looking out the huge picture window, as I puzzled over my life, what had become of it and what I was about to do. "I honestly have no idea."

"I meant the painting," he said, pointing at it. He dug his other hand deep into his black leather jeans. The jeans were complemented by a denim shirt that I could have sworn I'd seen at Barneys New York the week before.

Vanessa and I had taken our newly painted fingers and toes down to Tribeca for "Texarkana 1985"—the new exhibit opening at Vanessa's mother's gallery. Millie's gallery was in a huge penthouse loft in Tribeca, with fourteen-foot ceilings and views looking out to the water that made you feel as if you were in a movie. All exposed brick and original wood, it was framed perfectly by its many picture windows on each of the four walls. Rather than sacrifice the natural beauty of the space, Millie hadn't touched an inch of the original architecture and instead had the gallery set up with eight-foot white walls, arranged like Stonehenge, on which the art was displayed. Elvis was playing faintly in the background.

"Oh, yeah, I knew that," I quickly covered. "What does it all mean? Hmmm. What does it mean? I think that it is a statement about peace in the Middle East."

"Peace," he repeated solemnly. "Yes. Peace. To me," he said as he continued pointing to the painting like a professor, or at the very least, a very, very good tour guide, "it's saying something about the genocide taking place in the Sudan." I nodded in agreement as he pointed to the speakers—Elvis's "Don't Be Cruel" offering the support he needed for his argument. We were looking at a painting of a small child holding a green apple.

"Ah, yes, I got that, too," I said. His dark eyes bore into me as he listened intently. "I mean, I knew that it was a statement against something really, really bad."

What? I had to say something. I didn't want him to think I was stupid. I read the *New York Times* every day just like every other New Yorker. Okay, well, the Styles section at the very least. Okay, okay, so maybe I don't always read the *Times,* but I always read the *New York Post* from cover to cover. Well, maybe not cover to cover, but every last word of Page Six, to be sure.

"Well, I think that it means that we need a drink," Vanessa said, coming up from behind us and grabbing me. We walked over to the bar. "I hate it when people ask me about the art at these things."

"Tell me about it," I said as I grabbed two champagne cocktails off the bar for us.

"Are you holding up okay?" Vanessa asked me as she licked the powdered sugar off the rim of her champagne glass.

"Fine," I replied. "Absolutely fine." A waiter walked by with a plate of tiny pieces of filet mignon on toast. They had fancy mustard painted on top in a swirl design that looked like a question mark. We each took one. "Why on earth wouldn't I be fine?"

"Are you about to cry?" she asked me.

"Cry?" I asked. "Me?" Why on earth would she be asking me that? It *may* have been because she'd caught me in my office earlier that day crying to one of the guys from the mail room about my breakup with Douglas. Or perhaps because the day before I'd started to cry when I saw that Douglas's deodorant was on sale at CVS.

What? Don't you love a bargain, too?

"Oh, please don't do this at my mother's thing," she said, grabbing a tuna tartare on potato crisp as a waiter flew by.

"Do what?" I asked. I hoped that she noticed that her accusation had made me—unlike her—too flummoxed to even grab a piece of tuna for myself.

"Embarrass me," she whispered, eyes darting around the room as she put the whole crisp into her mouth. "You know how high stress these things can be for me."

"I'm not going to embarrass you!" I said, laughing. Please! Me, embarrass her? How could *I* possibly embarrass Vanessa? I was just about to ask her that very thing when her mother walked over to greet us.

"Where's your husband?" Millie asked, in place of hello. She kissed each of us on both of our cheeks as if she were French. Her hair was pulled back in a very severe chignon and she wore little to no makeup. As she always did, she looked more like the former model she used to be than the art gallery owner she currently was.

"Marcus is working," Vanessa said, already looking around to see who else was there. Millie's art gallery openings usually attracted an eclectic and altogether fabulous crowd. I stood around and tried to look fabulous myself, as if I'd actually been invited because of my said fabulousness, or fabulousity (or whatever the word would be that would mean that I was totally, completely fabulous) instead of the fact that I was merely there because I was friends with Vanessa.

"Working?" Millie said in a tone that I was pretty sure wasn't meant to pretend that she wasn't judging her daughter. "Just like your father."

"Yes, Mother," Vanessa said. She always called Millie *Mother* when she was upset. "Working. What men our age have to do."

"Jack managed to make it," Millie said, looking over our shoulders. We turned to see Jack walking in. He checked his briefcase and two huge Redwelds full of documents at the coat check set up by the front door. Clearly, he had chosen to bring his work home with him and do it later so that he could leave work early and make it to the show. "I see you met Christian Locke."

"We did?" I asked.

"The young man with the dreadlocks," Millie said, pointing in his direction. He was still intently studying the painting of the child with an apple.

"He's single," Millie said in Vanessa's general direction as she waved him over.

"Hi, I'm Christian," he said, shaking both of our hands. "And apparently, I'm single," he said with a laugh.

"Too bad she's not," Jack said as he swept in and gave Millie the requisite kiss on each cheek.

"Millie, are you misbehaving again?" a voice from nowhere asked. A man in a navy pinstriped suit joined our group and gave Millie a hug.

"Always, sweetheart," she said, returning the stranger's embrace.

"This is Sidney Locke," Millie said, introducing him to us. He made eye contact with each of us as he shook each of our hands, the way I'd seen Bill Bradley do once at a political fund-raiser. When Sidney reached out to shake my hand, I couldn't help but notice his monogrammed gold cuff links.

"Hi, Dad," Christian said, giving his father a hug.

"Sidney is a diplomat," Millie said, as Sidney feigned embarrassment over the introduction. "The work he does is truly amazing."

"I'm sure these kids don't want to hear about the work I do," Sidney said, smiling broadly at us. "It's after hours."

"I'm sure they do!" Millie said. "These are lawyers at one of Manhattan's top firms." Vanessa groaned. "What? I can brag about my daughter, can't I?"

"Then they *definitely* don't want to hear about my work!" Sidney said.

"They do! Actually, Brooke's boyfriend is from Scotland, so I'm sure that she would be *particularly* interested in what's going on across the pond."

"Mother," Vanessa began. "Stop." How could it be that she hadn't told her mother? I tell my mother what I have for breakfast each morning. I certainly would have mentioned it if my best friend had been callously thrown out of the apartment in which she had been living in sin with her boyfriend and was bunking with my handsome doctor husband and me. I must be such a wonderful houseguest that she never even needed to complain to her about me!

"Is Douglas coming, sweetheart?" Millie asked me, completely ignoring Vanessa. For the record, Douglas had never once made it to one of Millie's art openings.

"No," I said, trying to smile and act normal. "He's not."

"These young men!" she said, facing the group. "They all work way too hard, if you ask me! Brooke, sweetheart, what is he working on that he couldn't be here?"

"He's not working," I said. I smiled my fake smile and everyone else smiled their fake smiles back at me, like deer caught in headlights.

"Oh, okay," Millie said, breaking the silence with a nervous smile creeping onto her lips.

No one moved. Christian and his father were smiling so hard I thought that one of them might actually hurt themselves, and Millie and Vanessa were staring hard at each other, seemingly trying to communicate to the other through their clenched teeth. Jack looked as if he was about to say something to me.

"Douglas broke up with me," I said. Okay, granted, maybe it wasn't the sort of thing you just blurt out in polite company, but everyone knows that when confronted with a deer caught in your headlights, you are supposed to speed up and hit the deer really fast. It's a fact.

"Oh, Brooke," Millie said as she inched toward me for a hug.

"It's okay," I said, tearing up slightly as Sidney tried to put a diplomatic arm around me. "I'm okay."

"Of course it's okay," Sidney said, and as soon as the words left his diplomatic mouth, the waterworks began. Full force. Running down my face uncontrollably. Hoover Dam breaking style. I couldn't hold back. The tears just came and came and came and there was nothing anyone could do to stop them. I began simultaneously gasping for breath and wiping my running nose with my already used cocktail napkin. I tried wiping the tears away with the back of my hand to no avail—the tears just kept on coming and they wouldn't stop. Sidney offered me his handkerchief and I blew my nose into it. I thanked him and tried to blow my nose delicately and all ladylike, but it instead came out sounding more like a foghorn.

"I'm fine. I'm totally fine. I mean, all men cheat, don't they? So, it's really not that big of a deal."

"He cheated on you?" Christian asked, clearly incredulous that a man had cheated on a goddess like myself. He handed me his own handkerchief and I blew my nose into it. Loud.

"Yes, he cheated. But, who doesn't, right? Didn't Halle Berry's husband cheat on her?" I asked the group. Sidney nodded his head yes sympathetically as only a diplomat could. "And, she's the most beautiful woman on the face of the earth. You can't compete with Halle Berry. And didn't Marc Anthony leave his wife for J. Lo? That guy was married to Miss Universe! You can't get better than Miss Universe! And look at me! I'm just a mere mortal!"

"But she's J. Lo," Vanessa said.

"I know," I agreed. "But this is just a minor setback in our relationship. You see, it's no big deal. Because I'm okay and it's okay. I'm going to get Douglas back. Yes, sir-ee-Bob. I'll get him back. You don't have to worry about me. Not one bit. We are going to get back together. Possibly not until after my ex-boyfriend's wedding, but what does that matter? Right?"

"You're going to your ex-boyfriend's wedding?" Christian asked. I blew my nose into his handkerchief again as I nodded my head yes.

"Yes," I said, louder and more forcefully, as if I were about to announce something like, "With God as my witness, I'll never go hungry again," or "Tomorrow is another day," or something of similar import. "I am going to my ex-boyfriend's wedding. And then I'm going to get Douglas back."

"Of course you are," Millie said.

I tried to give Sidney and Christian their handkerchiefs back, only to have Vanessa intercept my reach, saying, "Why don't we have these cleaned before we return them to you?"

"I'm so sorry I made a scene," I said, turning to Millie.

"Not a problem, everyone here will think that it was performance art," she replied with a wink as she walked to the middle of the room to introduce the artist.

"So, this is some exhibit," Christian said and everyone quickly nodded their heads and brought their drinks to their mouths for a sip. "Jack, we've all been talking about what we think this exhibit means. What do you think the exhibit's all about?"

"Oh, yes. The exhibit," he said, looking around quickly at all of the paintings. "It just looks like kids growing up in Texas to me."

Christian and I laughed at Jack's pedestrian interpretation as Millie introduced the artist—a twenty-something woman with her hair tied into a loose ponytail and ripped jeans. She had long bangs that fell into her eyes and a piercing just below her lower lip.

"When I began creating this collection," she said, "I was looking to make a statement."

"Good thing you didn't embarrass me," Vanessa said through clenched teeth as the artist spoke. I wanted to apologize to her for making a huge scene at her mother's art-exhibit opening, but all I could think about was: *Please say peace in the Middle East. Please say peace in the Middle East.*

"It's really just all about my upbringing in Texas back in the eighties," the artist said. "The pure unadulterated childhood I had before computers ruled the world and everyone had a cell phone."

"Did you ever study art history?" Christian asked Jack.

"Afraid not," Jack replied.

"Then how did you know what the artist was trying to say?"

"Some things are just up-front and uncomplicated," Jack replied as Christian nodded his head.

"And, of course," the artist said, concluding her speech, "it's a statement about peace in the Middle East."

I smiled to myself and grabbed a tiny piece of caviar on a potato pancake to reward myself for being so damn smart.

"You're getting back together with him?" Jack asked me in a whisper.

"Of course I am," I said, dabbing my cocktail napkin at the sides of my mouth.

"But I thought that *I* was coming with you to Trip's wedding?" he said, brushing his shaggy brown hair from his eyes. His eyes seemed bluer than usual.

"You are," I said, and he looked back with a puzzled look.

"So, I thought that meant that you changed your mind," he said.

"About what?" I asked, tearing the cocktail napkin in my hand into two pieces.

"About getting back together with Douglas. I thought, I mean—the costume shop—wasn't something going on there? You know, between *us?* Why are you still talking about getting back together with *him?*"

"You're coming with me to the wedding, Jack, but it's not like I'm ready to throw away two years of my life just like that."

"He did," he said.

"I know that, Jack," I replied, pulling him closer to me so that the people around us wouldn't hear. "You think I don't know that?"

"Does he want to get back together with you?" he asked.

"He does," I said. Jack looked back at me, expecting me to say more. "He does. He just doesn't know it yet."

"He doesn't know it yet?" Jack asked.

"So, are you two enjoying the show?" Millie asked, swooping in from behind us, glass of champagne in her hands.

"It's really amazing," Jack said.

"Peace in the Middle East," I said.

"That's what I love about art," Millie said, her eyes melting into the painting we were standing in front of. "Just when you think it's one thing, it merges into something else. Something familiar can become something entirely different right before your eyes."

"My first impressions are usually dead on," I told Millie. I mean, come on—peace in the Middle East, people! "And I find that I usually don't change them."

"Well, sweetheart," Millie said, slowly sipping her drink, "then you probably miss a whole lot."

12

"You need to turn off all mechanical devices so that we can be cleared for takeoff," the stewardess said, leaning over Jack. He turned off the DVD player that he was playing *Trainspotting* on and I handed him a book on Scottish royalty.

"Hand me that movie and I'll put it away with *Rob Roy* and the Sean Connery DVDs," I said, reaching down to put them away.

"Why are you putting those in that?" Vanessa asked, referring to the litigation bag I was using. A litigation bag is not really a bag, and it's certainly not your typical carry-on luggage. Rather, it's a hard case used by litigators when they go to court. Now, the casual observer may have thought she was asking me this because junior associates at a big firm, even those who are litigators, rarely, if ever, go to court, but I knew that she meant, "Why do you have that large eyesore on a plane?"

"Because I narrowly escaped death trying to get out of the office tonight," I explained.

It was a little trick Jack had taught Vanessa and me when we were first-year associates. Whenever you are sneaking out of the office early (read: anytime before 9:00 p.m.), do so with a legal folder or large box of documents or even a litigation bag in your hand, so as to give off the appearance of your intention to work at home. I had used this trick mere hours earlier on my way out of work and discovered that my litigation bag actually made a very handy carry-on bag for the flight.

There I was with my suitcase in my hand, trying to make my escape for the weekend, when one of the partners on the Healthy Foods case came to my office to ask me to do some research that he needed for Tuesday morning. (He thought he was being a hero by making it due on a Tuesday instead of a Monday. As if I couldn't figure out that the assignment entailed weekend work either way.) I told him that I could not do it since I was traveling out of town, thus, the suitcase in my hand. He explained to me my duty to the firm and to the case and a whole host of other things that I didn't hear because I was already tuning him out. When he finally started to tell me how I was the only person who could do this assignment, I managed to grab a litigation bag that was filled with papers (from my last narrow escape from the office a week and a half earlier) to show him that even though I was going out of town for the weekend, I would actually be doing work on another case the whole time, so even if I really, really wanted to, I was not going to be able to get his work done for him by Tuesday. He grumbled something about "Wednesday, then," and left my office.

Vanessa got off from work scot-free, but as she suspected, her husband got stuck at the hospital on an emergency shift.

Once we got in the air, it was back to all things Scotland. Jack watched DVD upon DVD to start perfecting his accent while Vanessa and I brushed up on our research, finding out more things about Scotland and Scottish culture in general. Vanessa was really focused on learning all that she could and I wasn't sure why. Other than the fact that she's a great friend, that is. And a kick-ass researcher, I might add. One time, a partner called her from oral argument in federal court to get contrary authority for a case that opposing counsel had just cited. Before the judge's ten-minute recess was over, Vanessa had five cases for the partner that enabled her to win her oral argument. See, that's the difference between Vanessa and me: a partner calls screaming and demanding case law on a ten-minute deadline and Vanessa is completely unfazed, whereas I would have been—well, completely fazed.

I myself was using my credit card to call Douglas in his office from the airplane phone in the seat in front of me. I had to lie to Jack and Vanessa and tell them that I was calling into office voice mail, so when Douglas's secretary picked up, I had no choice but to dial random numbers into the phone as if I were entering my security code. It was then that I realized that one could not fake a phone call to her ex from a middle seat.

Our plane touched down in L.A. five hours and twenty-seven minutes after takeoff. We were all exhausted, and looking forward to getting to our hotel as quickly as we could. Vanessa's mammoth Louis Vuitton case was the first to come off the conveyor belt at baggage claim, with Jack's army-green duffel following close behind. I hate it when my bag doesn't immediately come off the conveyor belt. I always get that overwhelming feeling of complete dread.

"Oh, my God, my bags are lost," I said to Jack and Vanessa. Vanessa was so tired that she was sitting on top of her suitcase.

"Your bags are not lost," Jack said matter-of-factly, while his eyes betrayed him, darting around the baggage-claim area furiously. "They just haven't come off of the plane yet."

"Yeah," Vanessa chimed in, "the laws of karma would not allow it. There is no way in hell that, on the way to your ex-boyfriend's wedding, your bags could possibly get lost."

Vanessa was right. I was overreacting. I was probably just jittery and nervous about the whole perpetrating a fraud on the Scottish community thing. Which is totally natural.

One hour later, two flights from Houston and one from Miami had already landed and gotten their luggage. Vanessa told me that I must have been a very bad person in my former life.

"Thank you for flying Northeastern Airlines. How can I help you?" an airport employee asked me as if reading off a script. Her monotone voice matched her monotone…well, everything else. She wore the blankest expression I had ever seen.

"My bag never came off the conveyor belt," I explained, smiling a big smile. (The same look you employ at the post office can also be conveniently used at the airport.)

"So your bag is lost," she droned, seemingly on autopilot, "You can fill out—"

"No, it's not lost," I explained like a kindergarten teacher to her four-year-old students. "Of course, it just hasn't come off the conveyor belt. It can't be lost. It must be somewhere. Could you please just help me find it?" Don't these people know anything about customer service?

"So your bag is lost. You can fill out—" she repeated. I guess they don't. Perhaps the look is better kept for post-office use only.

"No," I said, pushing away the paperwork, "I don't need to fill that out. My bag cannot be lost. It cannot. My ex-boyfriend's wedding is tomorrow night and I need my dress and shoes, not to mention my makeup and hair stuff…."

She looked back at me with that same blank stare. Judging by her own lack of makeup and hair, I could tell that this was not a compelling argument for her.

"See, this is why people hate L.A.," I said to Jack and Vanessa. Jack shook his head in an "I told you so" manner.

This cannot be happening to me. This. Cannot. Be happening. To me. Okay, be cool. You can make this happen. You're a big-time lawyer at a big-time law firm. You've faced much tougher foes. In litigation, you always need to know what the other party needs in order to give you what you want. Now, this should be easy enough. This is clearly a very disgruntled airport employee. She just needs someone to be nice to her. And give her a makeover, but let's fight the battles that we can fight, shall we? Just be kind to her and watch how you get more flies with honey than vinegar.

"Listen to me, lady," I said. "I am *not* fooling around here. Let me make one thing clear—I'm not leaving this airport until I have my suitcase in my hot little hands."

13

"No, I do not have any bags," I said to a very blond, very tan, very smiley man behind the reception desk of the Beverly Wilshire. "No bags at all."

"We have two bags here," Vanessa chimed in.

"And we are very hopeful that the airline will recover the third bag shortly," Jack said. Very optimistically, I might add. Unfortunately, I was in no mood for optimism. Optimistic people suck. I never had that problem with Douglas.

"The airline lost mine," I explained to the Ken doll at reception, "on the eve of my ex-boyfriend's wedding. Can you believe that?"

"And we were escorted out of the airport by security," Vanessa added. "Can you believe *that?*" I guess she's still upset about the whole me threatening the airport employee, jumping over the counter in an alleged play for her neck, getting escorted out of the airport by security, and then getting a police escort to the hotel thing. You think she would have been more appreciative about getting a free ride to our hotel.

"Well, miss, that is absolutely terrible, but I am sure that they will locate your bag for you," Ken doll said to me. That optimism thing rears its ugly head again. Is everyone going to be like this in L.A.? "And I can assure you," Ken doll continued, "that we will take very good care of you at the hotel. Are we still four in the suite?"

"No, actually, we're three," I explained to Ken. "My friend's husband had to work this weekend. Is that going to be a problem?" Take that, Ken. You see, in the real world, real people have real problems. The real world isn't beautiful and blond and tanned and buff and smiley with really, really white teeth and…. Where was I? Oh, yes, the real world. Take that, Ken. We are real people here with real problems. And we have real spouses who have to do real work over the weekend. Really.

"It's no problem at all," Ken said, smiling back at me, typing furiously into his computer. "But," he said, leaning over the counter in a whisper, "I'm still going to give you a suite big enough for four, and only charge you for three." He is?

"You are? Thank you so much," I gushed. Ken's so nice. Now I feel bad that I said all that mean stuff to him. Well, I didn't say it to him—I only thought it—but still.

A bellhop appeared out of nowhere with our two bags and whisked us to our suite. Now, I fancy myself a real tough New Yorker. Completely jaded, unimpressed by most everything. But, when Jack opened the door to that suite, I gasped. I actually gasped. An actual sucking in of my breath and uncontrollably moving my hand to my chest. Everyone did. The suite was absolutely breathtaking.

"Welcome to the Vice Presidential suite," the bellhop said, with the requisite pageantry such an announcement deserved.

"Do you think we could have gotten the Presidential suite if all three of us had lost our bags?" Vanessa asked.

"Vice Presidential. Sweet," Jack said, in full surfer mode. He even made some strange hand gesture when he said it.

It looked fit for a queen. Or a vice president, as the case may be. The white columns in the entranceway served as the perfect invitation to the suite's living room, beckoning you to come in. As you did, you couldn't help but be struck by the windows that reached all the way to the ten-foot ceiling, framed by drapes with fabric so rich, they practically poured onto the tan marble floor. It felt as if you looked out those windows you could probably see the whole world.

It was just as perfectly regal as the lobby. Well, I didn't actually *see* the lobby, what with being all infuriated about my bags and all, but I remember the lobby from the pictures I saw of it on the Internet when I booked the hotel. And it was very regal, I assure you.

The living room itself was bigger than the first apartment I had in New York. I practically fell over myself in my rush to see the bedrooms. As I walked toward door number one, Jack was already behind the mahogany bar, taking drink orders from Vanessa. He popped the bottle of champagne that was the centerpiece of our complimentary fruit basket and I could tell that it was expensive from its very pop—a polite pop that sounded like a delicate song.

"What can I get 'cha, little lady?" he asked me, already pouring champagne and orange juice into a glass for Vanessa. Vanessa started downing her mimosa, picking up the phone on the bar to call Marcus.

"What have you got?" I asked him.

"For you?" he asked. "Anything." The phone rang as Jack and I locked eyes.

"Our hotel room has two phone lines," Vanessa informed me, downing her mimosa as she spoke to her husband. She pushed the glass over to Jack for a refill.

"How freaking cool is that?" I asked, turning to her. She put Marcus on hold and picked up line two.

"The airline is on two for you," she said. I ran to the sofa to pick up line two. The furniture was all deep reds and navy with just the right amount of gold strewn in, set in dark mahogany. I melted into the pillows and, for a moment, forgot that I was there to pick up the phone.

"Hello?" I said.

"She's living in our apartment and now she has to be on our calls, too?" Marcus said. Holy bad mood, Batman. I slammed down the phone and shot Vanessa an apologetic look.

"Just ignore him, Brooke," Vanessa said into the phone. "It's what I do." I picked up line two.

"This is Brooke Miller," I said, brushing my hands across the sofa's fabric. "Oh, my God, you did? That's fabulous! I can come over right now to pick it up!" I practically cried. My bags! My beloved bags! They're here! Come to mama!

"Shall we deliver them to your hotel, Ms. Miller?" a decidedly *non*disgruntled airport employee asked me.

"Deliver it? Why, yes, that's right," I said, suddenly becoming more articulate with each passing moment I spent in the suite and its luxurious surroundings. "You certainly *should* deliver it after all that I have been through."

"In the past sixty-five minutes…" Jack said, joining me on the sofa with a mimosa and a beer in his hands.

"It was a very *traumatic* sixty-five minutes, thank you very much," I whispered to Jack, holding my hand over the phone.

"That would be fine," I said in a very ladylike manner after removing my hand from the receiver. "Thank you very much." This joint was really classing me up.

Vanessa and I hung up our phones at the same time. We did a little dance and started to cheer.

"Delivering the bag first thing in the morning!" I said.

"Phew!" Vanessa said, dramatically brushing her hand across her forehead. "That would have really sucked if we had to run around L.A. like complete idiots looking for a new dress and shoes!"

"Not to mention hair products and makeup," I added. "My God, if my bag had actually been lost, it would have taken me a week just to get ready for this stupid wedding!"

"Well, actually, I wanted to surprise you, but I guess that I can tell you now that we're celebrating anyway," Vanessa said, holding up her glass of champagne. "Remember my cousin Damian?"

"The one that dresses like a woman?" Jack asked.

"Yes. Well, he's working as a stylist now, and he agreed to come over and help us get gorgeous!"

"Really?" I asked. "He does hair now?"

"And makeup!" Vanessa cried, suddenly a kid in a candy shop. "I figured it would be fun to get the Hollywood treatment before going to the Hollywood wedding. He's coming at four o'clock."

"Perfect. That's perfect. Thank you," I said, giving Vanessa a hug.

"Well, ladies," Jack interrupted, reaching his arms over the both of us to join in on the hug, "I'd say that this calls for a celebration!" And with that, we were off into the L.A. night.

14

An hour later, we found ourselves at a perfectly fabulous L.A. hot spot. Or what seemed to be a hot spot, anyway, what with all of the beautiful people walking around. I somehow thought that L.A. would be much different from New York, being on the other coast and all, but there we were, at a sleek new bar with the same eighteen-dollar martinis that we get in New York. The only difference was that this bar was on an outside terrace, so you could chase your eighteen-dollar martini with a breath of night air. That, and the L.A. locals seemed to be much blonder as an overall population and wore flip-flops a lot more than New Yorkers.

I felt as if I had a scarlet *NY* on my chest—dressed in black from head to toe, from my black wrap sweater (complimented perfectly with black pants) down to my black pointy-toed shoes. Vanessa was similarly attired in her own black pants and black sleeveless top, with an Hermès scarf tied around her waist and black D'Orsay pumps. Actually, a scarlet *NY* might have been a very nice fashion accessory—Californians seem to experiment quite a bit more with color than their New York counterparts.

"Now, remember, it's not an English accent. It's very distinct," I instructed Jack. We had found a table right in the center of the terrace and were sitting down.

"Why, Trip, old boy, old chap, nice to meet you," he said in a very bad English accent. English accent? Didn't we just cover that?

"Okay, that was really bad," Vanessa said, reading my mind.

"Yeah, he doesn't talk like that," I explained. "He says *fuck* a lot, so try to say that. But not in front of Trip's mother. Or grandmother."

"Well, no one's ever actually met Douglas, so I don't have to sound like *him,* I just need to sound Scottish, right?"

"That's true," I said, and felt an unexpected stab of sadness as I said it. I let the feeling pass. "But I think that Scottish people say *fuck* a lot in general."

"That's kind of a sweeping generalization. Do they really?" Vanessa asked. What is she, the accent police? Can't she see that we're working here?

"I think so," I abruptly answered.

"Well, did his mother say *fuck* a lot when you met her?" she asked. Sometimes it's annoying when all of your friends are litigators.

"Bond, James Bond," Jack said, this time with a perfect accent. A perfect English accent.

"No!" I said.

"I thought it was pretty close," Vanessa said. "Anyway, who's really going to notice the difference anyway?"

"Do you think that just because they live in California," I asked her, "they're stupid?"

"You think that just because they're from Scotland," Vanessa explained, "they say *fuck* a lot." Who brought the lawyer?

"Sean Connery is Scottish," Jack said.

"But James Bond is English! Jeez! More Braveheart than Bond." This was getting to be worse than when I used to tutor the Nelson twins in Spanish. (Twin no. 1: Why can't we just put an *o* on the end of everything? Me: Because in Spanish, they use masculine and feminine forms of their words. Twin no. 2: Well, we're going to just put an *o* at the end of everything. Me: If you do that, it will make you sound dumb. Twin no. 1: Mom, Brooke just called us dumb!)

"But they—can never take—our freedom!" Jack cried out so loud that the people around us began to stare. At least he did it with a Scottish accent, though.

"Please don't say that at the wedding," I instructed him.

"They're magically delicious!" Jack said, sounding a bit like the Lucky Charms leprechaun.

"Was that Irish?" Vanessa said.

"Are you making fun of me?" I said.

"You know what, I just need to do some of my acting exercises. I'm not warmed up," he explained. And with that, he began to make strange sounds with his throat. It was like something out of the Animal Channel. Vanessa and I sat very still, so as not to be eaten alive or anything. A waitress approached our table and I feared for her life.

"What can I get you to drink?" she asked, not thinking twice about the strange throat noises Jack was emitting.

"May we see your martini menu, please," Vanessa said.

"They'll take a look at the martini menu," Jack interrupted, with a Scottish accent no less. "I'll have a Scotch on the rocks, please." The waitress nodded and it looked like he really had her.

I was impressed—he had actually fooled our waitress! As a smile came to my face, Jack said, "For fuck's sake!" and the waitress walked away looking confused. She probably went to go and spit in our drinks.

"Could you please not say *fuck* this much around me?" Vanessa asked.

"Jack, that was really good!" I said. Positive reinforcement. Another thing I learned from the Animal Channel. "That sounded, like, totally Scottish! Soon you'll be eating haggis and talking about World Cup soccer!"

"Football?" he asked with a full Scottish accent. "You mean football? Ah, you Americans…"

"Now he's on a roll!" I said, looking to Vanessa like a proud parent.

"Put another shrimp on the barbie!" he cried in a perfect accent. A perfect Australian accent.

"And now he's not," Vanessa said, as the waitress returned with our drinks.

"Cheers!" Jack said, back in full Scottish accent. He also did a slight head tilt thing that I'd never seen before.

"Cheers," the waitress said with a flair. I think that she may have winked, too. Either way, it was an unequivocal flirt.

"Oh, my God. I think that you actually had her fooled," I said, my hand accidentally reaching for his leg. I must have gotten a bit carried away with the whole positive reinforcement thing.

"No, he didn't," Vanessa said. "Maybe she was just turned on by the throat exercises."

"Okay, *cheers* was good. Use that," I said, slowly removing my hand from his leg, as quietly as a gazelle, so as to not let anyone notice that it was there.

"I think that that's English, though, not necessarily Scottish,"

Vanessa said, seemingly oblivious to what was going on under the table.

"Well, I don't know what it is, but it sounds good, Jack, go with it," I said.

"I thought that we were going more Braveheart than Bond?" Jack asked, grabbing for my hand once it was almost detached from his leg.

"We are, but when in doubt, default back to English," I instructed, pulling my hand back to my own lap.

"I think that we're just confusing things now," Vanessa said, looking down like a child who has just caught her parents kissing.

"No, I'm a professional. You forget. I can handle this. I thrive on good direction," Jack said, arms flailing about, presumably to demonstrate what a wonderful thespian he was.

"You are not really thriving, thus far, on our direction," Vanessa pointed out.

"I said *good* direction," Jack countered.

"Just—whatever you do—do not lapse into that Australian accent," I said.

"A guy makes one mistake…." Jack said to no one in particular.

"I just don't even know where that came from," I explained. "I mean, they are, like, totally separate continents."

"I would like to see you try to do better," Jack challenged.

"Okay, point taken," Vanessa refereed. "But so was Brooke's— more Braveheart than Bond. But Bond is acceptable in an emergency. And never, ever, resort to Crocodile Dundee. Understood?"

"Got it." Jack was practically panting and ready to begin.

"Now, go grasshopper, and make us proud," Vanessa said.

Jack hopped up from the table like a lion let out of his cage and started circling his prey. It was actually fun to watch. I could practically see the wheels turning in his head as he decided which group of lovelies to approach. Men are so predictable. He'll probably start with some easy conquer—one of the lonely lambs seated at the bar. The sure thing, the easy pounce.

I watched and waited until he finally made his move. He sat down at a table with three women. Impressive. Now, this is a man who clearly loves a challenge. I waited for the pack to eat him alive, but, within moments, it was clear that these women were completely charmed by him. I could have sworn I heard one woman ask, "So, like, do you know how to play a bagpipe and stuff?" To which Jack nodded his head in a knowing way as if to say, "But of course!"

Women really do love an accent. I should know—I used to be one of them. One of those naive, unsuspecting women who thought that a man with an accent meant a mature, sophisticated man. Not a man who would cheat on you and get engaged to another woman and leave you boyfriend-less for your ex-boyfriend's wedding.

I mean, look at these women—they were practically drooling all over him and they didn't even know him. He's not even that good-looking! Well, not really, anyway. Well, I mean, unless you go for that sort of look. Which I don't.

"My, my, Brooke," Vanessa said, interrupting my thoughts, "I didn't take you for the jealous type."

"Jealous? Vanessa, please! Why would I be jealous!"

"You tell me. What was with the little hand thing under the table? And why can't you take your eyes off of him and his minions?"

"I don't know what you're talking about," I said, quickly snapping my head back to face her.

"I don't know what he sees in those girls, anyway," Vanessa said. "They are so L.A. I've never seen so much pink clothing before in my life."

"I know," I said, taking off my wrap sweater to reveal the white wife beater I had on underneath it, "it's pathetic." Vanessa nodded her head in agreement, adjusting her D'Orsay pumps. "So," I casually asked, "do you think that I should call Douglas later?"

"Why on earth would you do that?" she asked.

"Because he's my *boyfriend*," I said.

"He's your *ex-boyfriend*. Emphasis on the *ex* part. Your heart-breaking, two-timing, lying, cheating—"

"Okay, I get it," I said, cutting her off.

"Good," she said, taking the apple slice out of her martini to nibble. "Okay, now, back to important things—does that woman over there realize that the hair color she's got is not found in nature?"

"I know. It's really sad," I said, twirling my own long locks, which I had blown the curl out of to perfection that morning. "Just so we're clear, though, you *don't* think that I should call Douglas?" I asked.

What? You would have wanted to clarify things, too.

We watched Jack as he approached another group of women. And greeted them with a hearty "G'day mate!" He seemed hor-rified at his slip, but the women didn't even seem to notice, in unison saying back, "G'day!" Jack quickly excused himself to return to our table.

"So, how'd it go, loverboy?" I asked him. "All ready to forsake New York for L.A.?"

"It went quite well, actually," he said, tucking my pink bra strap into my wife beater. I looked down as his hand brushed against my bare shoulder. "I think that I had them all fooled. Either that, or they didn't care—because I got tons of phone numbers!" Vanessa couldn't control herself, eyes widening in disbelief. I myself stayed cool, as if I couldn't care less. Or could care less. Don't those two mean the same thing? Okay, well, just use whichever one means I didn't care at all. Because I didn't.

"You cad!" Vanessa said, smiling. Why the hell is she smiling? Those girls were massive bimbos! That, and the fact that he has no time to take any of them out since we are only here for the weekend. Although, if he moved anywhere as quickly as Douglas did, maybe he would. Anyway, what self-respecting women would all give their phone numbers to the same man? Maybe they thought they were on one of those reality dating shows. You see, this is why people hate L.A.

"The only problem is," Jack explained, "for some reason, that Australian accent keeps rearing its ugly head."

"Don't worry about it," I said, "just don't do it at the wedding."

"Goddamn Crocodile Dundee," Vanessa muttered into her drink.

After Vanessa and I had sampled every specialty martini on the menu (including one called the Mulholland Drive that was built for two and equipped with a very, very large straw), we managed to drag Jack away from his admirers and stumble back to our hotel suite.

We sprawled out over the Louis XVI furniture and feasted on all the minifridge had to offer. Snickers, Milky Way, Butterfingers, Hershey's Kisses…no candy was shown mercy. After the first round of candy bars, we didn't even look at the price list as we dove into the chips and mixed nuts. We were way too busy discussing matters such as: Why is the room spinning? Was it spinning before? And who can we call to make it stop?

Jack and Vanessa went out to the balcony to get some fresh air while I excused myself to use the ladies' room. And wouldn't you know it—our hotel suite is so fancy, we even have phones in our bathroom! I, of course, took this as a sign from God that I should give Douglas a call. Now, I know that Vanessa disapproved, but the last time that that girl was single was sometime in the 1980s. What did she know? And I'm sure, if given a vote, Jack would also have said that I shouldn't call, but he's a man, so what does he know? And at any rate, I'm sure that he was still very much turned on from the whole "hand on the knee/touching my shoulder" thing, so he couldn't really be an objective voter, now, could he?

I sat on the edge of the cream-colored marble whirlpool bathtub and dialed the number. As the phone rang, I realized that I hadn't taken the time difference into account. While I was still puzzling over the time in New York, counting back the hours on my fingers, the answering machine picked up.

"Douglas," I said after the beep, trying very hard to sound sober, "it's me. Things have been really crazy, but I'm just calling to tell you that I forgive you. I'm in California right now for Trip's wedding, but I want you to know that the second I get back to New York—"

"Hello?" a very sleepy female voice answered, picking up the phone. Oh, my God. Oh. My. God. When I was busy calculating New York time, I instead should have thinking about the fact that Beryl had already moved in, thus, making the plan of drunk dialing Douglas in the middle of the night very, very stupid. Even more stupid than the name Beryl. Okay, nothing's more stupid than the name Beryl, but you know what I mean.

There was no mistaking that voice. Even half-asleep, it still had a whiny "Daddy, will you buy me that?" quality to it. With just a touch of screech. It was a half an octave away from being a pitch that only dogs could hear.

A voice like that could only belong to a woman named Beryl. And I was quite certain that the sound of it was making me even more nauseated than I was before. "Hellooo?" she said, now sounding more awake and more annoyed. I immediately hung up the phone. What on earth was I thinking? How was making a complete fool of myself in the middle of the night taking me any closer to my goal of getting Douglas back?

Anyway, I thought in my drunken stupor, I just had to wait until Douglas cheated on Beryl (which he undoubtedly would) and she would leave him so that I could swoop in and reclaim my man and my apartment. There was one flaw with this plan that I refused to see at the time but now in hindsight is crystal clear: it relied on the irrefutable truth that Douglas was, and always would be, a cheater.

The room still spinning, I decided to shelve all further plans for getting back together with Douglas until I was decidedly more sensible, sound and sober. Now, it was time to go to bed.

But first, I walked across the gorgeous marble-encrusted bathroom and threw up.

15

I was dreaming that I was at Trip's wedding, talking to Trip. As I spoke to him, my teeth began to fall out of my mouth, one by one. I hoped that no one would notice, but the more I spoke, the more my teeth fell out. As I introduced Jack as Douglas to Trip, one of my teeth went flying out of my mouth and hit the floor with a thump. I fell to the ground, trying to pick up that tooth and the rest of my teeth, but the thumping continued. The more I tried to pick up my teeth, the more thumping I seemed to hear. I woke up in a cold sweat.

I sat up in bed, thanking all that was holy that my teeth were still in my mouth, but the thumping continued. Dull and far away. Almost like a knock. I finally realized that there actually *was* knocking on our hotel suite's door, and jumped out of bed to answer it.

I walked into the suite's living room, past Jack and Vanessa, both passed out and drooling all over our eighteenth-century inspired throw pillows, to the door.

My eyes still drunk with sleep, I could barely see the man

standing at the door, but I was almost positive that he was an airport employee delivering my lost luggage. I thanked him and tipped him and practically danced over to the coffee table to put the suitcase down to open it.

For a minute, I thought that I was still drunk I was so happy, but if I wasn't already sober, I immediately sobered up. I opened the suitcase and looked at a set of very lovely clothes. Very lovely men's clothes. Even in my very hungover state, I was pretty sure that they were not mine.

"This is why people hate L.A.," I said to Vanessa and Jack, who were still fast asleep. "The people are so phony. Here's living proof right here. They lied about my luggage! That disgruntled airport employee probably knew about my predicament and wanted to torture me because of my fabulous hair and makeup." Vanessa and Jack were still playing dead.

I jumped on top of Vanessa and woke her up.

"Five more minutes, Mom," she muttered as I began to shake her by the shoulders.

"Do you remember last night when you said that it would really suck if we had to run around L.A. like complete idiots looking for a new dress and shoes?" I asked her.

"Don't tell me," she said.

She was right. I shouldn't tell her. After all, this weekend is kind of like a minivacation for her, too, so I wouldn't want to stress her out. So, I didn't tell her. Instead, I reached over to the suitcase of dashed dreams and lifted a pair of silk boxers out.

"I'm guessing that those are not yours?" she asked.

A half hour later, we were out on the mean streets of L.A., hitting boutique after boutique, finding nothing. From Melrose to Rodeo, we hit every imaginable store in search of a black-tie gown suitable for a glamorous red-carpet wedding. Most of the stores only seemed to stock size-six gowns, so not only was I tired and cranky from all of the searching, I was also feeling a bit insecure and fat.

By my estimation, we'd hit over twenty-five stores, and still could not find a stitch to wear. Things were starting to look hopeless.

Hopeless, that is, until we came to a beacon of light. At first, we thought it was a mirage, we were so tired, but there it was. The unmistakable sign of all that is good and true in a harsh and unforgiving world: Barneys New York! Located conveniently for us right here in L.A.!

Barneys New York—my favorite store of all time. Barneys is to me what Tiffany & Co. was to Holly Golightly. Nothing bad could ever happen to me once I was inside. Except for this one time last year when I walked into the housewares department asking for some help in locating an anniversary gift for my parents. From across the floor (and at Barneys, it is a big floor, I assure you) the salesperson called out, "Are you one of our brides?" It seemed as if the world had stopped and everyone was staring at me, on pins and needles, waiting for my response. It was as if they were all a bunch of spies for my old Jewish grandmother. ("You're not married *yet?* Can't you just pick one and marry him?") I meekly whispered back, "No," to which the salesperson yelled, "Well, then, I can't help you." *What is this?* I thought. *You only help engaged people? Why, this is discrimination of the worst kind! Call the Anti-Defamation League! Call Alan Dershowitz! Call the Supreme Court of the United States of America—this calls for the ordaining of a new protected class under Title VII!* Even if she meant that she only worked the bridal registry and was unable to assist people in other departments, I still thought that I had a case.

But other than that little incident, Barneys is still my favorite store. What can I say? I'm very resilient.

Like two schoolgirls, we were giddy with excitement as we got into the elevator.

"Do you think dresses are on the same floor here as in New York?" Vanessa asked as she looked at the listing of what departments were on what floors.

"More importantly," I said, "where are the shoes?"

"You always do that," Vanessa remarked, pushing the button for the second floor.

"Do what?" I asked, checking my reflection in the mirrored wall of the elevator.

"Take your eye off of what's important," she said as we exited the elevator. "We're here for a dress. Not shoes. And here you are, still pining over Douglas, a man who treated you horribly, while you ignore Jack, a man who treats you like a princess."

"Jack doesn't even like me," I said as we reached the racks, convincing not even myself. "Remember we tried this once before—South Carolina—and he put the brakes on it?"

"That is not my recollection," Vanessa said. "Anyway, how many years ago was that?"

"We're staffed on every case together," I further reasoned. "Do you want me to get fired or something?"

"And give up the twelve-hour days and constant weekend work?" she countered. "What on earth was I thinking?"

"And even if he did like me, he's totally on the rebound, anyway," I said as I began to flip through the dresses. "He just broke off an engagement."

"Six months ago," Vanessa said, eyeing the racks.

"He'd never set a date," I said, fingering a pale yellow cowl-neck column dress.

"Well, look at you," she said, placing both hands on the rack as she stared at me. "I was just saying to give him a chance. You've gone and got yourself engaged to the guy already."

"Anyway, he's Jack. Now, be a good friend and look for dresses."

I held up a beautiful black satin number that I clearly could not afford. Vanessa shook her head *no*.

"I would find it sexy, you know," Vanessa said, holding up a short red dress to her frame. "Man travels three thousand miles to make a fool of himself all for a girl."

"It really isn't like that," I explained, showing Vanessa a black-and-white off-the-shoulder gown. She shook her head *no*.

"Then what is it like?" she asked, putting down the red dress she was holding, waiting for an answer.

"Brooke?" a salesperson asked, seemingly on cue. Saved by the bell. Or salesperson, as the case may be. "Is that you? Brooke Miller?" I politely smiled back, even though I had no idea who this woman who knew my name was.

"Brooke, it *is* you! Oh, my God, it is so good to see you!" she cried, throwing her arms around my neck. As she did so, I threw Vanessa a very confused look. "How *are* you?"

"I'm great. Thanks," I said. "How are *you?*"

"You don't remember me, do you?" the woman said.

"I remember you," I protested a little too quickly.

The salesgirl turned to Vanessa. "Well, could you expect the captain of the cheerleading squad, editor of the yearbook, etcetera, etcetera, to remember little old me? Senior year, voted most…"

"Of course!" I interrupted, "South Bay High! Yes!" Anything to make her stop reliving my glory days.

"You were a cheerleader?" Vanessa asked.

"Cocaptain," I said. "And I only did layout on yearbook."

"What were the etceteras?" Vanessa asked. She was having fun with this.

"Let's see," the salesgirl offered, "there was homecoming queen junior year."

"And life has been downhill ever since…." I said to no one in particular.

"We were in Spanish class together for all four years of high school," she explained to Vanessa. "You look exactly the same! You still have the same long hair—"

"Yes, of course! Spanish!" I knew that this was the part where I was supposed to show that I knew who she was, but I still had no clue.

"Nina Mitchell?" she said, making it more of a question than a declaration.

"Yes, of course!" I cried out. "Nina!" I was sure that if I said it emphatically enough she'd believe that I knew who she was, even though I was still piecing it together in my mind.

"And this girl, of course," she told Vanessa, "dated the hottest guy at school for a million years!"

"Hot stuff! Go Brooke!" Vanessa said.

"He wasn't anything special, I assure you," I said to Vanessa and the moment the words came out of my mouth, I totally regretted them. In an instant, a thousand memories came flooding back to me from the ninth grade. How could I say that about Danny? I was talking to "Nina, Pinta, Santa Maria"—the girl who was totally, madly, deeply in love with him from the time we all met when we were fourteen. Nina, Pinta, Santa Maria: an unfortunate nickname that Danny himself had thought up, seemingly to relate to her large size. (What can I tell you, he wasn't the brightest boy….) Now that I think of it, she wasn't even that large back then, she just wasn't as skinny as the rest of us were.

The braces may have been removed, the hair bleached blond, the waistline shrunk and the skin cleared up, but I knew that she was still Nina, Pinta, Santa Maria inside. I knew it because I'm still the girl I was in high school on the inside, too.

I remembered that I used to feel sorry for her because she always looked so sad. Like a kid with her face pressed against the candy-store window—always on the outside looking in. In the eleventh grade, at the homecoming dance, Danny and I were crowned king and queen. I was having the time of my life and there sat Nina, at a table in the corner, all alone. Looking at her, I thought I knew just what would cheer her up. Entirely against his wishes, I made Danny dance with her. I thought that I was doing a good deed. As he approached her, she looked so happy. Her face lit up like I'd never seen it before as she told Danny yes, furiously shaking her head. They hit the dance floor and all eyes were on them as he held her tight for a slow song. Halfway through "Careless Whisper" he leaned down into her and, while whispering something into her ear to distract her, pulled the back of her skirt up to reveal her enormous pink granny panties and control-top panty hose to the entire eleventh grade. Laughter erupted in the school gym and it took her quite a while to realize what was going on. I had sprinted halfway across the gym by the time she began pulling her skirt back down, arriving just in time for her to tell me, with her eyes fighting back tears, "You have ruined my life."

Thank God telekinetic powers only exist in novels.

I think.

I remember that after it happened, her mother was so infuriated that she called my mom and I was grounded for a month. Even though I had nothing to do with it. Not really, anyway. My mother said, "Either you did it or you are dumb enough to be hanging around with a boy who would. Either way, you should be ashamed of yourself and either way you're grounded." I guess I had great taste in men even back then.

"I was, like, totally in love with Danny for all four years of high school," she said. The final irony of Danny's life is that he wrote in his yearbook that his goal was to "leave Long Island or die trying" and he now lives on Long Island with his wife and four kids. And his wife is very, very fat. And Nina is very, very skinny. Should I tell her that?

"I'm sorry," I quickly said instead. "He…he was kind of special. He was special. He really liked you back then, I remember."

"Yeah, right, Brooke," she said, "I wish. I was a train wreck back then. Anyway, it is so good to see you! Speaking of hotties, I heard that you used to date Trip Bennington during law school or something."

"Actually, I did."

"Was *he* nothing special?" she asked.

"Well," I said with a laugh, as I twirled a lock of my hair, "he's the reason why we're here for the weekend. We're here for his wedding."

"Oh, my God," she said, as if time had actually stopped. "You are going to *the* wedding? I would kill to go to *the* wedding! It is going to be *the* event of the year."

"It's really not that big of a deal," I said.

"Not a big deal?" she asked Vanessa. "Does this friend of yours think that anything is special? All of Hollywood will be there! A-list only! And Ava is, like, the most beautiful creature on the planet. One time she came in here and I got to dress her. She is, like, the nicest person on earth."

"So I've heard," I said.

"And she's royal," Nina continued. "Do you think *that's* special?"

"Believe it or not, Nina, we're here to get a dress for the wedding," I said.

"But the wedding's tonight," Nina told me.

"Don't get her started," Vanessa instructed. "We actually had this whole airport-lost-baggage thing, and so…"

"Say no more," Nina said. "We've got a million dresses here."

"We've got about an hour," Vanessa told her.

"I'll be right back," she said, as she rushed off to find me a dress.

"You've got a major fan club," Vanessa said. "Was she like that back then?"

"We called her Nina, Pinta, Santa Maria," I said.

"What's that supposed to mean?" Vanessa asked.

"Because she was as big as three ships," I explained, looking over my shoulder to make sure she wasn't coming back.

"Okay," Vanessa said. "That makes no sense whatsoever."

"We were fourteen," I said, as Jack swept in with a tray of coffees.

"I figured that you could use some coffee," he said. He had been hitting the tourist spots while we were shopping and had a "Star Map" tucked under his left arm.

"You are an angel," I said. I clearly needed coffee by now. Nonetheless, Vanessa shot me one of those knowing looks. A raised eyebrow kind of look. One of those "He's Jack, you say?"

looks. "In a platonic way," I quickly said. That should allay everyone's confusion about the matter once and for all.

"Yummy," Vanessa said, laughing at me. "Thanks, honey—don't tell the partners that I drank this. It's not Healthy Foods coffee."

"Please tell the partners that I drank this," I told him. "Maybe it'll get me thrown off of the case."

"Will do," he said. "Now, where's the chair?"

We pointed across the floor to a few chairs set up just outside of the fitting rooms. He walked past Nina as she came back with a dress.

"This will be the only one that you need to try on. I promise," she said. "Brooke, is that your boyfriend?"

"Jack?" I asked. "No! God, no! I mean, he is, of course, very special, but, no, we are not dating."

I rushed off to try on the dress before I could get myself into any more trouble with Nina.

Outside of my dressing room, I overheard Nina approach Jack.

In a low, sultry voice that she hadn't used with Vanessa and me, she asked, "Is there anything that I can help you with?" Help him? Does he look as if he shops for women's dresses?

"No," Jack answered, "I think that I'll just sit here and wait for Brooke."

"Perhaps you would like me to try something on for you?" she offered. Oh, *help* him.

"Um, uh, no thank you?" Jack answered, kind of like a question.

"Very well," she said.

I put on the dress that Nina had picked out for me. A haze of pale pink organza with delicate ruffles strewn about, it had tiny spaghetti straps and a fish tail that was meant to float on the floor behind you.

I took a look at myself and immediately fell in love. With the dress, not my own reflection. It was really perfect. She did a great job picking it out. It just goes to show you, we all grow up and the past is forgotten. Nina's all grown up and she's skinny and pretty now and has an amazing eye for clothes. Turns out we *can* all just get along. A smile crept onto my face as I came out of the dressing room.

"So," I asked, effecting my best Audrey Hepburn, "how do I look?"

"Brilliant, darling," Jack said with a Scottish accent and I smiled.

"We'll take it," Vanessa said to Nina.

16

We ran back to our hotel just in time to see a very pissed off former cross-dresser waiting for us in the hotel lobby. Even if you hadn't seen him there, you would have felt him—his presence filled the entire lobby. There he was, sprawled out on a couch, taking lots of room with his long legs crossed and his massive bag of hair and makeup supplies sitting beside him.

He happened to look great. As a man, I mean. Last time I saw him, Damian was in New York, dressing and performing as a woman. Don't laugh. He did a really mean Diana, and his Barbra wasn't too bad, either. His face has a very feminine quality to it, so with the right hair and makeup, you would swear he didn't have an Adam's apple.

Damian now had cut his hair short and was dressed in form-fitting black pants with a black button-down shirt, which framed his six foot four very, very tall, very, very thin body perfectly. To complement the look, he had his shirt unbuttoned halfway down his chest (no chest hair, of course) and was wearing a Louis

Vuitton belt that had little *LV*s all over it. He looked as if he could be in an ad for something expensive.

"We're late," Vanessa said. "Damian looks pissed."

"We're not late," I told Vanessa. "We are on time."

"Correction," Jack said. "We would have been on time if we hadn't stopped for shoes."

"Okay," I said, "first of all, there is always time for shoes." What kind of talk is this coming from Jack? Even if we *were* running late to my ex-boyfriend's wedding, I still would not stand for such blasphemy.

"That you can't really walk in," Jack persisted.

"What does that have to do with anything?" Vanessa asked.

"I don't know," Jack said, "walking, shoes... Do you see where I'm going with this?"

"You are so naive," I said as we approached Damian. He rose from the couch slowly and stared at us disapprovingly. And he did *rise,* mind you; he didn't stand up or get up or anything that we normal people would do. Rather, Damian rose deliberately, like Moses parting the Red Sea.

"Okay, running like that—not attractive," Damian said.

"Dame, you remember Brooke and Jack," Vanessa said, still out of breath from the mad sprint from the taxi to the lobby. "And you had better not have been talking about me just now."

"Good to see you, girls," he said, looking us up and down. "We don't have much time." And with that, he began to walk toward the elevators. Because of his height, he moved as if in slow motion, gliding down the hallway, while the three of us followed quickly in his wake.

"Did he just say 'pleased to meet you, *girls?*'" Jack asked, grabbing my arm. I laughed as we all got into the elevator.

"We're cutting your hair today, Brooke?" Damian asked me. My hand instinctively flew to my head, the way a mama bird protects her baby birds.

"No," I said. "I am not cutting my hair."

"Damian," Vanessa said.

"Brooke can't cut her hair," Jack said, "it's her trademark."

"Thank you, Jack," I said, "I've had it this length all my life. And anyway, Douglas loves my hair."

"Chop it off," I could have sworn I heard Jack say under his breath just as we got to our floor.

Entering the suite, Damian got down to business. "Okay, first things first," he commanded, "get that booty into the dress you'll be wearing for tonight. I need to see it to figure out a hair and makeup concept." He waved his arms out like a magician and gave a dramatic pause before saying the word *concept*—as if he should have been accompanied by a lone spotlight beaming down on him as he said it—and pronounced the word *concept* as if it were two: *con-cept*.

As I ran into my bedroom, giddy with excitement, Jack's cell phone rang.

"Hello?" he answered. "Oh, hi there…. No, I'm actually not available today to do some work on that case…. Maybe you could get Michael to do it?… Well, I *would* come in today, but for the fact that I'm in L.A. for a wedding…. Yes, I *am* aware that we have an L.A. office…. Yes, I understand," he said, making a play for our *USA Today*. Grabbing and ripping its pages, he brought the phone down to the newspapers he was tearing up. "Uh, Ronnie, you're starting to break up…. I think that I'm losing you…. Oh, you can get Michael to do it? Great! Hello? Hello?" And with that, he slammed the phone shut. "Ah, technology," he said. "It has made our lives infinitely easier."

"This is why I love being a lawyer," Vanessa said. "What case was that on?"

"The Healthy Foods case," he said. "I'm going to order some snacks from their competitor from room service. Anyone want anything?"

"No, thanks," Vanessa said. "Some of us are actually loyal employees."

"You just had their competitor's coffee an hour ago," Jack said.

"No one said being a loyal employee was easy," she replied.

Taking the dress out of its Barneys garment bag, I felt just like a little kid with a brand-new toy. I slowly unzipped the bag as carefully as a child opening a Christmas present (not like I would know what that's like, being Jewish and all, but I unzipped the bag as carefully as I *would imagine* a child opening a Christmas present would). I admired the dress for a moment. It was just as beautiful as when I first laid eyes on it in the store. Sliding it on, I was beaming as I zipped myself up. I did a little spin in it before moving on to the shoes.

I removed my new shoes from their box and admired them, too, for a moment before sliding them onto my feet. The salesperson had called the color *blush* and the model name *beauty*. They were satin open-toe three-and-a-half-inch heels with enormous rhinestone detailing just above the toe. They were like an outfit in and of themselves.

I was sexy. I was sensational. I was elegant and refined. It was me, on the best day of my life. I walked out, ready for the compliments to wash over me.

"Very funny, girl," Damian said, dismissing me with the turn of his head. Not the reaction I was going for.

"What's funny?" I asked Damian, who was already walking toward the windows to take in the view. "What's funny?" I then asked Vanessa, practically tripping over the fishtail as I spun to face her.

"Nothing, honey," she assured me. "My cousin here is just being a Hollywood prick. See, this is why everyone hates L.A."

"Don't nothing me, girl," he said.

"Shut up, Damian," Vanessa said.

"For the love of God," I cried out, "What. Is. FUNNY?"

"That dress," Damian said. "That dress is funny. It's a copy of the dress that Miss Ava wore to the Golden Globes last year."

"That dress costs more than most people's rent," Vanessa said. "How can it be a copy?"

"Oh, my God," I said, suddenly breathing much quicker than before.

"And it's not even a good copy," Damian said.

"So," Vanessa said, "then maybe no one will notice that it's a copy."

"Oh. My. God," I said, grabbing at my stomach to make sure that I was still breathing.

"It's nothing," Vanessa said. "Brooke, you'll wear my dress and I'll wear this one."

"Not with that caboose, she won't," Damian said.

"Who the hell do you think you are talking to?" Vanessa demanded.

"I meant her," Damian said, pointing to me.

"Oh," Vanessa said.

"OH. MY. GOD," I said, falling onto the couch and putting my head between my legs the way they tell you to on airplanes in case of a plane crash.

It was just like that scene in *Rebecca*. When the mean old maid makes the new wife dress up just like the dead first wife and go to a party with all of the dead first wife's friends and everyone looks at the new wife and is, like, totally appalled. It's like Nina is that mean old maid and Ava is the dead first wife and I'm the new Mrs. Winter. Or deWinter. Or whatever the hell their name was.

Maybe if I'd remembered Nina's freaking name this afternoon this wouldn't have happened! I am a bad person. I am a very bad, bad person….

"Everyone, shut up!" Jack said from the other side of the room, taking control of the situation. It was the way I'd seen him take control with tough adversaries, reluctant witnesses and difficult partners. For all of his constant joking around, when Jack meant business, people usually listened. The room was silent as we all sat waiting for what Jack would say next.

"Damian," he said, "didn't you bring other dresses with you? I heard Vanessa specifically ask you to bring an extra dress or two in case we didn't have any luck shopping."

"Well," Damian said, "I brought one dress."

"It's fine," Vanessa said. "It's gorgeous."

"We haven't seen it yet," I pointed out to her, looking up from my lap.

"Right," she said. "Show us the dress."

"Well, what size does little Ava over there take?

"Don't be mean to her," Vanessa said, "she's having a total crisis here…girl!"

"Don't say *girl* if you don't know how to use it," Damian said. "It doesn't become you."

"Um, let's see," I reasoned. "Usually I'm a ten, but I haven't really eaten much in the past few weeks what with the breakup and all and then the stress about finding a date for the wedding…. So, I guess that makes me about an eight now."

"Girl, this is L.A. I've got a six."

"We'll take it," Vanessa said, and Damian walked over to his bag of tricks. He pulled out a dress—delicately, carefully—holding it as if it were a Fabergé egg.

It was a vintage Halston. I'd never seen one before. It was gorgeous. The epitome of what glamour is, was and always should be. Miles of whisper-thin black fabric perfectly cut to be more like a work of art than a dress. He put the dress in my hands and I, too, handled it carefully, as if it were a baby, as I walked back into the bathroom. I hung the dress onto the back of the bathroom door and couldn't help but notice the superior work-manship, holding together a design so timeless that it was relevant even now.

It was a floor-length column dress, with a slit cut from the pool of fabric at the bottom to where I imagined the very top of my thighs would be (and Vanessa thought that no one would see my freshly waxed bikini line). There was a slit on top to match. I wasn't sure which slit made me more nervous. The fabric bunched into an elegant knot right in the middle—I needed to suck in my stomach just to look at it.

I put it on. Well, I tried to put it on, anyway. I squeezed as much of me as I could squeeze and walked out for Damian's harsh judgment. Parts of me were spilling out from every bare angle of the dress. I held my hands over my breasts, which were pouring out (and not in a sexy way). Damian motioned for me to remove my hand and I shook my head no furiously. We danced this little dance a few times until, reluctantly, I moved my hand.

"I can't wear this," I said.

"I beg to differ," Jack said, turning around from across the room. "You are *wearing* that dress."

"Never fear. Just a little bit of this and you will be all set,"

Damian said. He was holding up a roll of something that re-sembled tape.

"What the hell is that?" Vanessa asked.

"You are not putting that on me," I said. I wasn't quite certain exactly what it was, but I did know one thing for sure. It was going nowhere near any of my important body parts.

"Double-sided tape," Damian said, just as naturally as if he were saying "an antique broach" or "a safety pin" or some other thing that did not entail adhesive material latched on to my most delicate areas.

"You are not putting that on me," I said again, just in case he'd missed it the first time.

"Don't be ridiculous," he said. "All of the actresses do it."

"Do I look like an actress to you?" I asked him.

"No," he said, "you do not." And then, as if that were not insult enough, he began to put his hands into the dress to move things around. He was about two inches away from touching parts that I didn't even let Douglas touch.

"Hey!" I screamed out.

"Please," he said, "don't be so parochial, Brooke. Jack, get your mouth off the floor and divert your eyes."

"Well, I'm going to watch just in case something happens with the tape," Jack said. "Like, if it becomes un-taped or something."

"Yeah, no," Damian said. I suppose you can't blame a guy for trying. "So," Damian said, "with the tape, it's going to look like this."

He surprised even me. I looked amazing. If I do say so myself, that is. Which I do! Maybe I really *am* a size six!

"So, that's just to give you an idea of what the dress will look like once I tape you into it," he explained. "Eliminates all of the sagging that you've got." Sagging? Did that man just say *sagging?* So, maybe I'm not a size six.

"Dame!" Vanessa screamed. "Be nice to her. She's practically having a nervous breakdown over here."

"Nervous breakdown?" I asked, trying to be cool. Or as cool as one can be with a former cross-dressing gay man's hands down one's dress.

"Girl," he said back, "that is a vintage Halston I'm about to tape your friend into. I *am* being nice."

"Point taken," I said. I thought it best not to infuriate the man who was now holding my breasts and later would be taping them into a dress.

"Anyway," Damian said, hands out of the dress and now smoothing it out for me, "I knew that if *I* could fit into this dress, *she* could fit into this dress."

"He can fit into this dress?" I mouthed to Vanessa. She shrugged her shoulders.

"Now," he asked, "who's ready to get gorgeous?" Vanessa and I both raised our hands.

Damian blew my long hair out straight and then put it in enormous rollers the size of cantaloupes to give it body and a bit of wave. He told me that he was going for a Rita Hayworth thing. For Vanessa, he went Jackie O, adding extensions and smoothing her locks into an elegant upsweep that defied gravity. He even put a bit of pomade into Jack's shaggy hair to give him a look that could only be described as dangerously debonair.

He then dove into his bag of supplies to do makeup. I should have watched to see what he was doing, but instead, I just sat back and enjoyed the pampering. He started by air-brushing foundation and blush onto my face. Yes, air-brushing—the newest thing in makeup. All of the actresses are doing it (and, no, I did not fall into the trap again of protesting and asking Damian if he thought that I looked like an actress). It felt like a cool breeze being blown onto your face and was helping to relax me for the big night.

For eyes, he gave me Marilyn Monroe white eye shadow contrasted with black liquid eyeliner. On Vanessa, he opted for a smoky forest-green look that brought out the flecks of color in her eyes. Damian gave us both false eyelashes—each applied lovingly lash by lash—which, quite honestly, could have gone to the party by themselves. I worried for a second about how on earth we would be getting the glue off our eyes at the end of the night, but then chose to focus, instead, on how they made me feel like a goddess each and every time I blinked. I began practicing my slow deliberate blink in the mirror, imagining myself saying seductive things like "You know how to whistle, don't you? You just put your lips together and blow."

Damian gave us each a lipstick and matching gloss to bring with us to the wedding—a pale beige lipstick with a glossy nude finish for me, and a baby-pink lipstick and pink lip gloss with a touch of glimmer for Vanessa.

When he was done, Vanessa and I looked positively heavenly, with just the right amount of eyes and lips to be innocent and sexy all at once.

And then, of course, there was more double-sided tape. Which I really came to embrace after a while.

We were buffed, beautified and beaming. We were ready to go Hollywood.

17

As we walked up the steps to the Viceroy, on our way to my ex-boyfriend's wedding, I had a feeling that nothing could go wrong. You know that feeling you get when everything seems to be right with the world? When the planets seem to be in alignment? That was exactly how I felt as I walked up the steps. I was wearing an impossibly sexy vintage Halston dress (if only two sizes too small) and brand-new stiletto heels (that I could almost even walk in), flanked on either side by my two best friends. Nothing could go wrong.

Well, sort of. My feet failed me, or I should say, my brand-new three-and-a-half-inch heels failed me and I tripped up the steps in my haste to get to the wedding in time.

"I'm okay," I said, as Jack held me up. Always the gentleman. As he stood me upright, I turned to face him and Vanessa.

"First," I said, "I just want to thank the two of you for hauling yourselves out to L.A. on such short notice."

"You know we'd do anything for you," Vanessa said. "And, also, I was invited, so I was coming anyway."

"Right," I said. "Then, Jack, especially you. It really means a lot to me that you're here and that you're helping me to perpetrate a fraud on the Scottish community."

"Anything for my girl," he said, putting his hand on my face. "You know that." And I did.

"Okay, so try to remember your Scottish accent," I said. "Don't do that English one or that Irish one. Focus."

"Got it," he said. In a perfect Scottish accent.

"And do not slip into that freaking Australian accent," I said, "because, A—I will kill you and B—you're just not very good at it."

"Right," he said back, still in character with accent in tow.

"And say lots of Scottish stuff like I taught you."

"For fuck's sake!"

I smiled like a proud parent. What I was about to say next was "Try to be more like Douglas," but I knew that it would hurt Jack's feelings. "Okay," I instead said, "try to be more good-looking." Vanessa's mouth fell to the floor. In hindsight I tend to think that maybe I should have just said the Douglas thing.

"For fuck's sake, Brooke," Jack said.

"Sorry," I said, "I'm just nervous. I meant…"

"Maybe this will make you less nervous," he said as he pulled something out of the inside pocket of his jacket.

It was the fake engagement ring—I hadn't even realized that I'd forgotten it.

"Thank you," I said and kissed Jack on the cheek.

We walked up the stairs to this fabulous Los Angeles hotel, and I felt like a movie star. Maybe that's because my ex-boyfriend Trip is a Hollywood agent, and most of the guests actually *were* movie stars, but I digress.

Quietly decorated in creamy white and beige tones, the hotel looked more like a spa than a hotel. Delicious fabric hung from everywhere and soothing music surrounded you as you walked in. I even detected the faint smell of vanilla mixed with spice—the familiar infused with the exotic. This being L.A., I went with it. Like the guests arriving for the wedding it was hosting, the hotel was fabulously elegant. Every inch of it, every last detail, was hopelessly chic. Even the bellhops' uniforms were glamorous. I wondered what the rooms looked like.

There was a delicate pond in the center of the lobby and the sound of the water trickling down its tiny waterfall had the intended effect—I immediately felt serene and at peace. There were black stones all along and inside of the pond, which created a striking contrast to the stark white that enveloped most of the space. The reception desk was hidden in a corner—the couches and tables that boasted cocktail service were the centerpiece of the lobby. That it was a hotel seemed only incidental to the "see and be seen" atmosphere that was before my eyes.

The hotel was beautiful, my friends and I looked beautiful, and at that precise moment in time, I felt as if the world were beautiful.

Amid the crowd of movie stars and movie star wannabes, I saw a tall figure that seemed to be the center of attention. His dirty-blond hair had gotten lighter in the Los Angeles sun, but even before he turned around, I knew that it was Trip from the very way he stood. Back straight and shoulders at attention, he looked like the prep-school graduate that he was. Wedding guests were approaching him and hugging him and kissing him from every angle and I could see a line of people, three or four deep, jockeying for position.

"Maybe we should wait until we see him at the cocktail hour," I said to Vanessa and Jack. "He looks too busy now."

"Good call," Vanessa agreed.

As we tried to make our way through the lobby, Trip turned around and made eye contact with me. For an instant, I didn't recognize his face. I realized that we hadn't seen each other since our law-school graduation. It struck me as sad that it was possible to barely even recognize someone with whom you had shared three years of your life. Someone with whom you had shared your bed.

"Brooke?" he called out from the eye of his tornado of wedding guests.

"Trip!" I said and walked toward him. He broke away from all of the other guests to greet us.

"Brooke, I almost didn't recognize you," he said as he gave me a kiss hello.

"Me, too," I said.

"Vanessa, you look exactly the same," he said as he gave her a kiss. "Gorgeous as ever. When are you going to come out here so that I can make you a movie star?" She giggled and all I could think was *Why doesn't he want to make* me *a movie star?* I would have to clarify that with him later.

"Trip," I said, "I would like to introduce you to my fiancé, Douglas," I said, as he shook hands with Jack/Douglas. Trip smiled at us with a million startlingly white teeth and I realized that I had forgotten how good-looking he was.

"Ah, Douglas," Trip said, "nice to finally meet you. I've heard a lot about you."

"G'day mate," Jack/Douglas replied, Crocodile Dundee triumphantly returning to our midst.

Now, does that sound Scottish to you?

Trip looked at me in confusion and I looked back with one of those smiles that says "I know you think my fiancé is Scottish and he's speaking like an Aussie, but really, there is a very logical explanation for this." You know, *that* look.

As I stood there with my mouth gaping open, horrified that Jack had given up the game before the game had even begun, a thought ran through my head for the very first time—maybe this would be harder than it had originally seemed.

18

"Chhhhhh! Hmmm. Ahmmm…"

Jack began to do his acting exercises, making strange noises with his throat. As he gargled, Trip began to look around for other, more normal, wedding guests to greet.

"Right," Jack quickly recovered in a Scottish accent. "Just kidding, there, chap. Did our girl here tell you that I'm part Australian? Damn pleasure to meet you," he said, shaking Trip's hand furiously. I smiled and tried to recover, but not before Jack then said: "For fuck's sake!"

While I looked around for a cliff to throw myself off, Jack continued speaking, with his Scottish accent now under control: "Uh, congratulations, I've heard a lot about you."

"And I you," Trip said as a waitress approached us with a tray of champagne. We all quickly grabbed a glass. "Glad you could make it."

"I hope you've got some haggis here," Jack said. "I could really go for some haggis."

"Maybe at the cocktail hour, honey," I said, downing my champagne in one gulp.

"Trip, dear," Trip's mom called from a few feet away, "could you please come and say 'hello' to the Hendersons?" She looked right through me. It was as if she didn't even see me standing there, even though I knew that she did. Trip excused himself and I overheard her whisper to Trip, "Who invited that Jewish girl?" It's comforting to know that some things never change. Who said you can never go home again?

"That went well," Jack said, putting his arms around Vanessa and me. "I don't know if you noticed, but for a second there I sort of lost the accent."

"You don't say?" Vanessa said.

"Yeah, I think that I might actually be a bit nervous about this whole thing. For a second there I was all Australian, but I don't think that anyone noticed," he said looking down at me. "You don't think that Trip noticed, do you?" Now, my mother is always telling me that you need to be gentle with men, that they have fragile egos that need constant massaging, so I knew what my mother would have said in this situation.

"You said *G'day mate,*" I said. (Unfortunately, that was not what she would have said.)

"So, you think Trip noticed?" Jack asked. I wasn't sure whether Jack was asking me if I thought that Trip noticed that he was nervous or that Trip noticed that his accent was all wrong, but since the answer to both questions was an unequivocal *yes,* I didn't think that I really needed clarification before answering. Vanessa shot me a dirty look.

"No, honey," I said and smiled. That *was* what my mother would have done. Vanessa smiled back at me and nodded.

(Married women always seem to know what to say at times like that. They must get a handbook on it or something after their ceremony.)

After about a half an hour of milling about, drinking champagne (or downing it in my case), we were ushered into the Grand Ballroom. It had been transformed into an ethereal space. The untrained eye would have no idea that one week earlier, the very same room had hosted the Dungeons & Dragons annual convention. Jack did, though, because he, like my dad, feels it necessary to strike up conversations with anyone and everyone within ten feet of where he is standing. Apparently the general manager of the hotel had told him about the convention in response to Jack saying, "Beautiful wedding so far, huh?" (To Jack's credit, my father would have then added, "Wonder how much this little baby set them back?")

White lilies and roses filled the Grand Ballroom, and tea lights were lit everywhere you looked, giving the feeling of an intimate atmosphere, even though the room itself was bigger than an entire Manhattan block. There must have been over five hundred guests coming into the room, each taking a perfectly dressed chair along the candle-lit aisle. Trip's ushers walked us to three seats directly across the aisle from a famous celebrity photographer who had shot everyone from the Artist Formerly Known as Prince to President Bush.

The string quartet began to chirp and the bridal procession began. First, Trip came out, escorted by his parents on either side of him. He smiled an enormous smile and walked down the aisle, stopping every few steps to greet wedding guests and shake their hands as if he were the pope. When he reached the aisle of a prominent Hollywood producer and his twenty-four-year-old wife, he actually stopped for a brief instant. I could have sworn I saw him shake hands on a deal. Was I the only one who saw it? Or was I the only one who noticed because this was just what they did at Hollywood weddings?

"If that man just made a deal, I hope that it was at least on the bride's behalf," Vanessa said, matter-of-factly, as if there were a Miss Manners chapter dedicated to the etiquette involved with making deals while walking down the aisle to one's own wedding.

Next, members of Ava's family came out, one by one, in what I could only assume were their traditional outfits of royalty. A cloud of red and gold fabric surrounded each family member as they walked down the aisle—slowly, somberly. I frantically checked my program as each person passed, anxious to see who they were and where they fell into the royal scheme of things.

Then came the Hollywood bridesmaids and ushers. Each bridesmaid paraded down the aisle in her red-and-gold satin gown as if she were on a red carpet. The groomsmen, dressed beautifully in white dinner jackets, all mugged for the wedding photographers as they walked. Vanessa told me that all of the major fashion designers were fighting over who would design the bridesmaid dresses. She said rumor had it that Karl Lagerfeld actually came to blows with Ralph Lauren over the dresses, but I don't believe that for an instant.

I was about to make a catty comment about the royal bridesmaids out-glamming the glamorous Hollywood actress bridesmaids when the quartet began to play an achingly beautiful melody. Everyone spun around and rushed to their feet as Ava walked out with her father. She was wearing a delicate off-the-shoulder gown that framed her petite figure beautifully.

I wondered if I would ever walk down an aisle as I turned my fake engagement ring around my finger.

"Dearly beloved," the priest began.

"Sorry about before," Jack whispered, leaning into me.

"No problem," I whispered back. I was too busy feeling bad for myself to give Jack any grief.

"I think that I covered well, though," he said, eyes beaming like a little boy. I didn't have the heart to tell him that he hadn't.

"Is it cold in here?" he whispered.

"I'm fine," Vanessa whispered.

"It's because your legs are exposed," I told him, observing that his legs were covered in goose bumps.

Stop looking at Jack's legs. Stop looking at Jack's legs!

"Now you know how we feel," Vanessa whispered to Jack.

"I guess you should have put on some hose with that skirt," I said.

"A—it's a kilt," Jack said, "and, B—that wasn't even funny."

"Okay," Vanessa said, voice getting a bit louder as she laughed, "A—yes it was, and B—I feel, like, totally vindicated as a woman now. It's like, if just one man can feel our pain for an evening, it's all worthwhile." A couple sitting in front of us turned around and we all looked ahead, pretending that we hadn't been the ones talking.

"You'd better watch out," I warned Jack, "before Gloria Steinem over there signs you up for a bikini wax."

The woman in front of me caught me on that one and quietly shushed me. But really, how could I be expected to listen to all of this? The priest went on to detail Ava's life and all of her mar-tyrlike pursuits: Ava works with the blind; Ava works with the homeless; Ava works with children stricken with cancer. He just droned on and on about how Ava did this and Ava did that and just generally explained how Ava is a saint and I'm evil. Except he didn't come out and say the part about me being evil, he just inferred it.

You know the way religion tends to do that? Makes you feel guilty? I asked a friend once what a Catholic mass was like and she said that it could be summed up with a simple topic sentence—the point of just about every sermon—you're bad, try to control yourselves. We really bonded over that because I told her that rabbis practically use the same sermon. They must all get it off the Internet or something. Or at least I *think* they all use the same sermons, because, truth be told, I really only go to temple on the High Holy days. And I don't even go to the whole service.

Actually, now that I think about it, Mormons aren't really based in guilt (I guess that Mormons don't really have the time for such things as guilt what with having so many wives and all). When I was sixteen, I went on a cross-country tour and spent a day at Temple Square in Salt Lake City. We were led around for the day by a missionary named Ted. He taught us tons of fun facts about Mormons such as the fact that they have a living prophet. Can you believe that? An actual living breathing prophet. You would think that in today's day and age of cynicism that people would doubt you if you claimed to be a prophet sent from God, but apparently not. How do you get that gig? And exactly how does one announce that he or she is, in fact, the living prophet? Who would have the gall to think so highly of themselves to think that they were a living prophet? Come to think of it, most of my ex-boyfriends thought that they were God. So did their mothers. Does that count?

Missionary Ted was so dreamy—all blond hair and blue eyes. I was so lost in his eyes that when he told me about his love for Jesus Christ and how he wanted to scream it from the rooftops,

I wanted to tell him that I would go with him to scream. I hoped that my brown hair and dark eyes wouldn't betray me. I was afraid to tell him that I was Jewish for fear that he would scream out "Jewess! There is a Jewess among us and she is trying to seduce me!" But, he didn't. Instead, he led our tour group into the visitor's center where an enormous statue of Jesus served as the centerpiece of the room (and I mean *enormous*—this thing made the statue of David in Florence look, well, small). Ted sat beside me as the lights went dim and an elaborate presentation began. I was so excited that he chose to sit next to me that I barely even noticed when Jesus began to speak à la Disney's Hall of Presidents. I was so disappointed when the lights came on and Ted quickly got up. He didn't even try to hold my hand or brush against my knee or some other completely innocent Mormon-esque gesture of affection. He thanked us all for coming and told us to enjoy the many exhibits about the life of Jesus Christ on the way out, helpfully pointing out that restrooms could be found between the crucifixion and the resurrection.

"Ava actually became an actress to overcome her severe shyness and now uses drama therapy with handicapped children at Mount Sinai…."

Enough with her good qualities already! I don't hear anyone talking about Trip's wonderful qualities up there. Maybe that was because Trip would never do anything unless there was some form of reward, monetary or otherwise, in it for him. But, I never heard them go on and on about one's qualities this much at a wedding before. Granted, I never attended the wedding of someone quite so saintlike before, but still. I mean, I billed over two thousand hours last year! I sincerely doubt that my parents' rabbi would be talking about that at my wedding.

This is why I much prefer a Jewish wedding ceremony. Twenty minutes long. You're in, you're out. Bring on the kosher cocktail franks.

"This can't be real," I thought but didn't say. Or, I should say, I thought and meant not to say, but said. Oops.

"Actually, it is," Jack whispered. "When I saw her on *Entertainment Tonight,* she took Mary Hart to this shelter where she—"

"You are a litigator in a big firm in Manhattan," I said to Jack. "How do you get home in time to see *Entertainment Tonight* every night?"

"I think that the better question is why do you watch *Entertainment Tonight* every night?" Vanessa asked.

"What's wrong with *Entertainment Tonight?* I used to be an actor, you know," Jack said.

"Let's just put it this way," Vanessa explained, "you're about one step away from watching Lifetime Television for Women."

Vanessa and I snickered as the priest announced that it was time to kiss the bride.

Trip and Ava kissed as the audience stood and applauded.

19

Finally, some cocktail franks. Kosher or not, those things always hit the spot.

The cocktail hour was amazing. Now I know the meaning of "rubbing elbows." The room was filled with Hollywood's best and brightest, and there was little old me, rubbing elbows with them. Literally. Brushing by them elegantly and then smiling to say "hello." Or, I should say, bumping into them very ungracefully and then checking my boobs to make sure that they were still in my dress, but you get my point. Glamorous actresses, brilliant directors, rich producers, the most successful agents and even a few sports stars had turned out for the wedding of the season. And I seriously doubt that it was the sushi bar that brought them there. Even though that was where my date had parked himself all night, I was sure that for the Hollywood folks, it took more than a spicy tuna roll to get them excited.

Vanessa and I, on the other hand, had parked ourselves at the caviar station. It was perfectly situated to the right of the vodka slide, but to the left of the kitchen doors, so that as the waitstaff came out with hors d'oeuvres, we missed nary a shrimp skewer, vegetable dumpling or smoked salmon on toast points between the two of us.

I left Vanessa over at the caviar station with a football player who had mistaken her for a famous model while I met Jack at the prime-rib carving station. He was being quizzed by old family friends of Ava's parents.

"Where in Scotland are you originally from?" Mr. Martin was asking Jack.

"Who me?" he asked in a perfect Scottish accent. "Ah, yes, Perth. Perth. Lovely Perth." He looked at me for approval, and I stood beaming from ear to ear. I was so happy I could have kissed him right then and there. In a platonic way, of course.

"Ah, yes, Perth! We've heard that it's so beautiful there," Mrs. Martin said.

"Beautiful," Jack said as he sipped his drink.

"We were just there!" Mr. Martin said.

"You were?" Jack said, his vodka straight up practically coming out of his nose.

"Why yes!" Mrs. Martin explained. "We just got back from Scotland last week, you see."

"You did?" Jack asked. I signaled for the waitress. This was going to be a very long cocktail hour.

"Yes," Mrs. Martin explained. "But I'm afraid we never made it to Perth."

"No, I'm afraid not," Mr. Martin chimed in. "Is Perth near Edinburgh?"

"Edinburgh. Edinburgh, uh…no?" Jack guessed as he brushed his hand through his hair. I could tell he was trying to visualize the map from www.visitscotland.com in his mind, but I didn't know how much that would help, since the map wasn't drawn to scale. I offered nothing to the conversation as I stood next to him smiling like an idiot—I hadn't studied where cities were in relation to each other, either, so I really couldn't be mad at Jack for not knowing the answer himself. "Uh, well, Edinburgh is where Paris ought to be. Yes, that's what I always say."

Where was that cocktail waitress? Can't she see that we're thirsty over here?

"Oh," Mrs. Martin said.

"Ever played St. Andrews?" Mr. Martin asked. Jack nodded and shrugged knowingly so as to say: "Don't I always?"

"So, what's your favorite part of Scotland?" Mrs. Martin asked.

"Ah, yes, well, that would be my own hometown," Jack said. I put my hand on Jack's shoulder as a show of support. He was recovering from the Edinburgh incident quite nicely.

"Well, isn't that sweet?" Mrs. Martin asked.

"Yes, it is," Mr. Martin agreed. "But come on, there have to be some other places you could tell us about. Tell us about some of the places that the tourists miss."

"Uh, yes, of course," Jack said as Mr. and Mrs. Martin looked on with anticipation. "Well, there's Aberdeen, also known as the City of Roses, did you see that? It's beautiful. And then there's Stirling, the smallest city in all of Scotland, that's quite beautiful, too. And then, of course, there are the famous lochs. Did you know that Loch Ness is actually the second largest loch? Not the first?" He was spewing off information quickly and in short snippets, as if he were a contestant on a game show.

"We did not know that!" Mrs. Martin said, clapping her hands together with excitement.

"What else do the tourists miss?" Mr. Martin asked, a big smile on his face.

"What else?" Jack said. "Did you know that over 790 islands make up the country of Scotland?"

"Yes, our tour guide told us that," Mrs. Martin said. "What else?"

"Did you know that Sir Arthur Conan Doyle, author of the *Sherlock Holmes* series was a Scot?" He was sounding more and more like Alex Trebek with every tiny fact he offered.

"Yes," Mrs. Martin said, eyes wide with anticipation for Jack's next tidbit of information.

"Yes, of course, what else? What else, indeed. It's just, god-damn. I'm sorry. I'm afraid that I can't really talk about it. It's times like these when you really think of family, you know. I just miss me mum so damn much!" And with that, he started to cry. While I stood in wide-eyed horror, it looked as if Mr. and Mrs. Martin really bought it. I guess he really is a pretty decent actor.

"Let's make a toast," Mr. Martin cried out, throwing his arms around Jack's shoulders and walking him toward the bar. "A toast to Scotland!"

"Yes, of course!" Mrs. Martin said. "A toast to Scotland. To your mum! I'm sure she misses you as much as you miss her!" Mr. Martin put his arm around Jack and Mrs. Martin took my arm. They walked us to the bar as if they were our chaperones.

"We should get some sort of traditional Scottish drink," Mr. Martin said to Mrs. Martin.

"Douglas, what should we get?" Mrs. Martin asked as we caught up with Jack and Mr. Martin at the bar.

"Traditional Scottish drink, ay?" Jack said. "Well, of course—that would be—Scotch!"

"Yes, Scotch!" Mrs. Martin cried as if it were the most natural thing in the world. "Of course! Bartender, four glasses of Scotch on the rocks, please!" We all lined up at the bar as the bartender set down our drinks.

"The water of life," Jack said as he grabbed his glass.

"To Scotland!" Mr. Martin cried out.

"To your mum!" Mrs. Martin said, tipping her glass to Jack.

"God save the queen," Jack said, downing his Scotch. Not knowing what else to do, I downed mine, too. It burned my throat, but I was careful to stay cool, as if I downed Scotch all the time with my handsome Scottish fiancé. "Now, if you good people would excuse me, I should be spending some quality time with my fiancée now."

"Well, yes, you should," Mr. Martin said. "Lucky girl."

Jack turned to leave and, like the gentleman he was pretending to be, put out his arm for me to take.

"Close call," I whispered to Jack, just as we were approached by a waiter.

"My fellow countryman!" the waiter called out in an accent I couldn't quite place.

"Excuse me?" Jack asked in his American accent.

"I don't meet too many fellow Scotsmen out here in La La Land. This is a real treat for me!" the waiter told Jack. Jack nodded his head, clearly doing his best not to speak, for fear of the real Scotsman hearing that his accent was a fake. "Do you run into many Scots in New York City?" the waiter asked Jack. Jack nodded again and used some hand gestures as if to say so-so. "That is where I heard you were from, isn't it?" he asked, looking at Jack's kilt. Jack vigorously nodded yes.

"May I please borrow my date?" I interjected. I felt it best to get the fake Scotsman away from the real Scotsman.

"Why, of course," the waiter said. "Right then. I'll see you later." Jack and I both nodded and smiled and walked away.

"Thank you. Thank you. Thank you," Jack said to me, once we were safely out of the Scotsman's earshot.

"Oh, my God," I said. "I had to get you away from that guy. He's Scottish."

"I'm aware," Jack said.

"But you're not," I whispered back.

"Again, duly noted," Jack said.

"But you're pretending to be," I whispered.

"Okay, Brooke, where are we going with this?"

"So, I just wanted to get you away from him. You obviously don't want to be speaking in front of him."

"That's why I was nodding a lot in lieu of speaking."

"Good move," I affirmed, adding a thumbs-up signal for emphasis.

"So, what's our plan?" he whispered, brushing his shaggy brown hair from his eyes.

"Plan?" I asked. Didn't he just see me deftly get him away from the real Scotsman? How much more of a plan can a girl be expected to have?

"Yes, plan. I mean, I can't keep nodding all night and you certainly can't keep excusing us every time he comes by."

"That *was* my plan," I said.

"Oh. Works for me."

"I really had no idea that all of these guests would be so well traveled and educated," I said. "I mean, I thought that Americans were supposed to be ignorant about other cultures."

"Well, I think that it's clear that you and I are the only ones who are ignorant about other cultures."

"True," I said. "Okay, I think that it's safe to say that we should drop the whole title thing. I mean, if we can't even handle the basics of being a Scotsman, we certainly can't take the pressure of pretending that you have a title."

"Agreed. Okay, do you know where Edinburgh is in relation to Perth?" he asked me. I looked back at him blankly. "Well, then, did you bring the outline?" he asked me, eliciting yet another blank stare. My outline was fifteen pages long. Did he really think that it would fit into my tiny evening purse that could barely fit my lipstick and gloss?

"How long did you date this freaking guy that you have no idea where he is from?"

"I know where he's from," I said. "He's from Perth."

"Yes, I've got that part."

"Well, I'm sorry that I didn't spend more of the relationship brushing up on my Scottish geography!"

"I just can't believe that you know nothing about where this guy is from," he said.

"Where was Penny from?" I asked.

"Penny?"

"Yes, remember her? The woman you were dating that summer I met you?" I was quite certain that he couldn't have forgotten Penny. No man could forget Penny. All long legs and pouty lips, even I couldn't forget Penny. All she ever wanted to talk about was her so-called love of sports and how much she hated shopping. As if she could fool me. Please! I made up that whole "I love sports" trick! Not like I was jealous of her or anything.

"Yes, I remember her," he said. "Cleveland."

"Cleveland, Ohio?" I asked.

"Yes," Jack answered, as if I had just asked him if the capital of

the United States was Washington, D.C., or something equally as
obvious to a big-time lawyer like him.

"Cleveland, huh? And, how close is that to Columbus, Ohio?"
I asked. Didn't I tell you that sometimes it's annoying when all of
your friends are litigators? My razor-sharp wit and amazing sense
of irony was completely lost on Jack.

"Are we at a wedding pretending that you are from Ohio?"
he asked me.

"Aberdeen is where Paris ought to be," I said through clenched
teeth. "Aberdeen!"

"What are you talking about?" he asked.

"You said Edinburgh," I said, "but the quote is Aberdeen! The
quote is 'Aberdeen is where Paris ought to be!' I told you to study
your cards!" Jack looked back at me and began to laugh. It made
me begin to laugh, too.

"Well, I didn't attribute it to Stevenson, so maybe the Martins
just think that I feel very strongly about Edinburgh," he said, still
with a chuckle in his voice. "Anyway, how did you know that I
needed rescuing?" he asked.

"You looked a little squirmy in that skirt of yours," I said. He
shot back a look. "More so than before," I clarified.

"This was much easier last night with the girls, you know,"
he told me.

"Brooke, my dear!" I heard calling from just a few feet away.
I could practically hear the theme song to *Jaws* as the voice got
closer. "Why, hello, Brooke."

"Hi, Aunt Muffin," I said, putting on my fake country-club
smile that I reserved strictly for my opposing parties in tough litigation and members of Trip's family. It was Trip's aunt and uncle.
Decked out in South Sea pearls the size of golf balls and a ball

gown the circumference of which rivaled any Southern debu-
tante's, Trip's aunt very much looked every bit like you would
imagine a "Muffin" would look. Blond hair arranged like a
football helmet and heavily made up so that you could barely tell
whether or not there was an actual face underneath, she matched
Trip's uncle perfectly, with his capped teeth and cheeks that were
red from one too many prewedding martinis. I used to joke with
Trip that the only reason they called her Muffin was that Buffy
had already been taken.

I could barely lean over and air kiss her because of the massive
amount of floor space her dress was taking up. Uncle John, clearly
drunk since picture taking earlier that afternoon, had his crisp
white dinner jacket already wrinkled and looked as if he was mere
minutes away from being ready for a nap.

"John, you remember Brooke, don't you?" Aunt Muffin said
to Uncle John. "The one who dated Trip during law school?"
She was speaking very loud, as if he couldn't hear her.

"The Jewish girl?" he asked Aunt Muffin. I wondered if he
thought that I couldn't hear him, or if like his sister, Trip's mother,
he simply didn't care.

"Shalom," I said, which gave Jack a bit of a laugh.

"Oh, yes, Brenda!" Uncle John said. "You were the funny one,
weren't you? You were very funny, right? This new one's not so
funny. Very nice, though. But not funny."

"Brooke, dear," Aunt Muffin said. "It's Brooke."

"What?" Uncle John asked. I was certain that he would be
calling me Brenda for the duration of the evening.

"Aunt Muffin and Uncle John, please let me introduce you to
my date. This is my fiancé, Douglas."

"Nice to meet you," Uncle John hiccupped.

"Fiancé? You're not married?" she said, glancing down at my hands. Her eyes immediately flew to my left hand and she took a quick peek at my faux engagement ring. Thankfully, her dress took up so much square footage that she was unable to get close enough to me to realize that the ring was fake. She nodded her head. "Oh. Well," Aunt Muffin said, grasping her hands together in a way that I was pretty sure she thought showed that she cared, "this must be a very hard day for you. No offense," she said, turning to Jack. And then, turning back to me, she asked: "Does he speak English?"

"None taken," Jack said.

"Actually, Muffin," I explained, "Trip and I are still very good friends."

"Trip asks you to move to California, you say no. He asks Ava, and look what happens," she said, waving her arms to indicate that she was talking about the wedding. Then, grasping my hand again, she whispered, "It's good that you're not bitter about it, though."

"Bitter?" Jack asked under his breath, "No. Insane enough to make her best friend dress up as a Scotsman and pretend to be her boyfriend? Yes."

"What was that, dear?" Aunt Muffin asked him.

"He was just saying how very happy we are for them," I explained.

"Well, that's sweet," Aunt Muffin said. "See, my generation, we didn't really stay friends with former beaus. I wasn't really happy for any of them."

"Well, we're still friends," I said. "I even helped Trip get his first job out here as an entertainment lawyer. Working for one of my father's friends."

"Goddamn Jews control all of Hollywood," Uncle John said, waving his arms to indicate that he was talking about the wedding. "But I don't have to tell you that."

"No, you don't," I said. "I only *wish* that you wouldn't." And I was pretty sure that half of the guest list wouldn't want him telling them that, either.

"Are you Scottish?" Uncle John asked Jack.

Jack looked down at his kilt. Uncle John didn't say a word and simply continued looking at Jack for his answer.

"Yes," Jack said.

"So, tell me about this tartan of yours," Uncle John said.

"Well, it's blue for starters."

"I know that the Scots are particularly proud of their tartans," Uncle John said. "Family thing, and all. I do business with tons of Scots."

"What type of business is that?" Jack asked.

"So, tell me about yours," Uncle John said.

"Me? Well, I'm a lawyer."

"About your kilt, silly, not your business," Uncle John said.

"Well, it's also got some red in it," Jack said.

"Used to have this one business colleague of mine who was a Scot," Uncle John said. "Asked him about his kilt once and he talked about it for damn near a half an hour! So, don't be shy. You can tell me all about yours."

"Well, it all started centuries ago when my family—"

"Will you two please excuse us?" I said, cutting Jack off. "I see some old friends that we absolutely must say 'hello' to." As we walked away, I heard Uncle John comment to Aunt Muffin: "Those Scots really love to talk."

We navigated the rest of the cocktail hour with relative ease, stopping only time to time to engage in such delightful exchanges as this:

Wedding guest: So, are you Scottish?

Jack: What gave it away?

Wedding guest: Do you know Evan McCullough?

Jack: He's from Perth, is he?

Wedding guest: No, Scotland.

Jack: It's a big country, you know.

Wedding guest: Oh, okay. You should get to know him, though. He's a nice guy.

Jack: Right.

Before we knew it, it was time to go into the main room for the reception. And we didn't even get a chance to sample the potato bar.

20

"Oh, my," I practically gasped as we walked into the room where the reception was being held. I looked in disbelief at the breathtaking space that was before me. It was another masterpiece—another cavernous banquet room, completely transformed. Like the room we had just left, this room was decorated beautifully with fragrant flowers, lush fabric and candles everywhere you looked. It was all at once formal, yet entirely comfortable—done up to the hilt, yet understated.

A wraparound balcony hovered above the two-story walls, tea lights lining its banister. Each table had a very complex, very beautiful floral arrangement floating on its tabletop. Huge glass candelabras held up miles of ivory roses and lilies, surrounded by tall, majestic candles, standing at full attention like the guards at Buckingham Palace. Somehow, I knew that the candles would not dare to drip. Each chair was magnificently dressed in a very thick, luxurious ivory satin with a bow tied around the back.

The dance floor had been painted white with Trip and Ava's

monogram elegantly adorning its center. I had never seen any-thing like it before in my life—I could have sworn I even saw a dove or two flying around the room.

"Do you think that this is what heaven looks like?" Jack asked, looking up and around as he walked.

"I hope so," Vanessa said, trailing off as she brushed her hand against one of the chairs.

"Speak like an Aussie just once during this reception and you will soon find out," I told Jack.

"So," a wedding guest asked Jack as we tried to find table eleven, "what do you think of the political situation in Scotland?" Jack and I shot each other blank stares. My goodness, a guy puts on a kilt and all of the sudden, everyone expects him to be an expert on all things Scottish....

"Well," Jack said, "what do you think I think of it?" The man nodded back at Jack knowingly.

"Ladies and gentlemen," the bandleader bellowed. His voice was equal parts Frank Sinatra and Tony Bennett. "Would you please give a large round of applause to Mr. and Mrs. Trip Bennington!"

Ava and Trip came gliding into the room, smiling. The band-leader stepped aside and made room for a singer wearing a little silver cocktail dress, covered in sequins. The band played "At Last" and the singer, giving Billie Holiday a run for her money, sang along.

"At last," the singer began to sing slowly, crooning about the end of her lonely days.

One more song to knock off my list of songs that I want played for the first dance at my own wedding. It seems that every wed-ding I go to, I lose one more. (Except for that one wedding I went to where the couple danced their first song to Guns N' Roses's

"November Rain." I think that the happy couple missed the fact that it was actually a sad song.) At the rate I'm going, if I don't get married soon, my betrothed and I will be dancing our first dance to "The Piña Colada Song."

After Trip and Ava had danced through about half of the song, the bandleader returned to the mike to invite guests to join the bride and groom out on the dance floor. I didn't make a move. It's an unspoken single-girl pact: you do not, under any circumstances, let your single girlfriend sit alone for the first dance. Even if you have a date, you sit with her. Now, Vanessa is married, I know, but I thought that the rule should still apply.

"Well, what are you waiting for?" Vanessa asked Jack. "Ask her to dance!" she said. Jack and I looked at Vanessa. "Yes, I'm all right. Go!" she said, with a smile on her face. I guess when you're married it makes no difference to you if you sit alone for a dance or two. You know that you've got a dance partner for life, even if he's not there to dance with you right at that very moment.

"M'lady?" Jack asked in his Scottish accent, taking my hand in his. He kissed it gently.

"How come you do the accent perfectly with me, but with everyone else you lapse into the Australian?" I asked him, spoiling the mood.

"Shut up and dance," he said as he led me onto the dance floor. He spun me around and I fell right into him. There was something very definite about the way he held me in his arms as we danced.

"This room is really beautiful," he said, looking around.

"Do you think that Vanessa is okay?" I asked, subtly spinning Jack around so that I could look over his shoulder to check on Vanessa at our table.

"She's fine," he said, leaning into my ear.

"I feel bad leaving her alone like that. I don't want her to feel lonely, you know?" I said. "It's such bad luck that Marcus had to work this weekend, don't you think?"

"Well, at least *she* was able to make it," Jack said, sounding like a man who often has to cancel his own weekend plans.

"That's true," I said, remembering a few canceled weekends of my own.

The singer continued on and Jack pulled me closer.

"What do you think your wedding will look like?" Jack asked me.

"Oh, you mean if I ever get married?" I said laughing.

"If you ever get married," he said, spinning me around, completely ignoring the self-pity. The dance floor was beginning to fill up with wedding guests.

"I don't really know. I never really thought about it."

"What do you mean you never thought about it?" he asked. "I thought that you wanted to marry Douglas?"

"I did," I said. "I mean, I do. I just never thought about what our wedding would be like."

"I thought that little girls always dreamt about what their weddings would be like?" he asked, dipping me down. We were face-to-face, Jack's arm behind my back being the only thing holding me up.

"Not me," I said as he brought me back up. "I never did. Now, don't get me wrong, I always dreamt about what the guy would be like, but not the wedding so much."

"So, what would the guy be like?" he asked, pulling me closer for a spin.

"Oh, I don't know—smart, funny, kind—wears pants, you know, the usual stuff," I said as I spun around.

"And Douglas was all of those things?" Jack asked, pulling me back to him.

"Well, as you know, the man was not a big fan of pants."

"No, seriously, the other stuff. Was he kind? Funny?"

"No, he wasn't. He wasn't any of those things at all," I said, suddenly realizing it for the first time.

"Oh," Jack said, looking down at me as if he wanted to say more. Our eyes were locked, but neither one of us said a word.

The singer murmured something about being in heaven and I couldn't help but agree.

I was sure that he was going to lean down to kiss me, but in an instant, the song was over and we found ourselves standing apart, applauding the band.

"Well, okay then," Jack said, "I'm going to go and get a drink. Would you like anything?"

"No, thank you," I said. I was beginning to think that I'd had enough champagne—I was tipsy and confused over what had just happened. Or what had just *not* happened. "I'm fine. I guess I'll go check up on Vanessa now." I stumbled back to our table.

"I didn't want to leave you here all by yourself," I said to Vanessa as I sat down next to her.

"I wanted you to go. You looked like you were having fun out there. Were you?" Vanessa asked me.

"Was I what?" I asked, tearing apart a dinner roll and taking a sip of my water.

"Having fun with Jack out there?"

"I don't know," I quickly answered. "I probably would have had more fun sitting at the table by myself, like you were, but knowing that I had someone in my life, rather than just having someone to dance with at that moment."

"Oh," Vanessa said.

"You're so lucky to be married. If I had married Douglas, none of this would have happened. Everything would be perfect. My life would be so much easier."

"Just because you get married, it doesn't mean that your life gets any easier, Brooke."

"Easy for you to say," I cried out, "you've been married for forever! You have no idea how hard it is to be single."

"You have no idea how hard it is to be married," she said quietly.

"Every wedding invitation is a torture test," I persisted. "You're either invited without a date and thus banished to the pathetic singles table, or you're invited with a date and it's a nightmare to find someone who will go with you. I should have just married Douglas."

"He didn't ask," Vanessa said, looking to me.

"Then I should have married Trip. Or at the very least, tried coming out to L.A. with him."

"Things with Trip weren't perfect, though."

"Then I should have married Danny, my high-school boy-friend. You don't know him, so you can't say anything nasty about him, can you?" I took a swig of champagne.

"You think that you would be happy if you had married Danny?" she asked, eyes still on me.

"Well, not even necessarily married to Danny, but just married in general. I should have just gotten married, period. If only I had gotten married already, my life would be so much easier."

"I'm sorry, Brooke," Vanessa said as she started to cry. "Would you excuse me for just one moment? I need to use the ladies' room," she said and bolted from her seat.

Dumbfounded, I followed her into the ladies' room, struck by the irony that we were at *my* ex-boyfriend's wedding, yet

somehow, Vanessa was the one who was crying. I burst inside and
she was nowhere to be found. Remembering how I used to hide
out in the bathroom to avoid the mean girls one very long summer
at sleep-away camp, I began checking the stalls. When I came
upon the one that had six-hundred-fifty-dollar gold Manolo
Blahnik strappy stilettos peeking out of the bottom, I knocked
on the door.

"Leave me alone," she said.

"No," I replied.

"Please, Brooke," she said, "I want to be alone."

"I think that being alone might just be your problem," I said
and gave the door a gentle push. "What happened just now?"

"What are you doing?" she said from inside.

"I figure if you're not coming out, I'm coming in."

"Back away from the door, Brooke," she said.

"Okay, I'll be waiting right here."

A minute or two later, she walked out of the stall, feet dragging
as if they carried the weight of the world on them. I had never
seen Vanessa break down like that before in the entire eight years
that I'd known her. She was always the strong one, the tough one,
but here she was, all dressed up in her dressiest black-tie dress,
with big fat tears falling down her perfectly made-up cheeks.

"Vanessa," I said, gathering her to me for a hug. She pulled
away and I watched her as she went to sit in front of the dressing-
room mirror.

"I don't know what's wrong with me," she said, carefully
dabbing away a tear from the side of her eye. I sat down on one
of the other chairs in front of the mirror. She continued to cry as
she fixed her makeup even though her face remained strangely
composed. She dabbed at each one before it fell down her cheeks.

I didn't know what to say. Seeing her cry like that, pretending that she wasn't, was making me want to cry myself.

"Honey, what is it?"

"Nothing," she said.

"Vanessa," I said, handing her a tissue.

"I just get very emotional at weddings is all," she said, taking out her engraved Tiffany & Co. compact and powdering her nose.

"Emotional is using a handkerchief to dab your tears of joy. You're about halfway into a box of Kleenex."

"Is it that bad?" Vanessa asked, checking her reflection in the mirror.

"Kind of, but you could never *really* look bad. So what is it?" I asked.

"No, this is your thing, Brooke. Your night. I'm totally fine," she said.

"Actually, it's Ava's night, not mine. And you're my best friend, so even it was my very own wedding, I'd still want you to tell me what was wrong," I said.

"Really?" she asked.

"Really. You're my best friend in the world. You know that. You can tell me anything," I said, handing her another tissue.

"Marcus isn't really working this weekend," she said.

"He's not?"

"He's not. I've asked Marcus for a trial separation," she said softly, looking down intently at her tissue. It was covered in her perfectly applied mascara.

"What?" I said. I couldn't believe my ears. Vanessa and Marcus were supposed to be the perfect couple. The beautiful lawyer and the handsome doctor living happily ever after. I grabbed a monogrammed guest towel off the counter and started tearing it in halves.

"It's been a long time coming," she said. "About a year ago, he had an affair and we just haven't recovered from it."

"I had no idea," I said, and was stunned that I hadn't. I can barely keep a particularly bad order of chicken parmesan to myself much less something that would affect my whole life like the breakup of my marriage. "I'm so sorry."

"*I* haven't recovered from it, I should say." Leave it to Vanessa to think of a detailed analysis on why she was still upset that her husband had cheated on her.

"I'm so sorry," I said again, handing her another tissue. It felt as if that were the only thing I could say. "I can't believe you were holding all of this inside."

"It's not exactly the type of thing that I want to talk about. I thought that everything was fine," she said and started to cry again. She had her head down and her shoulders were shaking. I leaned over and gave her a hug. Not one of those hugs that women give each other when they sort of grip each other's shoulders and delicately pat each other on the back. I gave her a real hug. One of those big bear hugs where you hold on so tight that you can barely breathe. I grabbed her and pressed her to me and didn't let her go. I could feel her entire body heaving and I could practically hear her heart beating. I didn't want to let her go until I could figure out how to make it all better for her.

"It's okay," I whispered into the back of her head. "It's going to be okay. I'm here for you. Anything you need. If you want to talk, we'll talk. Or, if you just want to cry, we'll cry. You know how good I am at crying."

Vanessa broke away and started to laugh. "How about this— we focus on me now and we cry about how your life is falling apart over dessert."

"Deal," I said.

"Actually, that's why I thought it would be a good idea to come here. Just put a little space between us and see what happens."

"And?" I asked. I noticed that she had barely called Marcus, but at the time I thought it was just because he was on call.

"I'm more confused than ever," she said.

I nodded.

"Do you think that you'd be able to forgive someone?" she asked me, and I honestly didn't know. I told her so. "Well, if given the chance, would you have forgiven Douglas?" she asked.

"Probably," I said. "But then I bet he would have done it to me again. In hindsight, I think that that's just the sort of guy that he is, you know?"

Vanessa nodded back to me, but I could tell that she didn't know. Of course Vanessa didn't know. She would never be stupid enough to be with someone for that long who wasn't a stand-up guy. To be with someone who you knew would do you wrong, but to be insecure enough to wait until it happened. To think that that's what you deserve, that you can't do any better, and then to not even have the luxury of being shocked when it *does* happen to you.

"Let's just put it this way," I explained to her, "when Douglas told me about it, I was angry, upset, and everything else you could imagine. But I wasn't surprised. I wasn't surprised that he'd done it. And there's something wrong with that."

And there was. Only I was just realizing it now. "With Marcus," I continued, "I'm pretty shocked. It just seems so out of character for him. Like a response to something, as opposed to a regular behavior. Like a little kid acting out almost. Not like I'm making excuses, though."

"I know, I know you're not. And I kind of agree," she said. "That's what makes it so hard. I feel like I can't turn my back on him, but I'm just so hurt. It's just so hard to get past. And the fact of the matter is that I can't decide whether I want to get past it or not. So, that's where I'm at. Don't tell Jack, okay?"

"Not a problem. Where is Jack?"

"Jack? I thought that your boyfriend's name was Douglas?" Ava said, looking decidedly unbridal, emerging from one of the bathroom stalls. She was pulling her dress back down with one hand, while balancing a martini glass and a cigarette in the other. She stumbled a bit on the way out in a way that made me think that this was not her first drink of the night. Nothing says class like a bride with a drink and a cigarette. Classy with a capital *K*. The only thing that would have looked better would have been if she were holding a beer bottle instead of the martini.

"It is! It is," I assured her. "I just sometimes like to call him Jack."

"Oh," she said, apparently unfazed. Or too drunk to actually be fazed. "Well, Vanessa, I'm so sorry that your husband wasn't able to make it."

Vanessa didn't say a word, apparently trying to decide whether or not Ava had heard our conversation. I couldn't tell, either, but I could smell the alcohol on Ava's breath from where I was standing.

"*There* you are!" a tiny little blond girl in a nondescript black strapless cocktail dress cried out, rushing into the powder room. She began alternately puffing up and then patting down Ava's dress, and then did the same with Ava's hair. "I've been looking for you *everywhere!*" she said, laughing nervously in our direction. "These brides, I tell you," she said, still with the nervous laughter, "you take your eye off of them for one little teensy tiny minute and look at what happens!" She was trying so hard to act as if all this was normal that it reminded me of the summer that my parents almost got divorced. The more my mother manically assured me that everything was okay, the more I got the feeling that I'd be spending weekends with Dad and weekdays with Mom.

Ava broke from the blonde's grasp and took a long drag from her cigarette, like a heroin addict getting her fix. The ashes were coming dangerously close to her gown. The tiny blonde held her hands out to catch them.

"Oh, my God," the blonde said in a panic, "Bev is going to kill me!" Beverly Lawrence—the name explained it all. I actually began to feel sorry for this little lackey of hers. Beverly Lawrence was the ultimate Hollywood public relations power player. She was as famous as her A-list clients in her own right. She even taught a class on it at UCLA. Beverly's reputation for being tough on her minions was the stuff of urban legends. Rumor has it that the last assistant who let her down couldn't even get a job selling (gasp!) retail once Beverly was done spreading the word about her in New York.

"Ava's really shy and gets panic attacks from too many people," the blonde said. "Please don't tell anyone that you saw this. It would really hurt her image with the kids," she said, with her eyes pleading and her arms lifting Ava up.

"Our lips are sealed," I said as the blonde began to spray Evian water on Ava's face. It seemed to do the trick because Ava was able to walk out of the ladies' room almost completely on her own.

"Alas," Vanessa said as they left, turning to me, "the emperor is wearing no clothes."

"She's an emp-*ress*," I corrected, reapplying the lipstick Damian had given me.

"No, I'm talking about the children's story, *The Emperor's New Clothes.*"

"You know, I never really understood that story. What kind of story are they telling to kids that ends with some pedophile running around town naked?"

"I think that you're missing the point of the story, Brooke."

21

Maybe Vanessa is right. Maybe nothing is perfect. Maybe nothing is what it seems. Relationships certainly aren't perfect. They're never even close.

Douglas wasn't perfect. Everything had to be his way or the highway, and even that wasn't good enough for him in the end. So, why was I still chasing him? Why was I spending all this time trying to get him back?

Trip certainly wasn't perfect. He had been so busy constantly trying to outdo me that he never really took the time to get to know me.

And Danny's idea of a fun night at home was torturing small animals. Not to mention the major mother issues going on there that it still hurts my brain to think about.

So, then, I suppose marriage can't be perfect. I mean, marriage is just one big relationship, so how can it possibly be perfect?

Jack grabbed my hand and took me out onto the dance floor the second I got back to the table. We danced and he was dangerously close. I could smell his aftershave and felt it go down my spine. I didn't pull away. The band played an old song that I didn't know and Jack sang along to it in my ear. My arms wrapped around him, I turned my faux engagement ring around my finger.

This time, I was determined not to spoil the mood. I just took it all in. The couples danced around the dance floor like tiny little tops, perfectly aligned, spinning around but never bumping into one another. The men, all dapper in black tuxedos and white dinner jackets, the women, splashes of vibrant color in reds and pinks and yellows and golds. As we spun around, the sweet smell of the lilies and roses hit me.

The moment was perfect. Maybe Jack was a little perfect, too.

"I'm having such a good time with you," I whispered into his ear.

"So, does that mean that I'm doing a good job trying to be more good-looking?"

"Wow," I said, taken aback. "How long have you been waiting to throw that one back in my face?"

"A long time," he said with a smirk.

"Yeah?" I said, trying to sound sexy.

"Yeah, most of the reception, I'd say," he said, pinching my waist. I giggled like a little girl. "And, don't think that it was easy to work that into conversation."

"Okay, I'm sorry," I said. "I happen to think that you are *very* good-looking."

"Is this the part where you say 'in a platonic way?'" he asked and my mouth fell to the floor. "That one I've been waiting to use since Barneys," he said. I laughed. "What's so funny?"

"Nothing, it's just that I'm not really accustomed to a man listening all that closely to anything that I say," I said, looking out onto the dance floor.

"I listen to everything that you say," he said, turning my face to his with his finger, suddenly very close to me again.

"You do, don't you?" I asked as he leaned into me. He shook his head yes slowly as he leaned in a little more. I couldn't believe it. We were going to kiss. I was going to kiss Jack. Or, Jack was going to kiss me! Either way, it was happening right this very minute—we were going to kiss!

I closed my eyes and lifted my head to his, but was abruptly brought back to reality by a familiar voice.

"May I cut in?" Mrs. Martin asked. Our faces simultaneously turned away from each other to look at her. "Douglas, dear, do you think that your fiancée would mind if I borrowed you for a dance?"

Mind? Yes, of course I mind! Don't I look like I mind? Couldn't she see that we were just about to kiss? Granted, she thinks that we are engaged and thus do that sort of thing all the time (or one should hope!), but the fact remains that we *are* not and we *do* not! I most certainly mind!

"Why, of course not!" Jack said, in his perfect Scottish accent. "Thank you very much for asking! Brooke, you remember Mrs. Martin from cocktail hour, don't you?"

"I most certainly do," I said.

"May I say, Brooke, you've got a real keeper here," she said.

"Yes, she does," Jack said, looking over his shoulder to me as he took Mrs. Martin's hand to dance.

"Don't you just love the accent?" she added in a stage whisper.

"Who wouldn't?" I stage whispered back as Mr. Martin took my hand.

"So, how did you two lovely young people meet?" Mr. Martin asked me as we began to dance. His hands were rough to the touch, like someone who has had to work hard his whole life, but his nails were neatly manicured, like a lady who lunches.

"We work at the same law firm," I said.

"An office romance?" Mrs. Martin said over her shoulder, spinning Jack around so that she could look at me. "My, my! Our daughter is always telling us that it's inappropriate to date someone in your office nowadays. That it's somewhat taboo."

"Funny you should mention that, Mrs. Martin," Jack said, taking back the lead. "That's the reason that Brooke and I didn't get together at first."

"You don't say?" Mrs. Martin asked, intrigued.

"Our firm had a silly little policy about interoffice dating," Jack said.

"It makes sense if you think about it," I said. "The office gossip mill could kill any good relationship, and if it doesn't last, then you have to see that person every day." Mrs. Martin shook her head in agreement as if she had heard this same line of reasoning before from her daughter. "And, of course, it's hard enough to be taken seriously as a woman." Mrs. Martin continued to nod.

"Yes, dear, I see your point," Mrs. Martin said, "but finding true love is worth the risk, isn't it?" I looked over to Jack and found him looking at me. I tried to formulate a response, but couldn't help but think that I agreed. All this time, I'd been wasting my time pining away for a cad like Douglas when I had a wonderful guy right here in front of me. What on earth had I been thinking?

"Well, with all due respect, Brooke," Mr. Martin said, "I always thought that working together was a stupid reason not to date someone." I looked over at Jack in his kilt and smiled. He was smiling, too.

It didn't matter *what* I had been thinking in the past. Now I had my head screwed on straight. I was going to go after what I wanted—what I deserved—from now on and nothing was going to stand in my way.

"I'm beginning to think the same thing myself, Mr. Martin," I said.

"Beginning to think so?" Mr. Martin replied. "You mean you *thought* so. You two are engaged already!" He and Mrs. Martin both laughed.

"Yes, thought so," I said, laughing along with the Martins. "I just meant that I couldn't agree with you more."

Jack and I locked eyes. The song ended and we all stood and applauded for the band. They cued up another number and Mrs. Martin grabbed Jack's arms to dance another dance.

"So, Douglas," Mrs. Martin said to Jack, "perhaps you can show me a traditional Scottish dance?"

"Yes, I would love to do that sometime!" he said.

"There's no time like the present, Douglas. Show me some moves," she said, grabbing his arms and moving them around as if they were going to start up some sort of spontaneous break-dancing wave or something. I could see Jack over Mr. Martin's shoulders and I gave him a hopeful smile. After all, he's a smart guy. He can improvise.

He began to do some salsa. Salsa? Maybe he can't improvise. Gosh, what does this guy do when he's in court? Thank goodness big firm litigators never really ever go to court, or this guy would really be in trouble. (Jack: "Your honor, I object." Judge: "Over-ruled." Jack: "Your honor, *por qué?*" Judge: "Sit down before I hold you in contempt.")

"No, Scottish moves, silly! Don't you Scots have any traditional dances?" she asked, laughing. I've laughed that laugh before. I could tell that in her head she was thinking, *Those crazy Scots!*

"Ah, yes, but I'm embarrassed to say that I don't know them very well," Jack said, taking a handkerchief out of his breast pocket to dab at his brow.

"You don't have to be shy with me!" she persisted.

"I'm just afraid that I wouldn't be able to teach them very well, is all. Scottish dances are very complicated, you see."

"But I'm a great dancer! Try me!" she said, and I tried to formulate a getaway plan. Perhaps now would be a good time to feign illness? Or pretend we just saw some wedding guests that we simply *had* to say hello to across the floor? Would the Martins buy it if I pretended that we'd just spotted Matt Damon and we absolutely *had* to go over and say hi since we were friends from high school? Or would Mrs. Martin know that Matt Damon was slightly older than me? Oh, my God, is that really Matt Damon?

Or, failing everything else, should I just simply grab Jack and run all the way back to New York? That wasn't sounding like such a bad idea right about now. After we said "hello" to Matt Damon, that is.

What? I wouldn't want to be rude.

"It's just that I don't want to butcher any of the moves," he said.

"It's not exactly like any of us are going to know the difference, now then," she said laughing.

I could see the lightbulb go off in Jack's head. I began looking around for the emergency exits. Clearly, this constituted an emergency situation.

Jack began to smile.

God, no. Please, no.

"Good point, Mrs. Martin," he said.

For the love of God, no! I was pretty sure I had told him that I was going for the whole "quiet-complacent-ex-girlfriend" thing, not the whole "loud-flashy-ex-girlfriend-with-the-hottie-in-a-skirt" thing. Certainly that excluded said hottie in a skirt dancing a ridiculous Scottish dance, didn't it?

"So, go on, then," Mrs. Martin goaded. "Show me what you've got."

And he did. He showed her exactly what he had. And it was not pretty. Depending on your point of view, that is.

Jack began doing a Scottish dance. Well, his rendition of a traditional Scottish dance, anyway. It was a crazy mix of the hora that they do at Jewish weddings and the Irish dancing that Lord of the Dance does. He began very slowly, very gingerly, and was clearly making up the steps as he went along. I wondered if Mrs. Martin could tell.

"That's right, Douglas!" Mrs. Martin called out. "Make your mum proud!" (I guess she *couldn't* tell.)

He continued dancing, and a few of the other guests began to watch. Within minutes, Mr. and Mrs. Martin were actually following along. I was having none of this, though. I slowly backed away from the dance floor and made my way to our table. By the time I'd edged away from the scene of the crime, even more wedding guests were watching Jack—cheering him on—following every move he made.

"Funny, I've never seen that dance before," the Scottish waiter said to me as I reached the edge of the dance floor. Oh, my God. We're busted. We are stone-cold busted. He's going to tell everyone that Jack/Douglas is not really Scottish! Everyone will know that I made my best friend dress up as my most recent ex for my other ex's wedding and it won't even matter that Jack wore a kilt, or that we almost kissed on the dance floor, or that I've finally come to my senses! I will be humiliated and never able to show my face in L.A. again! The whole west coast, really, if you think about it. Who would have thought that after all of this careful planning and plotting, in the end, I would get busted by the Scottish waiter? Damn the gods of coincidence. Damn these large banquet halls and their hiring of random Europeans all the time. Damn! Damn! Damn!

"He must be from Perth," the waiter said, shrugged, and walked away.

Damn.

I looked up and Jack was still doing his rendition of a traditional Scottish dance, now in full force and with most of the dance floor dancing along with him. Those who were too timid to try their luck dancing stood on the side of the dance floor, clapping along.

"Is that supposed to be a traditional Scottish dance?" Vanessa asked me, as she nibbled on a dinner roll. Our salads were being set onto the table.

"I don't know. I can't bear to look," I told her, turning my back to the dance floor and taking a swig of white wine from a glass that was sitting on our table. I hoped it belonged to someone we knew, although at this point, I didn't really care.

"Do the Scots even have a traditional Scottish dance?" Vanessa asked me.

"How the hell should I know?" I asked. "I think that we have established that I did not do the requisite research for this weekend. You think you've got an outline with colored tabs and some color-coded index cards with the name of a hometown and a kilt, and you're set. But you're not."

"Yes, I think that it's supposed to be a Scottish dance," Vanessa said, mesmerized by what she was seeing on the dance floor, unable to take her eyes away. "Only it looks like a cross between the hora and an Irish jig." Vanessa was intently staring, head tilted slightly to the right as she puzzled over what was before her eyes.

"I'm just warning you now, if he starts lifting people up in chairs, I'm walking out," I said, closing my eyes against the scene.

"Oh, my God. Do not turn around," Vanessa said, her head snapping upright. My God! Did that man start lifting people in chairs already?

"What?" I asked, starting to turn around. Vanessa grabbed my arm.

"Do not turn around until I've had a second to come up with a plan," Vanessa said, suddenly very serious.

"What on earth are you talking about?" I asked. "What is Jack doing now?"

"It's not Jack," she said.

"So, then *what* is the big deal?" I asked.

"It's not Jack. It's Douglas."

"What?" I asked. I stood up and turned around very slowly. There he was, walking to us, as if he didn't have a care in the world—the cad of all cads, the cheater of all cheaters—Douglas. Walking toward us, as if in slow motion. I sat there, completely helpless, like when you know you are about to be in a car accident, but it's too late to do anything about it but simply brace yourself and hope that you don't get too hurt.

I stared at him coming to us, closer and closer, looking absolutely gorgeous as always—like James Bond, only more handsome. Eyes flickering with that devilish look, mouth contorted into his David Addison smirk, with just the perfect amount of stubble on his face. I could just tell that if you got close enough to him, he probably smelled great, too.

As he walked toward me, I couldn't help but notice that he was impeccably dressed from head to toe. It wasn't surprising—he always had all of his suits custom made—but there was something unexpected to this evening's ensemble.

Pants.

"Is that man wearing a fucking tuxedo?" I asked Vanessa.

Stay cool. Stay calm, I thought to myself. *This is not a problem. This is nothing you can't handle. This isn't even that big of a deal. You are simply at your ex-boyfriend's wedding with your faux fiancé keeping your dignity ever-so-slightly intact. Piece of cake. Nothing can stop you now. Not losing your luggage. Not a run-in with your high-school nemesis. Not Vanessa having a nervous breakdown in the bathroom. Not even a Scottish waiter. The real Douglas showing up? Please.*

"Ladies," Douglas said, his voice dripping with sex, reaching for each of our hands to kiss.

And with that, I passed out.

22

It is a universal rule that the cad must always come back. I don't know why, he just does. Just read any Jane Austen novel and you'll see what I mean. And I should know. I've read a lot of Jane Austen novels. So why, then, do you suppose I was so surprised and confused when *my* cad came back?

I came to a few minutes after passing out, in a tiny little room with a tiny little waterfall trickling in the background. The first thing I saw was Jack's face, hovering over mine, looking very worried. He had a napkin dipped in ice water and he was dabbing it on my forehead as I lay sprawled out on a heavily upholstered love seat.

"Oh, God, Jackie. I just had the worst dream," I said, looking up to the ceiling. It was hand painted with an intricate deep blue pattern. "We were at Trip's wedding and out of nowhere, Douglas showed up. Not you Douglas—the real Douglas. I fainted and I could have sworn that I heard Trip's mother say, 'Who brought that Jewish girl?'"

Jack didn't say a word and kept dabbing at my forehead. I

looked down and was face-to-face with his kilt. "Oh, my God, it wasn't a dream."

"It wasn't a dream," he said, and as I turned to look at him, I could see that we were in the bridal suite. It was dimly lit, the only source of light being from the vanity mirror's lights. Jack had pulled up one of the chairs from the table next to the vanity to sit next to me.

There was a plate of pigs in blankets and sushi sitting on the table, half-eaten by Trip and Ava. Beside it, there was an ice bucket with a bottle of Veuve Clicquot turned upside down. I got a visual of Trip shoving spicy tuna rolls down Ava's throat as she chugged champagne by the glassful under the guise of a panic attack. Jack dipped the napkin back into the ice bucket and gently put it to my forehead.

"It wasn't a dream? You mean, we're really here?"

"And so is he," he said.

Douglas is here. And I'm here. And Jack is here, dressed up as Douglas. Who is here! And I just passed out and made a huge scene at my ex-boyfriend's wedding. Why, oh, why couldn't I have just cracked my head open and died like a normal person when I'd passed out and hit the floor? Life can be so unfair sometimes.

"I am so embarrassed. I can never go back out there. Let's leave. No, we can't leave. What will we say to everyone?"

"Already covered. Vanessa handled it quite well, I must admit," he said with a chuckle.

"Thank God for you and Vanessa. What did she tell them? Did she fess up? Tell everyone the truth?"

Yes, that's it. Maybe Vanessa just confessed. That would be easier at this point, wouldn't it? It would be a relief to stop playing this silly little charade. I mean, it's not as if I was really keeping my dignity intact—ever-so-slightly or otherwise—and the people whom I really cared about knew what a loser I'd been lately and seemed to love me nonetheless. (I think.)

"God, no," Jack said. "Are you insane? She told everyone that Douglas is Marcus."

Thank God she lied. Thank God my friend Vanessa is a big fat liar. Thank God she looked at them dead in the eye and told them a bold-faced lie.

"So, now you're pretending to be Douglas and Douglas is pretending to be Marcus?"

"Pretty much," he said, getting up to dab the napkin in the ice bucket again. "I can't wait to see Douglas try to do an American accent."

"He actually does a great American accent. He used to imitate me all the time. Well, mimic me, really, when he was annoyed," I said as Jack came back to the couch with the napkin. "Anyway, it was still pretty hysterical."

"I bet," he said, and I realized that it really wasn't all that hysterical. Douglas did it a lot—he would call it "the voice"—when we were hanging out with his European friends. Douglas would accuse me of speaking "American," not English, and it would tickle his European friends pink to see him bring me down. It tickled *him* pink to bring me down, too, now that I think of it.

They would pretend that they couldn't understand things I said with my "American" accent, really just an excuse to talk among themselves and completely ignore me. Which Douglas was rather good at doing.

"You guys are really the best," I said to Jack. "I am so lucky to have you."

"You know I would do anything for you," he said.

"That is so sweet. You really would?" I asked. He didn't respond, but just looked down at the kilt and his bare legs. Jack's not-so-subtle way of saying, yes, he really would. I smiled. I never had someone before who would do anything for me.

"Right," I said, propping myself up on my elbows to look at Jack.

"Right," he said, leaning in.

"Right."

And with no one there to distract us, he kissed me. And it was worth the wait. At first it was delicate, sweet, as if I were a fine piece of crystal that he didn't want to break. Then, more passionate, lustful, as if he had been waiting his entire life to kiss me.

His lips were soft and he tasted like Scotch and sugar. I put my hand on his right cheek and it was warm to my touch. When I finally opened my eyes, he was looking right at me. It was a look I had never seen before. Serious, earnest, burning—downright smoldering. I was beginning to melt. We kissed shamelessly for God knows how long when finally one of us realized that it might be bad form to spend the whole of your ex-boyfriend's wedding making out with your date in the bridal suite. It was probably Jack who came up with that realization, because I didn't seem to see a problem with it.

I stood up and smoothed out my dress as I made my way to the vanity mirror. I couldn't stop myself from giggling and looking back at him, still sitting on the couch. As I applied some lipstick to my pout, out of the corner of my eye, I could see Jack staring at me. He looked like an old-time movie actor, like Cary Grant or Humphrey Bogart reincarnate, communicating everything he felt with just one look. Except I don't think that Grant or Bogie ever wore a skirt. But you get where I was going with that one.

"Ready for some more lies and deception?" I asked, turning away from the mirror, hoping that I looked like an old-time movie star myself. Audrey Hepburn, I hoped, but I can't say that Audrey ever wore a number quite as revealing as my Halston.

"Let the games begin," he said, putting his arm out for me to take.

"Oooh, that was good," I said, marveling at the accent, which was maturing quite nicely. "You are getting really good at this. Admit that you're kind of enjoying doing the accent."

Jack smiled. I wished that I could have frozen time at that very moment. It was that delicious stage in a relationship where anything seems possible. I wished that I could take a photo of us right then and there—Jack looking at me adoringly with the smile of a man who knew how to get what he wanted, and me gazing up at him as if he were my hero. I was so happy at that precise moment. Such unadulterated happiness. That sort of thing never lasts, does it?

We should never have left the bridal suite.

We walked out of the room, holding hands, and the second we looked up, Douglas appeared and grabbed me like a caveman.

"Mind if I borrow her," Douglas said in his American accent, "dude?" He didn't wait for an answer, grabbing my arm and leading me out onto the dance floor. I was shocked that he didn't knock me on the head with a stone and drag me out to the dance floor by my hair. His grip was so tight, I was certain that it would leave a mark. Jack began to follow us, but I turned around, putting my finger up as if to casually say "I'll be back in just one short moment." Jack reluctantly backed away. I hoped that he knew that I just needed that one short moment to rid myself of Douglas so that I could get back to him.

"For fuck's sake, would you mind telling me what's going on?" Douglas asked.

"Obviously, you've figured it out by now," I said, keeping a smile plastered on my face so that anyone who saw us would think we were just two regular wedding guests, dancing around and having a pleasant conversation. Not a cheating cad and his ex having a most decidedly *un*pleasant conversation.

"And, obviously, you have completely lost your mind."

"I'm not the one who flew out to L.A. to stalk me," I said.

"I was invited to this wedding," he informed me.

"I kind of thought it was assumed that you were *un*invited when you announced that you were sleeping with someone else, were getting engaged to said other woman, and then threw me out of our apartment."

"I was trying to be romantic, coming out here and surprising you," he said, turning his eyes on. The earnest eyes. The "would I lie to you?" eyes. Did he really think that after all that we'd been through, I would fall for the eyes?

"Well, you've partially succeeded. I certainly am surprised."

"Aren't you at all happy to see me?" he asked.

"Well, seeing you again at least gives me the chance to tell you that I never want to speak to you again," I said with a smile. Mr. and Mrs. Martin could see me from across the dance floor and I didn't want to give them any cause for concern. Mrs. Martin waved at me. I smiled and waved back at her.

"Brooke, you can't mean that. There's not even a little part of you that's happy to see me?" He was obviously getting desperate, now turning the sad puppy eyes on. Once upon a time, that look used to work on me, too. I used to think that he really meant it and would forgive him for whatever he'd done. Now, I just saw it for what it was—manipulation to keep me under his control. I was surprised at how quickly he had lost his effect on me. It was as if I could turn it on and off the way you would change the channel on a particularly bad made-for-TV movie.

"You. Are. Fucking. Wearing. Pants."

"I thought that you wanted me to," he said.

"I do. I did," I quickly corrected.

"Well, then, better late than never, I say."

"Look, if this were only about the pants, this probably would be a very touching gesture, but the fact remains that it is not," I said.

"We've broken up," he told me. I wondered why he was informing me of this very, very obvious fact. Did he think that I hadn't noticed that we'd broken up? Did he think that I thought that people who were still an item kicked each other out of their apartments and got engaged to other people? Did he think that people who weren't broken up were busy making out with their best friends at their ex-boyfriend's weddings? Were people accusing us of still dating and this was why he was pointing out that we had, in fact, broken up to me?

"Yes, I'm painfully aware," I said.

"No, not us. I mean…" He stammered. Stammering. Poor lost little boy manipulative trick number 732. It's a matched pair with the eyes. I've been a bad boy. So bad that I can't even cough out the words. Hugh Grant—hooker—Jay Leno show—enough said.

"What?" I asked.

He continued stammering and batting his long eyelashes as Vanessa and Jack came up next to us, dancing.

"Mind if we cut in?" Vanessa asked. "I'd like a dance with my husband," she said, accentuating the word *husband* in case any other wedding guests could hear us.

"Of course!" I cried out before Douglas could articulate his dissent.

"Are you okay?" Jack asked the second I was back in his strong arms.

"Yes, I'm fine," I said. "Now that I'm with you."

"What the hell is going on?" he whispered, pulling me closer. "What is he doing here?"

"I have no idea," I said, taking advantage of the opportunity to put my face close to his. I could smell my own perfume on his neck and I smiled and thought about the bridal suite.

"Did you know he was coming?" he asked me, pulling his face back. Before I could answer (my response was going to be a very witty: "I didn't know what Douglas was doing when we were living together, so I certainly don't know what he is doing now"), we had somehow switched partners and I found myself face-to-face with Douglas again.

"Darling," he said. Douglas always called me *darling*. I used to love how it sounded with his accent: *dah-ling*.

"Don't call me that," I said, looking over his shoulder at Jack and Vanessa. Jack was looking over Vanessa's shoulder at me. I smiled at him.

"Look, we've called off the wedding. Brooke, darling, I've made a huge mistake. I only hope that it's not too late to fix things," he said.

Too late to fix things? It was too late to fix things when we were still *in* the relationship. Only I didn't know it then. The emperor really doesn't have any clothes on, but all along I was thinking that he had on a custom-made Italian suit.

Jack was right—I needed to concentrate more on what things really were, and not just what they looked like. Regardless of how Douglas looked, on the inside, he was a lying cheat. And I was too good for that. Jack, on the other hand, had a wonderful inside. It just *so happened* that he had a wonderful outside, too. Not like I care about that superficial stuff anymore or anything.

As Douglas stood there, faking tears and confessing his love to me, I realized that this relationship was never really real—it was something I had created in my head and had chosen to believe in. Even after two years of being together, living together, I have had more meaningful relationships with certain pairs of shoes.

"I love you," he continued. "I don't know what I was thinking. I never meant to hurt you. Marry me. Let's pick up where we left off."

I could hardly believe my ears. Douglas was coming back to me. And asking me to marry him, to boot. It was all I had ever wanted, only I didn't want it anymore.

"Have you lost your goddamned mind?" I said as he leaned in to kiss me, presumably to prove his deep love and affection. He moved back, the shock of a woman actually saying no to him registering on his face.

"Darling, I love you. Haven't you heard what I'm saying to you?"

"Yes, but it's that—"

Before I could finish the thought, he grabbed my face and kissed me. Hard.

No response to what I was trying to say, he just kissed me. Apparently he thought that a kiss from him would answer my questions. It did not. He kissed me and held me to him and it was a struggle to release myself from his grasp.

He had his hands on either side of my face and I couldn't pull away. My only thought was that Jack would help release me from Douglas's grip, but as I opened my eyes all I could see from the corner of my eye was Jack storming off the dance floor.

23

After what seemed like an eternity, I pushed Douglas and his cheating lips away from me and hit him in the chest. Hard.

The singer finished her song and the crowd stopped dancing to applaud. Douglas and I stood there like strangers amid the other happy wedding guests, the only ones not applauding. We were face-to-face, but neither of us said a word. The bandleader invited the crowd to sit down to enjoy the main course.

Douglas turned and grabbed Vanessa—who was standing behind us wide-eyed after witnessing the kiss—and made his way to our table with her. I spun around and tried to find Jack, but he was no longer on the dance floor and he wasn't at our table. As the dance floor cleared, I spotted him across the room at the bar.

I walked over to the bar where Jack was surrounded by what can only be described as a bevy of young women. Single young women. I wondered if they were all clients of Trip's or friends of Ava's. They were all clearly in the business, one way or another.

I completely stood out, like a man in a lingerie store, since I was the only one there with her original boobs, lips and nose. (Okay, so maybe it's not my original nose, but the boobs and lips are all me.) I wondered if Jack had told them that he was a producer. I knew for a fact that that used to be Trip's little party trick when he first got to L.A.

A five-foot-ten redhead was draped around Jack as if he were the sultan of Brunei. He didn't seem to mind at all. I could have sworn I recognized her from an episode of *Law and Order*.

"So, do you ever regret giving up acting?" a tall blonde wistfully asked Jack.

"Would you mind if I took back my date?" I asked with a laugh, nudging my way into the circle. The redhead didn't move. Neither did Jack. "Jack?"

"I saw you," he said, and turned back to his drink. The redhead didn't move a muscle. She stayed wrapped around Jack, staring at me intently.

"Jack," I continued, undeterred. "Our main courses are on the table."

"I saw you with Douglas," he repeated, louder, more aggressive. His bevy of women all began to glare at me. I couldn't tell if it was because he had told them about me and Douglas or if it was simply because they had all seen him first.

"I heard you the first time," I whispered, trying to take his arm. The redhead was still drawing her tentacles into him and I began to turn my faux engagement ring around my finger.

"I *saw* you with him," he said, turning toward me, looking me dead in the eye. His blue eyes looked darker than I had noticed before. The redhead stepped aside as Jack's voice climbed louder and louder. He walked out of the circle of women to face me.

"Can we talk about this later?" I whispered to him, motioning to the people around us who could hear.

"I saw you kiss him, Brooke, so why don't you just cut the crap," he said. He wasn't even trying to use the Scottish accent anymore even though there were tons of wedding guests around us. "Cut the crap right now." I grabbed his arm and led him out of the reception room. His feet stayed heavy and it was hard to get him to move.

He continued to rant once out in the hallway. "I know that's what you want. That's what you really wanted this whole time. So why don't you just go for it? Why don't you just take back what you want?"

"That's not what I want," I said and I could feel the tears starting to build up.

"Bullshit!" he snarled. I was so shocked that he had yelled at me that I felt my body jerk backward. "Sure you do," he continued. "You spent the better part of the weekend thinking, plotting ways to get back together with Douglas. And now he's here. So go and get him. You two deserve each other."

"I don't want him," I pleaded, tears swelling around my eyes. "I want you. I want to be with you."

"I was a moron to think that you would want me. In fact, you only wanted me when I dressed up and pretended to be Douglas. How sick is that?"

"That's not true," I said, hardly able to speak with the tears running down my face.

"I've been a fool for you for so long, Brooke. I don't really know what on earth I was thinking. But that's over now. And you should be thrilled. You have both of the men in your life here, making utter fools of themselves."

"No, that's not what I want at all. It's you that I want. I want you."

"Tell it to someone who cares," he said, storming off.

"Where are you going?" I called after him, tears still falling uncontrollably from my eyes.

"I'm going to eat," he said, opening the door to the reception and marching through. The sound of the band playing drifted out to me and then the door closed with a slam, leaving only silence surrounding me.

I stood there alone in the hallway, barely comprehending what had just happened. How could Jack know what I wanted when I barely knew it myself?

Douglas? I didn't want Douglas. Not anymore. Not since he'd been revealed for what he really is.

But married. I do want to be married. And that's what Douglas is offering. But what kind of marriage can you have with a man you can't trust?

I can trust Jack. But how could Jack say such hurtful things to me? I guess that was how much seeing Douglas and I kiss had hurt him. Could I have underestimated the feelings he had for me all along? I had underestimated the feelings I had for him all along, so why not?

The door from the reception began to open out into the hallway where I was still standing and I brushed the tears from my cheek. The music from the reception floated out into the hallway again and I could hear the band playing "Celebration." Jack was coming back for me. I knew that he couldn't stay mad at me, just the way I could never stay mad at him. He will come back and I will explain everything and tell him how I feel and everything will be all right. The door opened slowly and I began to smile.

"Brooke?"

"I'm right here," I said.

"Brooke, are you okay? My mother told me that you passed out." It was Trip. My smile all of the sudden felt forced, and I felt the tears beginning to build up again.

"I'm fine," I said as he reached out and gave me a hug. The nicer he was to me, the more it made me want to cry. Why is it that when you're sad, the simple act of someone being nice to you makes you want to cry even more?

"Good, I just wanted to make sure that you were okay," he said.

"Thanks," I said, forcing my lips to continue smiling.

"You don't look okay," he said. "What is it?"

"Nothing, Trip. It's nothing. This is a beautiful wedding. Thank you so much for having me," I said, wiping away a stray tear under the guise of fixing my makeup.

"It's my pleasure, kiddo. You're sure you're all right?"

"Sure," I said.

"Good," he said. "Because I have *got* to talk to that guy who just went into the can about a deal." He kissed my cheek and ran off to the men's room.

I walked back into the reception and found our table. Douglas, Vanessa and Jack were all in a row, with an empty seat in the middle. I took a deep breath and sat down between Jack and Douglas. Jack wouldn't even look me in the eye. Douglas couldn't keep his eyes off me.

"So," the wedding guest next to Jack asked us, "how long have you two been engaged?"

"Not very long," I said. I wondered how quickly I could eat my chicken and get Jack alone so that I could talk to him.

"Oh, really?" Douglas asked.

"Yeah," Jack said, "it's like we're barely even engaged at all." Douglas began to snicker.

"I'm Jenna," the wedding guest said, putting her hand out for us to shake. "I grew up with Ava. How do you know the happy couple?"

"She used to sleep with the groom," Jack said, turning to me. At least he looked me in the eye, though.

"Trip and I dated in law school," I quickly covered, forcing a laugh. "I sort of had to drag him here," I said, motioning to Jack, hoping we looked like a cute bickering couple and not a couple about to kill one another.

"My husband can be the same way," Jenna told me and smiled. "So, when's the big day?"

"We haven't decided yet," I said.

"You haven't?" Douglas asked. "See, and I thought that you had the whole thing figured out, Brooke. Or, at least completely made up in your own mind." I laughed and Jenna nervously laughed along.

"But we do know we want something small, don't we, darling?" Jack said, putting his arm around me and squeezing me a little too tight. "After all, after this weekend, Brooke plans to have a few less friends. Right, honey?" I laughed really loudly as if to say, "Isn't my faux fiancé funny?" I hoped that she would just laugh to be polite and not try to figure out why Jack was being so goddamned nasty to me. She did not.

"It's really about the relationship, though," Vanessa offered, sweeping in to save me from across the table. "If the love is there, it will just fill the room and it won't matter if it's a big wedding or a small wedding or a formal one or a casual one. It's just all about the couple, I think."

"Well said," I told Vanessa, reaching over to her and putting my hand on top of hers. Jenna nodded her head in unison.

"It's all about the trust, I think," Jack said. "If there's no trust, there's no relationship. No foundation to build anything meaningful on."

"You're so right," Jenna said, nodding. I sent a panicked look to Vanessa.

"Well, I think that it's about passion," Douglas said, "excitement and fire to keep the love alive."

"You would say that," Jack said. I saw Jenna looking at Jack with a confused expression. Jack and Douglas had resorted to their natural accents and looked as if they were about to jump across the table and tackle each other.

"It's about love," I said, trying to interject before things got ugly. "It's starting with friendship and letting it become something more. Even if that takes a little longer than it really should. It's about finally realizing that someone is the right person for you and looking to the future, no matter how confusing the past may have been. It's about forgiving mistakes and moving forward. As a team. If two people are in love, anything is possible and everything else will fall into place." I looked to Jack and tried to read in his eyes whether or not I had gotten through to him.

"And sometimes it's just about realizing you were wrong in the first place and cutting your losses," Jack said. Jenna looked down at her chicken.

Before I could utter another word, we were interrupted by the bandleader who announced that it was time for speeches as Trip's mother was taking the mike. Jack went back to avoiding my gaze and Douglas's eyes were burning into me.

"Thank you," Trip's mother said as she got to the mike, her

voice a bit uneven. It seemed that she, herself, had been nursing a little panic attack, too. "And thanks to all of you, for being here to share in this special, special day with us. As most of you know, my son, Trip, is the light of my life. I'm so proud of the man he's become—all of his accomplishments, all he has done. I love you, baby," she said, putting her hand to Trip's face. Trip smiled back at her. "It's so wonderful to be here tonight to celebrate the marriage of my son, Trip, to Ava. You know, I never even knew that he liked Oriental girls until he brought home Ava." Trip put his head in his hands as Ava stood and smiled stoically, sort of the way the other four actresses smile into the camera when they announce the winner of the Academy Award.

"Or working girls," Trip's mother continued. Trip's father whispered something in Trip's mother's direction. "I mean, girls who work. Who have careers. I never knew that Trip liked girls who had careers. But at least we know that she's not after his money!"

"Get to the toast, Ma," Trip said.

"Ah, yes. The toast. Would everyone please raise their glasses as we make a toast. A toast—to this blending of two cultures. East meeting West! Congratulations, Trip and Ava. Or, *kung-hsi*. As you would say, Ava, in your country."

"And you thought that she was just an anti-Semite," Vanessa said, clapping along with the crowd.

"Wasn't Ava born in New York City?" Jack asked in Vanessa's direction, still not speaking to me.

"And raised there," I answered anyway.

"Well, if you ask me, she sounds just like someone else I know. Intolerant of other cultures," Douglas said.

"For the love of God, are you still talking about the fucking skirt?" I asked.

"It's a kilt," Douglas said through clenched teeth.

"Would you just shut up already?" I said. Jenna turned away and was pretending not to hear.

"Would you please start using an American accent?" Vanessa whispered to Douglas. "Everyone is staring."

"Just drop it already," Jack said. "Both of you. Just drop the act. Who are you kidding? You two are a perfect match. You are both superficial, insensitive fools and neither one of you seems to be all that discriminating, in particular when it comes to where you put your lips," he said and stormed away from the table.

"There's my girl," Douglas said, as he slid over to me and put his arm around my shoulder.

"I am not your girl," I said, shrugging his arm away. "And I guess that I never really was."

"Well, for fuck's sake, Brooke, what's that supposed to mean?" That menacing look, the look I had spent most of our two years together trying to avoid, was back. Only this time I didn't care. I didn't back down.

"I couldn't possibly have been your girl when you were with someone else. I'd say, by definition, that would make me, at the very most, only one of your girls."

"Darling, don't be ridiculous," he said, "you are my girl. Always have been, always will be."

"Not anymore," I said.

"Let's do this the right way," Douglas said, not missing a beat, getting up from the table and dropping down onto his knee, "Brooke Miller, in front of God and all of these people, will you marry me?" He put his hand in his pocket to take out a jewelry box.

"Would you get up off of the floor?" I said, grabbing at his tuxedo jacket to bring him back to the table. I was slightly embarrassed by his making a scene, but since most of the wedding guests had since made their way back out on the dance floor, no one even batted an eyelash at Douglas's grand display. He got back onto his seat with a laugh, never once letting his eyes leave my face.

"So?" he asked, pushing the tiny little box over to my side of the table and picking up a glass of champagne. It was a teeny little square box—it was difficult to believe that something as big and important as an engagement ring could fit inside its diminutive walls. For a moment I wondered whether or not this was the ring he had given to Beryl, but realizing that it didn't really matter, opened the box and looked inside. It was a princess-cut diamond on an elegant platinum band. At first glance, it looked enormous and grand, all sparkles and fire, but when I looked a bit closer, I noticed that its cut made the diamond look large because it was all surface, with very little left underneath.

"I don't know what to say," I said, placing the ring back into its box.

"I asked you to marry me. Isn't that what you want?" he asked. I stared out at the dance floor. "Brooke, I'm speaking to you."

"No," I said, with my head still turned away.

"No, you won't marry me, or no, that's not what you want?"

"Both. Neither," I said, turning to face him.

"How can that be? Are you willing to throw this all away? Everything we had together?" I wondered why it was okay when he was the one throwing it all away—that when it was him, it was something that I just had to accept, but when it was me who was throwing it all away, that we had to discuss it. "Remember that time we went out for a casual Sunday-night dinner on the Lower East Side and we ended up dancing on the tables at that place until

4:00 a.m.? What was the name of that place?" he asked, running his index finger along the underside of my arm.

"Remember that time I had to have one of my wisdom teeth removed in an emergency surgery and you wouldn't cancel your dinner plans that night to take care of me?" I asked back. He took a sip of his champagne.

"I'd rather remember that time you were burned out at work and I surprised you with a week away in the Caymans," he said, twirling a lock of my hair with his finger. "Remember our little bungalow on the beach?"

"Remember that time Vanessa's grandfather died and you wouldn't come with me to the wake because you told me that you didn't like death?" I asked. He put his glass down onto the table.

"Why are you doing this?" he asked quietly. He looked down.

"That's not the question you should be asking me. The question is why did it take me so long to do this?"

"Darling," he said.

"Don't 'darling' me. That one isn't going to work on me anymore. You proposed to someone else, Douglas."

"But I've told you. That's over now," he said, as if it were the most natural thing in the world.

"Yes, Douglas, and so are we," I said with equal ease.

24

A *no* to his marriage proposal was clearly not what Douglas was expecting from me. I left him at the table with his mouth still wide open as I jumped up and walked out of the grand ballroom. I was walking a bit taller as I made my dramatic exit out of the reception, pushing the doors open with as much force as I could muster as I left. (Or as much force as my body would allow me to muster in three-and-a-half-inch heels, which were really, really beginning to hurt the balls of my feet.) When I got into the hallway, I didn't know where I should go, so I headed back to my unofficial headquarters for the night—the ladies' room. I sat down on one of the chairs in front of the vanity and looked at myself.

For a second, I didn't even recognize the reflection staring back at me. Who was I? What was I doing? What was I thinking? How did I manage to make such a mess of things? Careful not to disturb Damian's handiwork, I grabbed a monogrammed guest towel, dipped it in cold water, and dabbed it onto my neck and wrists.

"We are spending an inordinate amount of time in the ladies' room," Vanessa said as she walked into the bathroom. "I feel like I'm thirteen again at a bar mitzvah." I looked up at her. "What?" she asked. "I grew up in New Jersey."

"Then in that case, we should be burning a memory candle for Trip and Ava," I said, wondering if that particular Long Island party tradition was the same in New Jersey. Back then, we would spend hours on end during the receptions of our friend's bar and bat mitzvahs to burn memory candles for them: a strange concoction of monogrammed matches, napkins and anything else we could get our hands on, which we would then melt together by pouring the melted wax from a burning candle into a wineglass stolen from the caterers. We would then bestow this deformed *objet d'art* onto the guest of honor, oftentimes to have said guest of honor's mother toss it in the trash before ever bringing it home.

"Ah, yes," Vanessa said, "the sacred memory candle. I think it's not such a good idea to put anything flammable next to the bride right now. By now, I'd say she's 150 proof." She took out her lipstick and lip gloss and began to touch up her pout.

"Yes," I replied, "I suppose it would be very bad form to set the bride on fire at her own wedding." Vanessa and I laughed.

"After you ran off, Douglas stormed out," she said. "I think that he left."

"Good," I said, delicately massaging the temples of my head.

"It *is* good," Vanessa said, pressing her lips together to make her lip gloss even. "I just have no idea how I'm going to explain why he came unexpectedly, ate and then ran."

"He really likes chicken?" I offered. Believe it or not, I really was trying to be helpful.

"But he's on a diet, so he couldn't stay for dessert," she said, fiddling with her false eyelashes. I touched her arm to remind her not to unnerve Damian's handiwork and she sat down on a bench next to me.

"Am I an idiot?" I asked her.

"Yes," Vanessa replied. Without hesitation, I might add. I wondered if a real friend would have waited or if a real friend just tells it like it is. I haven't, in my life, had too many people who just told it to me like it was, but it dawned on me that maybe that's what makes real friends so rare.

"You're supposed to say, 'No, Brooke, of course you're not an idiot.'"

"But you are an idiot," Vanessa said. Not backing down, was she? Vanessa is either a really, *really* good friend, or just not a very nice person.

"But, tell me, Vanessa, how do you really feel?"

"Brooke, there is a man out there who is crazy for you. Has been since the day he met you. And he has been making a complete fool of himself for you. And you have to ask me if you are an idiot?"

She was right. I *was* being an idiot. Jack was, like, totally, completely, madly in love with me. Who couldn't see that? And I was, like, totally, completely, madly in love with him. Why didn't *I* see that? I looked at myself in the mirror and took a deep breath. I put on some lip gloss (What? You have to look good for these major life moments!) and got ready to march out of the bathroom and profess my love to Jack. I was going to set things straight and make everything right again.

I would get up and march out and Vanessa would say, "Way to go, Paula!" like Debra Winger's best friend says to her at the end of *An Officer and a Gentleman* when Debra gets her man. Even though Vanessa isn't exactly your shout-out kind of girl. And I guess it would have been strange for her to call that out, what with my name not being Paula and all. But you get the general sentiment I was going for. Maybe when I found Jack and proclaimed my love for him, he would pick me up like Richard Gere picks up Debra Winger and carry me out of this godforsaken wedding just like Richard takes Debra out of that godforsaken factory. Even though Jack was kind of skinny and I was kind of, well, not skinny. But maybe my professed love for him would give him superhuman strength! And this five-star wedding certainly wasn't a godforsaken anything, but it would still be super romantic for him to lift me up and carry me out into the sunset. Or onto Sunset. Whatever.

"You're right, Vanessa," I proclaimed. "I'm going out there to tell Jack how I feel right now." All ready for her to shout, "Way to go, Paula!" or "Way to go, Brooke!" as the case may be, she said:

"You can't, Brooke, he already left."

"Oh," I said, freezing in my tracks. The door to the ladies' room swung open as a guest came flying in and I almost got hit.

"That doesn't matter," Vanessa said, as I walked back to the vanity mirror. "We can still have a great time. We are still going to salvage this night. Go out there and dance until our feet hurt."

"My feet already hurt," I said, slumping onto the stool next to hers.

"Okay," she said. "Then, we are going to dance until our feet hurt *even more*." I took off my shoes and began to massage the balls of my feet. "And drink too much and just have a blast."

"I drank too much last night," I informed her. "And I think that I already drank too much tonight, too."

"Work with me, here, Brooke," she said, and pulled me up by the arms. "No sulking allowed at your ex-boyfriend's wedding."

"Isn't that the perfect place to sulk?" I asked her.

"Let's go," she said, practically pushing me out the door.

And go we did, right back into the reception. We took a spin toward the bar, and ordered two glasses of champagne. Seemingly the only two single women there, we stood around and tried to look busy.

We went out onto the dance floor and danced for a song or two. I was totally distracted at first, only thinking about Jack and how he had left, but sometime into "Dancing in September" I started to get into it.

Just as Vanessa and I started to get into the swing of things, a slow song came on next. So as not to look like those old women you always see at weddings dancing to slow songs together, we retreated from the dance floor. I hate slow dances at weddings. It always slows the action down, just when things are heating up. And reminds me that I'm alone. Just when I think, as a single girl, that I'm okay being alone at a wedding, a slow song comes on to remind me that I am not. I suppose when I'm married, I'll come to embrace these romantic moments at weddings, but for now they flat out suck.

"And now," the bandleader bellowed, "will you all please take your seats as Trip and Ava cut the cake!"

All of the guests jumped up and circled around the dance floor to watch Trip and Ava. The cake was beautiful—ten layers of pure white frosting covered in roses and pearls made entirely of sugar. I turned to Vanessa and wondered if she was thinking of her own wedding cake.

Trip and Ava held a large sterling-silver knife and cut into the cake together, eyes glued to each other the entire time. Trip took a fork and began to feed it to Ava, slowly, gently, as if she were a baby eating whole foods for the first time. He leaned down and gave her a little kiss as she was still chewing. They both began to laugh and turned to the photographer for their Kodak moment. Through the haze of wedding guests, I could see Beverly's blond lackey looking on from the side, sort of the way Katie Holmes's Scientology "handler" seems to be ever-present whenever she steps out into public.

"Do you think they are going to last?" Vanessa asked me, and it caught me off guard.

"Oh, I—"

"I know," Vanessa said, "what an awful thing to ask as the couple is cutting the cake. But do you?"

"Yeah," I said. "I guess I do. But I always think that at weddings."

"Me, too," Vanessa said.

As Ava picked her fork up to feed Trip, I could see Beverly's blond lackey looking on with a panicked expression. I was sort of curious what Ava might do, too. Ava put the fork into Trip's mouth and got the tiniest bit of frosting on one side of his upper lip. The crowd all laughed and cheered and Trip posed for a photo before wiping the frosting off.

The band began to play some sort of traditional wedding song as waiters quickly began serving the cake. Vanessa politely shook her head *no* when a waiter came to us with pieces of cake.

"Isn't it supposed to be bad luck not to have a bite of wedding cake?" I asked Vanessa, as I longingly watched the waiter walk away.

"No," Vanessa corrected me, "it's only supposed to be *good* luck if you do."

"Either way, I think we need some of that cake."

"I'm not really hungry," Vanessa said.

"Get me some of that goddamned cake," I said as a waiter walked by with another piece. I politely nodded and smiled at him, as if I had not just cursed at my best friend over a baked good, and took a piece for Vanessa and me to share.

"None for me," Vanessa said as I handed her a fork. I ignored her and began eating.

"I think you only need *one* bite for the good luck to kick in," Vanessa said.

"Well, I need all the good luck I can get," I told her as I continued devouring the piece of cake.

"Yeah," she said, "Me, too. Save some for me." And with that, she began to dig into the cake. Within seconds, we were onto our second piece, adorned with a sugar rose (undoubtedly a symbol of *even more* good luck), which we split in two. I ate my half with my hands while Vanessa ate hers carefully with her fork.

After we finished, we took another spin around the reception—from the bar to the bathroom, meandering through some of the tables filled with the more famous faces in attendance. (I *knew* that was Matt Damon!) After a few laps, we finally found ourselves back at our table, all alone. Jenna was up dancing with her husband, and the other guests from our table were scattered about. It dawned on me that this may have been the first wedding Vanessa had ever attended alone. She fidgeted and looked unsure of what she should do. She began to pick at a dinner roll.

"Isn't anyone going to ask us to dance?" she asked me, looking around the reception with hope in her eyes.

"It doesn't look like there are any single guys here," I said. I thought but didn't say: "And even if there were, odds are they would be too insecure/immature/arrogant/flat out rude to even ask."

"So," Vanessa said, looking around the reception again, "I guess we're all alone now."

"Welcome to the world of the single girl."

25

Sitting at my table, I could see him from across the dance floor. Jack. He was still here. Jackie was still at the wedding, after all—I knew he couldn't leave me. I smiled to myself. He was dancing and as the crowd cleared a bit, I could see the redhead trying to wrap her tentacles around him once again.

Without thinking, I stormed across the dance floor, grabbed Jack and kissed him. The redhead jumped back and the rest of the crowd faded away as we kissed and kissed and kissed.

"So, does this mean that you think that I'm ridiculously good-looking after all?" he asked me.

"Well, you look ridiculous," I replied with a smile.

"Let's dance," he said, and took my hand. He gave me a gentle spin and I fell into his arms, slowly, as if it had always been meant to be.

"Let's just say that it means that any guy who puts on a skirt for me is something special," I said.

"It's about the legs, isn't it?" Jack asked. "I've got great legs, don't I? I knew you wouldn't be able to resist."

"You're right," I said, leaning into him. "I can't." He kissed me.

"But you're not going to make me dress up in it again, are you?" he asked as he pulled away slowly. "Like some bizarre, kinky sexual fetish?"

"God, no," I said, shuddering at the thought. I would never do anything crazy like this ever again in my life. I had learned my lesson. From now on, I will be honest and try to behave like the normal, well-adjusted big-time lawyer that I am.

"Damn."

"Don't worry," I assured him. "I have other tricks to get you to show me your legs."

"You dirty, dirty girl," he said, and gave me another peck on the lips. He spun me around and I fell into his arms again.

"So, is this the part where we would normally fess up everything and tell everyone the truth?" I asked him.

"Probably," Jack said.

"That we've perpetrated this huge fraud on the Scottish community but that we're sorry and then we all hug or something?"

"Probably."

"But, we're not going to do that, are we?" I asked.

"Hell, no," Jack said.

"Thank God," I said. "See, this is why people hate L.A."

"Yeah, all of the people are so phony," Jack agreed.

We kissed and it was perfect. Absolutely perfect. We kissed and kissed and kissed and we didn't care about who else was there or where we were.

"Brooke," Jack said.

"Yes," I said, eyes still closed.

"Do you have it?" Jack asked.

"Have what?" I asked.

"The initial research on likelihood of confusion," he said.

I opened my eyes, and I was not at the wedding anymore at all—it was just a daydream. A positively delicious daydream, but a daydream nonetheless. I wanted to go back to the daydream where I was still at the wedding, kissing Jack and he had forgiven me for kissing Douglas and everything had been sorted out. Instead, I was in a conference room back in New York at a strategy meeting on the Healthy Foods case. Jack was there, only he didn't look as if he wanted to kiss me. He just sat across the conference-room table seething and silently hating me.

I sat up in my chair, hoping that I looked as if I were paying attention to the meeting, and not daydreaming about Jack and me kissing.

"Yes, of course I have that research," I said, knowing full well that Jack knew that I did not. It was the research project the partner on the case had tried to give me on our way out to California the previous weekend. Jack knew that I hadn't done any work on the case over the weekend and that I had been so tied up on my other cases that I hadn't even looked at Healthy Foods all week since I'd been back. And it was Thursday. For a minute I was actually nervous that Jack would tell.

"I think that Brooke can handle the follow-up research, as well, then," Jack told the partners. "By Monday, Brooke?" Jack said. Monday? Did he just give me a weekend assignment? Jack had just banished me to the office for the whole of the weekend. And he hadn't even tried to pretend that he hadn't by giving me a Tuesday due date. He was angrier than I thought.

"Not a problem," I said. "We're still set to go to the client together tomorrow?"

"Were you taking Brooke to Healthy Foods?" one of the partners asked Jack.

"I'll take Tina with me to the client tomorrow and Brooke can stay here and do the heavy lifting. Right, Brooke?" he asked.

"Of course," I said. I could not believe that he was going to take Tina Epstein, the first-year associate on the matter, to the client and leave me here to do research—all weekend long, mind you—when the first-year associate could easily have done it. And probably should have. I billed out at a much higher rate than a first-year associate.

I left the meeting in a daze and walked back to my office on autopilot. I couldn't believe that I wouldn't be going with Jack to the client. I was really counting on that time alone to talk to Jack. An hour's drive there and back were all I needed to apologize and make him realize that he was still madly in love with me. I even had a cute outfit planned for it and everything.

I walked back to my office and slumped into my chair. How was I going to get Jack back if he wouldn't even speak to me? He hadn't returned my phone calls or e-mails since we'd been back and my only hope at getting him alone was the work we'd been scheduled to do together.

The phone rang and I checked the caller ID. Jack's name came up. Jack was calling me! He must have been trying to act professional in our meeting so that neither one of us got fired. Surely, if he'd told the partners we were going to Healthy Foods tomorrow they would have noticed that the man is totally, completely, madly in love with me. I should have known it was all an act all along! Turns out, Jack really *is* a good actor!

"Are you back in your office?" he asked me.

"I'm right here," I said and a smile came to my face.

"Okay," he said, "I'm swinging by."

Of course he was coming to my office! Because Jack still loves me. So it doesn't even matter if I have to work all weekend or miss going to the client or any of it at all. Because I have what I really want—Jack. Well, truth be told, I'd rather not work all weekend, but...

I began to prepare for the big reconciliation. I shuffled through my purse for some lipstick and Listerine breath strips. Making up is the best. It's so good that it almost even makes up for the actual fighting. No doubt Jack will come up to my office, pull me into his arms while he says, "I was crazy to ever let you get away, even for a minute," and ravish me right there on my desk. Just thinking about it made me blush and smile even wider.

Then I began to panic. I reached for the pressed powder and blush, and even pulled my hair out of its bun and flipped my head upside down to give my hair a few good shakes.

Just as I was scouring my drawers for some perfume, he knocked on the door.

"Come in," I said as nonchalantly as I could, waving my arms above my head to make the cloud of hair spray and pressed powder dissipate.

"I'm so happy you're here," I said, getting up from my desk so that I could be at the right angle for him to pull me to him and ravish me.

"You left your legal pad in the meeting," he said, holding it out at arm's distance.

"Oh," I said, grabbing the pad. I flipped the pad over, hoping that Jack didn't see the front page where I'd scribbled *Jack, Jack, Jack* with little hearts all over it.

"Jack, we should talk," I said.

"Talk?" he said. "I don't think that there's anything left to say."

He turned on his heel and walked out the door before I even had a chance to formulate a thought.

26

When I got back to Vanessa's apartment after work that night, she was sitting on the couch, glued to the television screen, flipping through the channels. The apartment still smelled like cheap Mexican takeout. I could tell she had been crying.

"Bad day?" I asked her. She nodded her head yes.

"Do you want to talk about it?" I asked, throwing my bag down and approaching the couch.

"I don't think that I'm ready to talk about it yet," she said.

"Okay," I said, "when you are, let me know." She nodded and kept flipping channels. I picked my bag back up and went to the spare bedroom—my bedroom for the past few weeks—and threw my stuff down and took my shoes off. Unbuttoning my pants as I walked, I opened the closet door and grabbed a pair of pajama bottoms to change into. On the closet floor there was a basket that hadn't been there that morning. Trying as hard as I could not to peek inside (read: not at all), I saw a pile of picture frames with assorted pictures of Vanessa and Marcus. I knelt down and picked the first one up—a sterling-silver Tiffany picture frame filled with Vanessa and Marcus's wedding photo. I ran my finger along the side and felt a tear come to my eye. I could barely imagine how hard this was going to be for Vanessa if it was this sad for me.

"Did you eat yet?" Vanessa called out from the living room. I jumped up like a kid who had been caught with her hand in the cookie jar, almost dropping the frame that I was holding in the process. "There's some leftover chicken fajita if you want it."

"Thanks," I said, making a fast exit from the closet and changing into my pajama bottoms as quickly as I could, practically tripping out of my black work pants as I did so. I walked back to the living room in a walk-run to account for the time I'd been nosing around Vanessa's guest bedroom. "I'm not really hungry," I said, throwing a pillow against the side of Vanessa's lounging body and putting my head down. She continued flipping through the channels.

"I have some Lean Cuisine frozen pizzas," she said.

I jumped up from the couch and headed toward the freezer. I noticed that Vanessa had thrown out the carton of Rocky Road ice cream that had been there just this morning. Marcus's favorite.

"Did Marcus move his things out?" I asked, turning from the freezer to face Vanessa. Her eyes stayed glued to the television screen.

"Yeah," she said. "It's strange, though. He was never really here that much, so the place doesn't seem any emptier."

"How do you feel?" I asked, taking the frozen pizza out of its box and turning the oven on.

"Sad, mainly."

"Sad because it's sad, or sad because you did the wrong thing?"

"Does it matter?" she asked.

"It's never too late to change things if you did the wrong thing," I told her.

"Do you really think that?" she asked, turning to look at me. I answered her quickly. I didn't need to think about it at all—I really did.

What if when Jack had asked me, I'd considered for more than just one day whether one of us should leave the firm? What if I hadn't shrugged it off? Hadn't shrugged *him* off?

And why had I done that? For a job that I didn't really like? Not that I would have immediately quit my job for a kiss, but maybe if I'd taken him more seriously back then, I wouldn't have let the last few years just pass me by. Jack would never have gotten engaged and I would never have met Douglas and Jack and I would be together. Like I told Vanessa, you can't change the past, but it was never too late to change your future.

Those very words came back to haunt me the following morning.

"You can't change the past, but you can change your future," she sung, leaning over my bed at 6:00 a.m.

"Five more minutes, Mom," I moaned as I tried to pull a pillow over my head.

"No way!" Vanessa yelled as she pulled the pillow off my head, "You said that we were turning over a new leaf today!"

"That was really more for you than me," I said, eyes still tightly shut. "I meant that you should turn over a new leaf today. My leaf is just fine."

"What about all those changes you said you were going to make? You said," Vanessa reminded me as she opened the wood blinds, "that *you* were going to start training for next year's marathon with me?" As I turned over to face away from Vanessa, I vaguely recalled telling her the night before that I would begin training for the New York City Marathon with her. However, at the time, I was trying to convince her to let me eat raw cookie dough from the tube (she seemed to have some silly concern about raw eggs), and I really would have said anything just to get the goods.

"Statement made under duress," I said, opening my eyes slowly. It was so early in the morning that the room didn't get much lighter with the blinds open. "Not admissible."

"Well, I'm holding you to it," Vanessa said, grabbing the blanket off my bed and dragging it behind her as she left my bedroom. "Get up. We leave in fifteen."

A half hour later, we were out on the city streets—Vanessa looking great in skintight running pants and a snug fitting Howard University sweatshirt, and me looking as if I'd just rolled out of bed in yoga pants that I rarely ever used for actual yoga, but wore more for just bumming around the apartment, paired with the cashmere hoodie that I'd worn the night before and grabbed off my bedroom floor that morning.

"I feel better already," Vanessa said, jogging in place as we waited at the light to cross over Fifth Avenue to get into the park at the Seventy-second Street entrance. "Don't you?"

Now, I wish I could be one of those people who says something like "You know, once I got out there, I felt great!" I really do. But I'm not. Once I got out there, I didn't feel great. In fact, I felt worse. The sad fact was that I was absolutely exhausted by the time we'd jogged from Third Avenue to Central Park.

"Am I expected to go work a full day after this?" I asked Vanessa. She pretended not to hear me, continuing to run, nodding at other runners as we passed in a bizarre supersecret handshake sort of way. There was this weird subculture of runners in the park, a subculture that Vanessa was clearly a part of. A subculture of people who actually *enjoyed* getting up at daybreak.

These were not my people.

"So, do you want to talk about things?" she asked me, giving a brief glance in my direction.

"No," I said (between huffs and puffs). "Do you?"

"Well," she said, "running certainly clears my head. Helps me to think about things."

"Why can't you get that from taking a shower like regular people?" I asked her. "That way you don't have to get all sweaty."

"I think in the shower, too," she said.

"So, what are you thinking?" I said.

"This is going to sound crazy, but I'm so embarrassed about my marriage breaking up."

"That doesn't sound crazy," I said, still huffing and puffing. "That's totally natural. You know, you don't have to tell anyone for a while. It's your business. The whole firm doesn't need to know every little piece of our lives. You can take your time in processing it by yourself."

"Yeah, I guess," she said.

"And before you know it, you'll be back out there," I said. "You'll find someone even better."

"The thought of dating in Manhattan totally terrifies me. What if there are no men left?"

"There will be plenty of men left," I said with a laugh, even though that exact thought had gone through my mind more than once. "You should just take your time. It's also okay to be alone for a while."

"I don't know how to be alone," she said.

"Well, not completely alone," I said. "I mean, you still have your friends. We can go out for dinner all the time, go to the movies, shop…."

"We do that already," she said, stifling a laugh.

"I know," I said. "I just meant that you're not going to be alone, alone. If you want to, it's okay to give yourself time to be single and not looking for someone new."

"I don't know how to do that," she said.

"That's okay," I said, "I'll show you." Vanessa smiled at me and I smiled back. I knew that Vanessa would be just fine. It was just a matter of making her realize that she'd be fine, too.

She led us over to Writer's Walk, a beautiful tree-lined path with enormous sculptures of famous poets and writers. I took a deep breath of fresh air and decided that I would be just fine, too.

"Hey, Vanessa!" a voice called out from ahead of us.

"Hey!" Vanessa called out as the other runner approached us. She introduced me to a friend of hers from the Road Runners Club. Another woman who was similarly attired in skintight running pants and a fitted sweatshirt that she looked great in. I smiled and tried not to look completely winded as I shook her hand and she and Vanessa jogged in place and talked about next year's New York City Marathon. I had stopped jogging altogether, puzzling over what time the hot-dog vendors set up their carts. I know, I know, a hot dog would have been totally inappropriate this early in the morning, but I figured that a hot salted pretzel couldn't hurt. Purely for medical reasons, that is. What? A girl has to keep up her blood sugar, doesn't she?

"Brooke, you should keep running in place," Vanessa said to me, still immersed in her conversation about the marathon. I pretended not to hear and instead adjusted my ponytail.

A few minutes later, we were back to running through the park, Vanessa, still nodding at random other runners and me, trying to look as if I were not at death's door. I was getting the hang of it for a while, and as we began winding down, I was proud that I'd gone the whole time without dying. Vanessa slowed our pace to a "cool down" speed and I began to fantasize about the hot shower I would take when we got back to the apartment. Still quite a bit away, I could see the Seventy-second Street traffic light, beckoning me like a siren calling out to a tired sailor on the high seas. We got closer and closer, and a smile came to my face. I could even see the vendors beginning to set up their carts for the day, as I wondered if Vanessa had brought any cash so that she could buy me a congratulatory pretzel. I could hear the traffic roaring down Fifth Avenue and I silently patted myself on the back for a job well done.

Maybe this would be the new me. A healthier, more positive me who woke up early and went running and nodded to other runners as I ran. A motivated me who faces challenges head-on and tackles every obstacle in her way. The kind of woman who doesn't get flummoxed by the mere prospect of going to her ex-boyfriend's wedding. Who goes with her head held high, with a real-life boyfriend as opposed to a faux Scottish boyfriend, and behaves like the normal well-adjusted big-time lawyer that she is, as opposed to alienating the faux Scottish boyfriend she has realized she is in love with.

This was what turning over a new leaf was all about! I turned to Vanessa, all ready to tell her about my epiphany, and lost my footing for a brief instant. I felt something under my foot and it caused my entire body to jerk sideways. I heard Vanessa call something out about a hot dog, which really puzzled me, and then I went down.

My body hit the pavement with a thud, like a sack of potatoes, as I tried to break my fall with my hands.

"Brooke!" Vanessa cried out as she knelt down on the ground next to me. A crowd began to gather around us. The pain coming from my ankle was searing, and I grabbed it and bent my head down toward my knee.

"Is your friend okay?" I heard a stranger ask Vanessa.

"She tripped on that hot dog," Vanessa said. I looked up to see the offending hot dog rolling away as Vanessa began yelling at the vendor about how we were lawyers and she was going to sue him. I knew that hot dogs weren't particularly good for you, but this was ridiculous.

"I think I need to go to the hospital," I said to Vanessa as she helped me to my feet. Or, foot, as the case may be. I put my arm over her shoulder as I hopped with her to the curb.

"Should we get that vendor's license number?" Vanessa asked me.

"I'm in too much pain to think about possible future law-suits," I said.

"I'm taking you right to Mount Sinai Hospital," Vanessa said as a taxicab stopped to pick us up.

"Mount Sinai?" I asked. "That's thirty blocks away. We need to go to Lenox Hill, it's five blocks away."

"We can't go to Lenox Hill," Vanessa said, opening the cab door and gently helping me in. "Mount Sinai Hospital, please," she said to the cab driver. He wrote down our destination while we sat there at the red light.

"She means Lenox Hill, sir," I said, looking at Vanessa. "I'm in a bit of pain here." He shot me a dirty look in the rearview mirror as he erased our former destination and began to scribble down the new one.

"Marcus is at Lenox Hill," Vanessa said, looking down.

"We're not going to see him," I said, still clutching my ankle.

"It's a big hospital. If you want, you can even just drop me off and go home. Slow the cab down to a cool five and just roll me out. Lenox Hill, sir."

"It's a really small hospital and I can't leave you alone," she said. "She means Mount Sinai. Sorry for the confusion."

"*Marcus* is in surgery," I pleaded. "*We* are going to the emergency room. I don't mean to be insensitive, really I don't, but I don't think that I can make it till 100th Street. Sir, it's Lenox Hill."

"What if you *need* surgery?" Vanessa asked. "Mount Sinai, please."

"What if I need surgery? I need surgery?" I said as tears began to fall from my eyes. "I don't need surgery. Do I need surgery?"

"Ladies," the cab driver said, "what's it gonna' be?" The "Don't Walk" sign had come up and I could tell that our red light was about to turn green.

"Lenox Hill!" I said.

"She means Mount Sinai," Vanessa said.

"No, I don't!" I said. "Vanessa, for the love of God! Lenox Hill!"

The cab hopped the traffic light on red and took a sharp turn onto Seventy-second Street as Vanessa and I stared each other down. Neither of us even moved as the cab lurched as it turned. We were like Wyatt Earp and Doc Holliday at the O.K. Corral, even though we were actually in a taxicab and I think that those guys were on the same side. But you get the general point I was trying to make with that one.

"Ladies," the cab driver said, "we're going to compromise and take you to Weil-Cornell New York Presb on Sixty-eighth Street, okay?"

"Thank you," we called out in unison.

Our cabbie ripped across town to York Avenue and I was hopping into the emergency room in two minutes flat.

"Maybe your friend can help you to a seat so that you can fill out these forms," the admitting nurse said to me with a smile as she handed me a clipboard filled with papers.

"I'm here alone," I said to the admitting nurse as I steadied myself on a wall. "My best friend has absolutely no regard for my health whatsoever."

"She tripped on a hot dog in the park," Vanessa said, ignoring me completely. "And now she has blinding pain in her ankle."

"Can you walk on it?" the nurse asked me, silencing a laugh.

"It's not funny," I said to the nurse.

"She can't walk on it," Vanessa said.

"I'll take care of these two, Nurse Carlson," an English accent from behind us announced. "Are they checked in?"

"Yes, they are, Dr. Locke," the nurse said, smiling coyly at the doctor.

I turned around and recognized a set of immaculately groomed dreadlocks. They were held back by that same chocolate-colored bandanna he'd worn when we'd first met him at Millie's art gallery.

"Christian?" Vanessa said. "Brooke, you remember Christian from my mom's art gallery, don't you?"

"It was a week ago," I said, still clutching the wall, "so, yes."

Christian helped me into a wheelchair and walked us back to the examining area. He and Vanessa then carefully got me up onto a hospital bed where Christian pulled back the curtain to examine my ankle in private. Which was good since I hadn't shaved my legs since the wedding.

Oh, please. As if you shave your legs when no one's going to see them.

"So, how was your ex-boyfriend's wedding?" Christian asked as he poked and prodded my ankle.

"Fine," I said. "Ouch!"

"Okay," he said, "I'm going to put a little pressure on it. Tell me if this hurts."

"Ouch."

"So, everything worked out at the wedding?" he asked, still looking down at my ankle. "Are you and Douglas back together?"

"It didn't exactly work out the way I had planned," I said. "Ouch."

"Most things never do," he said. "But that's what makes life exciting, right?" Vanessa and I both stared back at him blankly. It was still before eight o'clock in the morning—my usual wake-up time—and I could do without my current "excitement."

"So, whatever happened with that other guy," Christian asked, now moving my leg around in circles, "the one who was at the opening with you two? He seemed very interested in you, Brooke."

"Oh, that didn't work out, either," I said as Vanessa grabbed my hand and smiled at me. Christian turned my ankle in a slow circle. "Ouch."

"I see," Christian said, looking up at me as he stopped poking and prodding my ankle. "Okay, Brooke, the good news is that it's not broken."

"Thank you," Vanessa said, taking on the maternal role, her hands clutching the metal bar of the hospital bed.

"You do have a nasty sprain here, though," he said. "I'm going to put you on crutches for a while."

"I can't be on crutches!" I said. "I live in New York City! How will I get around? I walk everywhere—how will I walk? Or the subway—how will I get down the stairs to the subway?"

"Think of it as a good excuse to take cabs everywhere," Vanessa said, and then added under her breath: "Which you sort of do anyway."

"Staying positive," Christian said. "That's good, Vanessa. I'm glad to see that. I hear from your mom that you're not having the best time of things lately."

"I'll be okay," Vanessa said. "At least I'm not on crutches."

"Ha ha," I said.

"Well, if you ever need to talk about it," Christian said, "you know where to find me." Is this man flirting with Vanessa while he's examining my ankle? The nerve! How is he going to give my ankle a proper analysis? This is why people are always complaining about the state of health care in the United States.

"I don't need to talk about it," Vanessa said, smoothing back her hair.

Even though the pain was maddening, all I could think was if Vanessa marries yet another doctor before I've had a chance to marry even *one,* my mother will die. I can just hear her now: "Your friend married *two* doctors and you can't even get a date!"

"So, I can't go to work today, right?" I asked Christian.

"No, you can go to work," he said, still preening in Vanessa's general direction.

"Are you absolutely positively sure?" I asked.

"Yes," he said, eyes still glued on Vanessa.

"Because I don't have to go to work," I said, ever the trooper.

"Brooke, you can go," he said.

"Can you check again?" I asked. He shook his head *no* to me without even looking my way. "Do I at least get some painkillers?"

"Let's start with an ice pack and some ibuprofen. I'll go get you a soft ice pack that you can use for the next forty-eight hours," Christian said as he pulled back the curtain and walked off to get me an ice pack, but not before he patted Vanessa on the hand before he did so.

"Don't worry, Brooke," Vanessa said. "Everything will work out."

"It's badly sprained, Vanessa," I said. "It's done. It's over. There's nothing to work out."

"I was talking about Jack," she said.

"Oh," I said. "I guess I feel the same way about Jack. I screwed up. It's done. It's over."

"No, it's not. With Jack, it is in no way done or over. With the ankle thing, you're just screwed."

"Thank you for that sensitive commentary," I said, grabbing at my ankle.

"I'm kidding!" she said. "It's going to be fine! It's not broken, and you'll be back on your feet within weeks. In the meantime, you have an excuse to not exercise and take cabs everywhere! I would think that that would be your secret fantasy or something."

"It would have been my fantasy if I also got a note saying that I couldn't go to work."

"I'll work on it when he gets back," Vanessa said, looking out past the curtain for Christian to return.

"Are you going to flirt with him some more?" I asked.

"I wasn't flirting with him," Vanessa said, toying with the zipper on her sweatshirt.

"Yes, you were," I said. "You know, it's okay if you were."

"I know," she said. "It just still feels like cheating somehow. I'm not ready to flirt with strangers just yet."

"You don't have to be ready yet," I said. "Just take your time. Everything is going to work out the way it's meant to."

"I was just about to say the same thing to you."

27

The following Monday, I marched right into Jack's office and brought him the research I'd done for him over the weekend. Well, more like *fell* right into Jack's office. I was still figuring out how to negotiate the crutches and the plastic boot I was condemned to wear on my ankle. ("Oh, my God, that thing is hideous, are you really going to wear that out of the house?" was Vanessa's reaction.) I wore my hair down for our big meeting and I kept catching pieces of it against the crutches underneath my armpit. Not the image I was going for.

"Thanks," he said, barely looking up from his computer. I'd worked hard on the research—I didn't want to give Jack any more reason to hate me than he already had—and I'd also drafted a comprehensive memorandum outlining the case law for him and highlighting future points for argument, which he hadn't even asked me to do. I was hoping to get more mileage out of my weekend's work than a mere "thanks."

"Is there anything else you need me to do?" I asked, hoping he would say yes and extend the conversation a bit further.

"Nope," Jack said, eyes still locked on the computer, "you're all set. Thanks."

"Tell me the truth," I said, trying to be cute, "is that really your fantasy football league that you're working so hard on?"

"No," he said, turning his screen to face me, "it's the survey for the Healthy Foods case."

"Oh," I said, still standing in front of his desk. In a false-advertising lawsuit like the Healthy Foods case, what must be proven is actual confusion—that consumers were actually confused into buying your product because of your false advertising. Jack was crafting a survey that would then be conducted out in the public to prove that consumers weren't actually confused into buying Healthy Foods coffee because they thought it was healthy. A case can be won or lost on a survey, a fact I knew acutely since Jack and I had drafted the winning survey on the last false advertising case we'd been on together. I couldn't help but feel a slight pang of disappointment that he hadn't wanted to work with me on the Healthy Foods survey.

"Don't you have other work to do?" he said, turning his screen back to face him and beginning to type.

You're losing him, I thought. *Get his interest back.*

"Yes," I said, hopping over to his visitor's chair and plopping myself down, crutches strategically placed against his desk for maximum sympathy, "but I think I'd rather consult the Magic 8-Ball to find out if we're going to win our case. Magic 8-Ball," I said, shaking it slowly in a manner that I was hoping would look seductive, "are we going to win the Healthy Foods case?"

Jack grabbed the Magic 8-Ball from my hands and threw it into his garbage can. I felt my body involuntarily jerk back into my chair from the sheer force that he had used to throw it down. I was certain that its contents were in the bottom of his garbage can, blue liquid oozing out everywhere.

"Stop," he said. "Enough. If you want me to find you some work to do, I can find you some work to do."

"For you?" I said, perking up. "Okay."

"No," he said, looking me dead in the eye. "Not for me."

"But we always work together," I said.

"Well, Tina and I worked really well together at the client's office last Friday, so I think I'll be working with her a lot more on a forward-going basis. You're getting too senior to be doing all of your work for me anyway."

"Oh," I said, immediately feeling the urge to cry. "Of course." I grabbed for my crutches and tried to steady myself as I stood. I pushed back the visitor's chair with one crutch and hopped around to face Jack's door. Jack sat at his desk staring at me.

"Anyway," he said once I'd almost made it to the door. "I'm sure you'll be too busy planning your wedding to Douglas to work on my cases anyway."

"My wedding? I'm not marrying Douglas," I said, turning to him quickly on my good leg and almost losing my footing. I hadn't heard Douglas's name in a week. He hadn't even contacted me in as long despite his declaration of love and marriage proposal at Trip's wedding, and I had a visceral reaction to hearing it spoken. "Where did you hear that?"

"Vanessa told me that he proposed to you in L.A. after I left the wedding," he said.

"But did she also tell you that I said *no?* That I stormed out on him?"

"Yeah, she told me that part," he said, looking me dead in the eye. "But I know you, Brooke, and you'll be back for him. I know what you like. What's important to you. You'll be planning that wedding to Douglas in no time."

"No, I won't," I said. "I won't, Jack."

"You know what, Brooke," Jack said, shaking his head, "it doesn't even matter anymore."

"But I love you," I blurted out. I didn't mean to say it—and certainly not like that—but the words just fell out of my mouth.

Jack stared at me in silence for a moment before looking back to his computer. "I wish I could believe you," he said as he began to type. Partners sometimes did this charming little trick when you were excused from their offices. They would bark out their orders to you, and before you could say a word, they would then pick up the telephone or begin to type or start reviewing a file without even telling you the meeting was over. Jack and I used to joke around about how unbelievably rude this practice was and report back to each other whenever a partner did it to us, putting them on a mental list of people we never wanted to work for again. I stood in Jack's doorway for a moment, staring at him, certain he would look back up at me and want to talk, but he kept on typing furiously.

"It's true," I said. Jack still didn't look up from his computer. I continued to ramble on anyway. "When you rejected me after that South Carolina trip, I couldn't stand it. I made up all of these excuses about why you weren't right for me, and it kept me away from you for all of these years. But now—"

"*I* rejected *you?*" Jack said. "*You* were the one who rejected *me*. I was ready to leave the firm for you—something I'd worked my ass off for—and you barely gave it a day's thought."

"I did give it a day's thought," I said. "In fact, it was the *only* thing I thought about until Danielle Lewis took me for lunch and threatened me with my job. I got scared and I ran away from you. I was wrong. I should have fought for you. But all of that doesn't matter anymore. What matters is now. What about now? Isn't now what's important?"

"There is no now," he said. "You're going to get back with Douglas."

"I'm not back with Douglas. I *will never* get back together with Douglas. I'm sorry about everything that's happened. I want to make everything all right now. I want to be with *you*. I love *you*." I began to hop back into his office, certain that he would jump up from his desk and hold me to him and tell me that he loved me, too, but he didn't even get up from his chair.

"Really?" he asked.

"Really," I said, my voice almost a whisper.

"See, Brooke," Jack said, pointing to his computer, "that's why I'm so good at crafting surveys. I'm very good at knowing that just because a product's label says one thing to you with a big beautiful smile, you'd have to be a fool to believe it."

I stood there frozen. I couldn't believe that Jack didn't believe me, didn't forgive me, didn't want to be with me. There was nothing left to say. As I turned around and hobbled out of his office, I could feel his eyes burning into my back.

I hopped back to my office, slammed the door shut and slumped down into my chair. I set my crutches down, leaning them on my desk next to me, but before I could stop them, they slid down and fell to the ground. I considered picking them back up for a moment, but the thought of reaching over and then getting back up exhausted me.

I was right. Vanessa was wrong and I was right. It was done. It was over. Jack and I were over. Before we'd even had a chance to really begin. Whatever Jack and I had built, I had broken. And it couldn't be fixed. Jack didn't want it to be fixed.

As I swiveled around to my computer, certain that work would take my mind off Jack, the telephone rang. I didn't recognize the number on caller ID, but I picked it up anyway.

"Hello?" I said into the phone, completely forgetting to be professional and answer the phone with a crisp "Brooke Miller."

"Hi, is this Brooke Miller?" a voice asked.

"Yes," I said, sitting up in my chair.

"My name is Michelle Berger and I do attorney placement. Do you have some time now to talk?"

I laughed to myself. *A litigator never has time to talk.* I looked at my computer, with the Healthy Foods memo I'd written for Jack still open in Word, and the assorted other case law and documents I still had to organize for the Healthy Foods case.

"As a matter of fact, Michelle," I said, clicking the Healthy Foods memo off my computer, "I do."

28

It's amazing how similar a job interview is to a date. As I hobbled on my crutches across town to each of the small law firms where Michelle had secured me an interview, I couldn't help but notice that all of the same benchmarks were there: you worry about your outfit; you stress out over what you will talk about; and everyone is trying to put his or her best face forward. There is little to no room for error; the slightest faux pas and you could be back at square one, jobless, or worse yet, single.

The screening interview is like a date over drinks or coffee—the other party hasn't committed yet to the idea of giving you more than thirty minutes of their time. If said other party deems you good enough, then you get to the real interview, where you meet four or five members of the firm, and you curse the fact that you wore your best suit for the screening interview and told all of your best anecdotes. But still, it's a second date.

All of the parties smile a lot and highlight their most positive attributes and leave out any negative ones. Everyone laughs at everyone else's jokes and keeps their elbows off the table. I tried hard to remember how to fold my hands in the ladylike way my aunt Myrna taught me to when I was younger. The same topics are taboo—no one discusses politics or sex—except in the job interview, you are encouraged to immediately express how much you love the firm and how you want to stay there until your dying day.

In both the job interview and dating, you hope and pray for the Holy Grail—the job offer/marriage proposal—and then soon learn that the courting was actually the fun and easy part.

Michelle had set me up on six screening interviews/first dates, which I then parlayed into three second-round interviews/second dates.

After interviewing at all three firms that had invited me back, I had secured offers from two of them.

I agonized over my decision for days, in striking contrast to the on-campus recruitment season when I was in law school. Back then, Vanessa and I sat in the Law Review office in the height of interview season and discussed our options:

"Which firm did you like the best?" Vanessa said.

"I was so busy trying to get them to like me that I wasn't really paying attention to them…." I said as I leafed through *The American Lawyer* midlevel associate survey. "Which did you like the best?"

"Gilson Hecht is on Park Avenue, is only three blocks away from Saks and has the most attractive lawyers," Vanessa said. "Probably because they're close to Saks and can get really cute work outfits."

"But," I asked as the managing editor of the Law Review walked into the office, "where do they rank on the *Law Journal* list? How much experience do junior associates get early on? Number of female partners?"

"Good questions, Brooke," Vanessa said, practically biting a hole in the side of her cheek as she tried not to laugh. We had decided early on in the on-campus interview process that all of the big firms were practically identical, so we were best off finding a place where we would just fit in and get along with the other associates. "I'm also curious to know the partner-to-associate ratio."

The managing editor nodded at both of us as she grabbed the mail from her mailbox and left the office. We both fell into hysterical laughter the second she walked out of the office.

This time around was different, though. I actually cared about things like level of responsibility given to associates and the partner-to-associate ratio. I paid attention when I was at each firm, to every person, every word uttered, the subtext in what they said to me, the way they interacted with those around them, their body language. Because this time, I would not make a mistake. This time, I would not make an important life decision for the wrong reasons.

My first offer came from Anderton Frommer, another Park Avenue law firm like Gilson Hecht, with a similarly long and illustrious history. Much smaller than Gilson Hecht, it was a small intellectual property "boutique" firm with about fifty attorneys. I felt immediately at home when I walked into its offices. Michelle told me that it was the sort of place that attorneys who want to leave big firm life gravitate to; it still had the creature comforts you were used to at your old big firm, and you still would get the same thrill out of telling people where you worked.

My other offer was from Smith, Goldberg and Reede. I'd never heard of them before, but Michelle told me that they were a relatively young up-and-coming firm whose reputation in intellectual property work was growing due to their excellent work product and high ethical standards. Lawyers who worked with them and litigated against them routinely praised them for the way they did business.

Their offices on Third Avenue weren't nearly as posh as Gilson Hecht's offices, or even Anderton Frommer's, for that matter, but somehow that didn't seem to matter anymore once I began to meet the people who worked there. There was no mahogany, no imported marble, and no room dedicated solely to supplies. More importantly, though, there was also no cafeteria—SGR attorneys weren't expected to work through dinner.

I met two associates whom I really liked. One was junior to me and the other would be senior, and I could see myself working with both of them. I also met one of the founding members of the firm, Noah Goldberg, and was immediately impressed that he would take the time out of his schedule to meet a prospective new associate. He wasn't as old as I expected him to be. None of the named partners were even still alive at Gilson Hecht, nor were they at most of the city's large firms.

As Noah talked about his vision for the firm and the type of lawyer he was looking to hire, I began to remember why I'd wanted to be a lawyer in the first place—I loved to write and I loved to work with people. He talked about helping clients and being creative and working with good people. Hearing him talk about intellectual property law and why he chose the field got me excited about the law in a way I hadn't been since my second-year Trademarks class. The work was what was important, not whether or not your case got into the paper. Having a life outside of work made you happy, not merely having the ability to tell people that you worked at a prestigious firm. As we talked about intellectual property law, I realized that I'd truly gotten excellent training at Gilson Hecht and that I was very much prepared for more responsibility and a new opportunity, which was what SGR was offering me.

Noah introduced me to my last interviewer of the day, a partner named Rosalyn Ford. Introducing the female candidates to a successful female partner was a trick the big firms used that I remembered from interviewing the first time around ("This firm is great for women, we'll prove it to you by dangling a female partner in front of you!"), but I still appreciated the effort.

"Brooke Miller," Rosalyn said as we shook hands and she helped me set my crutches next to my seat. "It can't be easy running around Manhattan with these."

"No, it's not," I said with a smile, noticing a picture on her desk of her and two toddlers.

"Now that I work here I actually get to *see* those little guys," she said, catching me looking at the photo. I smiled back at her. "But then again, my kids stay up until midnight."

"Oh," I said, trying to formulate a response.

"I'm kidding," she said. "Only kidding." She told me a bit about herself and her family and how different her life had become since leaving big-firm life. We both agreed that the big-firm lifestyle could be punishing, though I was cautious in my answers to let her know that I was not opposed to working hard when circumstances called for it.

"So, what attracted you to Gilson Hecht?" she asked. "Actually, no, that's a stupid question. I was seduced by the big-firm thing, too, right out of law school. It's hard not to be, isn't it? The offices are beautiful and state of the art, your clients are all famous and world-renowned brands, your cases are always in the paper, you have unlimited resources at your fingertips, and they pay you more than you really deserve your first year out of law school." I couldn't help but smile in response. She put it so succinctly, but she was right. Rosalyn reminded me of the sort of person I'd grown up with, down-to-earth and without airs, and I found her easy to be around. "And don't you love saying that you work at Gilson Hecht?" she asked. I was slightly embarrassed by the question because the fact was that I *had* loved saying that I worked there, and somehow that now seemed silly.

Rosalyn and I talked a lot about why I wanted to leave Gilson Hecht and her own decision to leave a big firm. She told me about the types of cases she was working on and the types of cases that I could hope to work on. As the interview wound down, she summed it up for me: "Offices aren't as fancy and the cases aren't as sexy, but you'll get better hours, and better experience. I'm happy I came here and I think that you will be, too."

I was sold. Within weeks, I was on my way to SGR. They didn't offer the big firm salary, but they did offer more substance, which seemed like an excellent trade-off.

I was off crutches by the time I gave my notice at Gilson Hecht and then spent the following two weeks wrapping things up on all of my active cases. The Healthy Foods case was wrapping itself up, actually, thanks to a successful survey Jack had crafted that showed that real consumers were not actually confused into thinking that Healthy Foods coffee was healthy, as the lawsuit claimed. The case would be disappearing in no time, due to Jack's good work.

It took me most of the two weeks just to clean out my office, throwing out some things and giving away others. It was a long-standing Gilson Hecht tradition that as an associate left, that associate would give away most of his or her things to those he or she left behind. A changing of the guards of sorts. I had quite a few things on my own desk that had been handed down to me from more senior associates whom I'd looked up to before they'd left themselves.

I had Stephanie Paul's old Gilson Hecht mug from before Trattner had become a named partner—a collector's item for sure. I also had Bernard Mitnick's old Etch A Sketch that he used to keep on top of his computer, still with the poorly drawn picture of a bird (a "free" bird) that he'd drawn for me on his way out. I took those with me.

I gave away my own Gilson Hecht mug that I'd received the first day I came to the firm as a summer associate and the stress ball that used to sit at the edge of my desk. I hoped that I wouldn't need a stress ball at my new firm. I put my take-out menu collection into a legal folder and gave it to the first-year associate I was assigned to advise. I told her who to ask for at each place, along with what to order and what to avoid.

Vanessa came in and took all of my office supplies, from the desk calendar down to the paper clips, which she claimed were in much better condition than her own (something about my not using my stapler as much as she did—I was pretty sure it was a not-so-subtle dig at my work ethic, but I let it slide). She also dragged out my two visitor's chairs. They were chocolate-brown distressed leather, whereas most of the associates all had the same standard fabric run-of-the-mill doctor's waiting-room chairs in their offices. I had gotten them when I was a first-year associate—stolen them really—from the office of a recently disbarred partner. I'd felt it only fair that I have first dibs on his office furniture—I'd been working on a case for him at the time, and had been the first to know of his impending disbarment. I felt Gilson Hecht owed me something for the pain and suffering I endured from having watched a partner being taken out of the office in handcuffs right in the middle of a meeting.

I shuffled through my top desk drawer for more things to throw away or give away when I came upon the faux engagement ring Jack had bought me. It still shone brightly with its tiny fake baguettes and fake platinum band. I picked it up and looked at it for a moment just as Sherry Lee, one of my favorite first-year associates, came into my office.

"I knew it was true!" she said, walking into my office and sitting down on my empty credenza. She crossed her slim legs and I remembered how Vanessa and I used to get dressed up and wear skirts when we were first years.

"What was true?" I asked.

"That you got engaged to Douglas in L.A.! It's why you quit, isn't it? Let me see the ring!" Sherry said, leaning over my desk.

"This isn't the ring," I explained. "I didn't get engaged to Douglas. We're not together anymore."

"Then what's that in your hand?" she asked me.

"This?" I asked, looking at the ring. "This is nothing."

"Oh," she said. "Sorry. Well, then, I'll see you at your going-away party tomorrow night."

I smiled at her as she walked out. I turned the ring over and over in my hands, unsure of what to do with it. I couldn't throw it out and I most certainly couldn't give it away. I turned it over and over again, remembering how much fun Jack and I had had together on the day that he'd bought it for me.

I put the ring into an interoffice envelope and put it in my *Out* box.

29

I didn't even know I was going to do it when I walked into the place, but the moment I got there, something overcame me and I just knew that the time was right. Something was different—somehow I was different—and I decided all at once.

"I usually don't recommend doing this after you've had a traumatic situation," Starleen said.

"I haven't had a traumatic situation," I said simply.

"Let's see," she said, "Douglas broke up with you and threw you out of your apartment after proposing to some bimbo, which left you dateless for Trip's wedding. Then, you realized you were in love with your best friend, but Douglas came back and ruined that, too. And now, you're about to start a new job. You're right, Brooke, that's no stress at all."

"Do it," I said, looking at myself in the mirror. "I'm ready."

"After you do this," she said, "you can't just go back, you know."

Actually, you could. As I walked into the hair salon that day, there was a huge sign advertising a summer special on hair extensions. You could cut all of your hair off one day, and then return to the salon the very next day and have extensions put in that would make your hair the exact same length that it had been. But that didn't matter. I wouldn't need to go back.

"Cut it all off," I said to Starleen, who had been my hairstylist for the last ten years. When I'd first started seeing her, she'd been a mere assistant to the namesake of the salon (read: charged really cheap rates), but she had worked her way up to become a senior stylist (read: so expensive that I'm actually embarrassed to admit the price). She'd seen me through Trip and Douglas and about a million other bad dates in between. So, I could understand her apprehension to change my style so drastically after such a long time.

"Here goes," she said, running a comb through my long wet locks and making the first cut.

I watched the first piece fall to the ground and felt a tear come to my eye. It wasn't so much that I was sad—I cried often enough to know the difference between cries—it was just a recognition of how hard it was to cut away a piece of yourself. A piece of yourself that has been there since you were just a kid. Something that's been *with* you for more of your life than it hasn't.

But maybe change is good. It certainly felt good to go out and get a new job, and I was excited about my new opportunity and the thought that it was up to me to make something of it. By letting go of what I thought I'd wanted, I had found an even better job than the one that I'd had, just as I'd recently found a new apartment that was even better than the one in which I'd lived with Douglas. I just knew that the new job was only the beginning of more new good things to come for me.

"I can stop right now," Starleen said, watching me looking down at my locks of hair in the mirror.

"No, I said, "I don't want you to stop."

So she didn't.

When all was said and done, Starleen had taken twelve and a half inches off—I knew exactly how much it was since she'd had to measure it before sending it on to Locks of Love, the charity that collects hair to make wigs for children with cancer.

Even with that much taken off, it was still shoulder length because Starleen said that she still wanted it to look like me, but just a better me. And it did. Most people would still consider it long (or medium length if you didn't want to be generous about it), and the cut made it look much healthier. It *was* healthier, lighter. The style had more movement, but it still knew exactly where it was supposed to go.

When she was finished with the cut, Starleen began to blow it out straight on autopilot. I told her that maybe we should keep some of the natural curl in it and she gave me bunches of subtle waves.

"Fabulous," Starleen said when she was done and I wasn't sure if she meant me or her own handiwork. Either way, I felt great as I walked back to my office to get ready for my official Gilson Hecht going-away party.

"Are you ready?" Vanessa asked me as she burst into my office.

"Yeah," I said, still sitting behind my empty desk, applying blush. I was excited about my new haircut and even though I knew that it was a more professional look for my new job and the next phase of my life, I was still making up for the resultant "naked" feeling by doubling up on blush.

"I told you to be ready at 5:00 p.m.! Let's rock and roll!" she said, brushing the ends of my hair as she walked past me. Vanessa had changed out of her tailored pantsuit and into tight black pants and a tan Nanette Lepore top that was bordering on being a bit too low cut for an office party.

"Shut the door," I said. "I haven't changed yet."

"Why aren't you ready?" she asked.

"Most of the people attending tonight aren't going to be able to get out of here until seven o'clock, the earliest, and even that's pushing it, so what's the rush?" I asked her, grabbing the outfit that was hanging on the back of my office door.

"I know!" she said. "We barely have any time! We need to get to the place and make sure that we have a little area sectioned off for just our group. Then we need to eat something and freshen up our makeup so that we look like we're just coming from the office, too."

"Do you think Jack's coming?" I asked, pulling down on the ends of my hair.

"It looks fantastic," Vanessa said, "stop touching it."

"Thanks," I said, as I began to put on my own black pants and pink little top that was definitely too low cut for an office party. Vanessa picked up my telephone and started dialing. With just a bra and one pant leg on, I dove for the phone. "Do *not* call him!" I screamed, slamming my hand over the phone. "I was just checking to see if you knew."

"I'll know once I call him," she said.

"If he wants to come, he will come," I said, my hand still firmly planted on the phone.

"But you want him to come. That's why I was calling him. Do you really care how he gets there?"

"Yes, as a matter of fact, I do. We haven't spoken for weeks. The last time we did speak he made it clear that he hates me. Anyway, he knows why I quit," I said, putting my other leg into my pants.

"Why did you quit?" she asked me, pulling up a chair to listen as if she were Dr. Phil.

"Now the ball is in his court," I said, putting on my top.

"No," she said, "I think that you're giving him way too much credit for having ESP and reading your mind. He probably just thinks that you were miserable here like everyone else."

"Let's go," I said, pulling Vanessa out of the office.

Seconds later, we were barreling in the door to Sammy J's, a dive bar around the corner from the office. Every Gilson Hecht associate since 1997 has had his or her going-away party at Sammy J's for sentimental reasons. Sammy J was a Gilson Hecht associate himself, toiling his nights away at the firm like most young associates do, dreaming about one day owning a bar. On the odd night that Sammy J wasn't working until midnight (and some that he was), you could find Sammy J at Fat Joe's, the dive bar that was then in the space that Sammy J's now occupies. He was there so often that the local pizza place used to deliver pizzas for him right to the bar. He was so close with Fat Joe, having spent so many late nights at the bar, that Fat Joe let him do it. Sometime into Sammy J's fourth year at the firm, rumors started flying around the firm about Fat Joe filing for bankruptcy and the next thing everyone knew, Sammy J was giving his two weeks notice and buying Fat Joe's place for pennies in foreclosure. It's considered good luck to have your going-away party there. And Sammy J will even order in the pizza for you himself.

We sat at the bar eating pizza with Sammy J when, just as I'd predicted, at 7:00 p.m., the crowd started rolling in. Vanessa and I had commandeered the best tables in the place—far enough back to be somewhat private, but positioned just right so that we could see the front door every time it opened.

I couldn't keep my eyes off that door. Every time it opened, I prayed it would be Jack coming in. But it never was. I wondered if Vanessa was doing the same thing, hoping that Marcus would show up. I asked her.

"Why on earth would I think that?" she answered.

"Not necessarily think it, but hope it," I explained.

"No," she said.

"Why not?" I asked.

"Marcus is not coming," she said simply. And at that moment, I knew that Jack wasn't coming, either. I would just have to accept the situation, much as Vanessa had. She and Marcus were separated, so he would not be coming. Jack and I were not together anymore—weren't ever, really, so he would not be coming, either.

Even though it wouldn't kill him to show his face at an office goodbye party. I mean, the man *does* want to make partner at this firm, doesn't he? My God, he could show a bit more office spirit, don't you think?

Vanessa went to the jukebox, dollar bills in hand, and began to select the soundtrack for the evening. "Born to Run" began to blast over the ball game Sammy J had up on the television screen and I couldn't help but smile. I knew that Vanessa thought she was being clever. I walked up to the jukebox and checked what other songs she had selected. Equal parts Tom Petty, The Pretenders and Liz Phair, I couldn't have picked a more sexy, kick-ass mix myself. She even had a few of my favorite eighties songs thrown in for good measure.

We greeted the other associates as they came in and talked about my plans for the future. None of the girls could believe I'd chopped off my hair. I heard some of the third-year guys talking about which way they liked it better, but I decided not to listen because I'd decided that *I* liked it better this way and that was all that really mattered.

I spoke to all of the associates who were there and told them all about the new firm, but even as I was talking, I couldn't keep my eyes off the door. Still hoping, praying, that with each swish of the door, it would be Jack walking in to see me. But it never was. I drank beer after beer, shot after shot, in the hopes that I would just start to relax and enjoy myself at my own going-away party.

"Okay, Brooke," one of the second-year associates told me, "now that you're leaving, you have to play one of my favorite games with me. It's called 'Death is not an option.'" A few other second years began to gather and sat me down at the back table. They lined up beers and shots of tequila and explained the rules to me. They would name two different people that we knew and I would have to decide which of the two I would sleep with.

"Dennis in the mail room or Tony in duplicating?" she began.

"Dennis weighs over three hundred pounds," I said.

"Do I hear a Tony?" one of the other girls asked.

"I'd rather kill myself," I said.

"Death is not an option!" they all cried out in unison.

"Then I guess it's Tony," I said. The other second years all nodded their heads in agreement. "That was a tough one," one of them said.

"Okay, Rich Harper in tax or that dude in the cafeteria whose hair net is always on crooked?"

"Rich Harper is a partner," I said. The girls all nodded, anxious for my response, "who wears a really bad toupee." The girls nodded again, practically falling off their seats, they were leaning in so close to hear. "I guess I'd have to take the dude in the cafeteria."

"Ewww!" one of the second years said. "Hair nets! I think that I got the cooties just from hearing you say that!"

"Yeah, at least Harper would buy you jewelry," another chimed in.

"Yeah, Brooke, that's kind of gross," the ringleader said. "Okay, Emmett in word processing or Jordan Levy in corporate?"

"Jordan's a girl," I said. The girls all nodded.

"Yeah, but Emmett has a mullet," the ringleader said. "And really bad acne."

"Good point," I said. "I guess I'd have to go with Jordan, then. At least we could share clothing and stuff." The girls all nodded along.

"And shoes," one added.

"Okay, here's a tough one—Jack, or…"

"Which Jack?" I asked.

"You know which Jack," the ringleader said.

"Jack in litigation or Jack in real estate?" I asked.

"You don't know Jack!" said the second-year to her left, giggling as she downed another shot from the glasses lined up in front of us.

"Is that what this whole game is about?" I asked. "If you wanted gossip, all you had to do was ask."

The Doors came on and all at once I felt suffocated. "Break on Through" blasted through the bar and I couldn't catch my breath. I had to get out of there.

"Oh, my God, I looove this song!" one of the second years called out and they all got up to dance around the bar. I got up, too, and started heading for the door. I grabbed a strand of hair to twirl and felt my eyes tear up as I remembered that I'd cut it all off.

I tried to grab Vanessa to tell her that I was leaving, but she was far too busy dancing on a table to pay me any mind. Yes, she was dancing on a table. She was dancing with Sammy J, though, so I was pretty sure that it was okay and that he wouldn't try to charge us extra for destroying his bar. Turns out, the single life agreed with Vanessa much more than I expected it to. Who would have thought? Either way, you've gotta hand it to that girl for making up for lost time, I suppose.

I walked outside just as a cab was approaching the bar. I put my hand out to hail it and it stopped for me right in front of Sammy J's. The door opened and out walked—well, isn't it obvious? Out walked Jack. Typical—the first second that I stop thinking, hoping, praying and dreaming that he will show, he shows.

"Am I too late for the party?" he asked. I couldn't tell by the look on his face if he was here to see me, or if he was simply here to make sure that I was really leaving.

"No, the party's still raging. You actually got here just in time," I said, pointing to the bar. The sound of the music and the laughter was pouring out into the street.

"Then, where are you going?" he asked.

"I think I've had enough. Goodbyes aren't really my thing," I said.

"I noticed," he said. "You didn't even stop by to say goodbye to me on your last day."

"I didn't think you wanted me to," I said, studying the sidewalk intently. I found myself unable to meet his gaze.

"Do you think you can stay long enough to have a drink with me? To celebrate with me," he said.

"I think that I'm completely celebrated out for the night," I said. "But half the firm is in there dancing on tables, so you'll have no problem at all finding someone to celebrate my departure with."

"I don't want to celebrate your departure," he said.

"Well…"

"They made me partner," he said. "Just this afternoon. There was this whole big meeting, and then we all went out to dinner to celebrate. That's why I'm so late."

"Congratulations!" I said, my guard completely down. "I'm so proud of you." I jumped up and hugged him without thinking, and immediately released my grip, hoping I hadn't overstepped my bounds.

"Thanks," he said. "It's been quite a day."

"I didn't think that you were coming," I said. "I mean, you didn't have to come. You must be exhausted. And have so many people to call, so many things to do."

"I wouldn't miss your going-away party," he said, moving a strand of my newly shorn locks behind my ear with his finger. "You know that. And, at any rate, I couldn't wait to tell you. In fact, amidst all of the excitement of the day, all the craziness, all I could think about the whole time was coming here and telling you. All I could think about was what you would think, whether you'd be proud of me…"

"I am so proud of you," I said, looking him dead in the eye. "I'm so happy for you."

"I'm really going to miss you when you're gone," he said, leaning in to me, his voice almost a whisper.

"I've missed you so much," I said, tears welling up in my eyes.

He put his arm around my waist and pulled me to him. He pressed his lips to mine, hard, and I didn't want to let him go. He ran his fingers through my hair as he kissed me and his touch drove me wild.

When I looked up, I could see half of the firm's associates with their noses pressed up to the window of the bar. Jack laughed.

"See," he said. "I told you that one of us had to quit."

"Well, then, aren't you glad that I'm gone?" I asked.

"Very," he said, and we kissed again. He pulled back and put his hand into his jacket pocket.

"I think that I have something of yours," he said. "I think that you misplaced this." He was holding the faux engagement ring. I took it and held it in my hands.

"Thank you," I said, looking at the ring.

"Why don't you hold on to that for a while?" Jack said. "Maybe if you're lucky, someone will replace it with another one, one of these days."

"Is that your way of asking me out?" I asked.

"Yeah, what'd you think?" he asked.

"I knew you couldn't stay mad at me for long," I said. We smiled at each other and he put his arm around my waist as we walked toward the bar.

We walked back into the party to a chorus of whispers and pointing. I announced to the crowd that this party just got converted from a going-away party to a "congratulations on making partner" party. All of the associates ran over to congratulate Jack, hugging him and shaking his hand, while Sammy J called out from behind the bar, "Why the hell would you want to do that?" The second years called out that shots of tequila were on them, and everyone gathered around the bar.

Vanessa joined Sammy J behind the bar to help him serve the shots. She was having so much fun back there, she decided to stay behind the bar to serve drinks with him for the rest of the night. It was great—it meant that everyone's drinks for the rest of the evening were free ("I'm a lawyer, I can't be expected to add up the costs of all those drinks in my head! Why else would you become a lawyer unless you were bad at math?"), but unfortunately, getting the actual drink orders straight was not Vanessa's strong suit, either. She gave her customers whatever she felt like they *should* be drinking.

Jack and I drank and danced and kissed until the wee hours of the night, and we finally closed the place down at 6:00 a.m., when a bunch of the second years suggested that we all go to the rooftop of the Gilson Hecht building to watch the sunrise. We all piled out of the bar and onto the roof, including Sammy J himself. He later said that it was the best going-away party in the history of Gilson Hecht.

Epilogue

As I walked back to my apartment, on my way home from work, I had a feeling that nothing could go wrong. You know that feeling you get when everything seems to be right with the world? When the planets seem to be in alignment? One of those days when you're actually running on time, your apartment is (relatively) clean, and you haven't gotten into an argument with your mother/best friend/boss/therapist in at least a week? That was exactly how I felt as I walked home that day. The previous spring, I had survived my ex-boyfriend's wedding with my dignity ever-so-slightly intact, and by fall, I was engaged to man that I loved (yes, Jack! Jack, Jack, Jack!), had a wedding date set for the following summer (which delighted both Jack's and my parents alike), and was planning the wedding of my dreams. (Well, okay, it was really the wedding of my mother's dreams. What, like your mother wouldn't get involved?)

I had picked up some flowers at the corner deli and some fresh parmesan cheese for the chicken parm I was cooking for Jack that evening. Yes, in my new job where they actually encourage you to leave the office in the evening, I had become quite the little domestic diva. You would have been so proud of me. Jack absolutely loved everything that I cooked for him. Except, that is, for the times where the food was too well done for him (read: burned). But most of the meals were nothing short of gourmet.

I rounded the corner, groceries in hand, and saw Jack standing on the sidewalk in front of our apartment building. I couldn't help but smile. This was what total domestic bliss was all about—fresh flowers, chicken parm and the man you love. No doubt we would go home, begin cooking together, glasses of red wine in our hands, and spend a blissful evening at home. No doubt we would become so overwhelmed with passion midway through the cooking, that after we put the chicken into the oven, he would pull me into his arms and kiss me fervently and pick me up and carry me to our bedroom where he would make love to me passionately. The chicken would burn and the smoke detectors would go off and the building's super would say, "Oh, those crazy lovebirds!" and Jack and I would laugh and order in pizza and cuddle on the couch together for the rest of the night. After we turned off the smoke alarms, that is.

I took a breath of the lilies that I had just picked up and was in heaven. The flowers were beautiful, the dinner would be beautiful, and at that precise moment in time, I felt as if the world were beautiful. I got closer and closer to Jack and saw him talking to someone. Someone who started to wave at me. Who was that talking to Jack?

I walked a few feet farther and stopped dead in my tracks. It was Trip. Talking to Jack. In front of my apartment building. I tried to smile and gain my composure before I walked the twenty feet that would lead me to my biggest nightmare. My ex-ex-boy-friend was talking to my fiancé, Jack, whom he thought was my faux fiancé, Douglas, whom he most certainly was not! What would I say to Trip? Should I just lie? Should I just pretend that Jack was still Douglas? What if the doorman came out and said hello to Jack? What if one of our neighbors passed by? Damn those tight New York City quarters. If this were upstate New York, I could totally get away with this!

I got closer and closer and could see that Jack and Trip were deep in conversation and laughing, even. Maybe Jack had just confessed the whole thing and they were having a good laugh over it? I could hear them now: "That Brooke! She's a real firecracker, isn't she?"

"Trip!" I cried out, as naturally as I could muster, throwing my arms around him. The bag of groceries hit him dead in the back and he lurched forward a bit into me. "What are *you* doing here?" Didn't he know that New York was my town? How dare he come here without asking me first!

I gave Jack a quick peck on the lips as Trip began to answer. I wondered to myself if I had to keep my engagement ring hidden. Jack's grandmother's ring looked nothing like the faux engagement ring I had been sporting for the whole of Trip's wedding. Since no one at the wedding had even noticed that it was fake I thought I was safe.

"Ava and I have some meetings in town this week. I've been meaning to call you so that we can all get together," he said with a smile. I smiled back. Just act natural, I told myself. He doesn't suspect a thing.

"How are you two newlyweds?" I asked. See? Totally natural.

"Absolutely wonderful," he said. "Married life is great. Which you two will most certainly find out soon enough." I had a vision of Trip and Ava at home—she, with martini and cigarette firmly in hand, he, too busy making deal after deal to notice.

"Yes, we will," I said, inexplicably giving Jack a little jab in the ribs to punctuate my point. Jack grabbed my hand.

"So, how about dinner this weekend? I barely had any time at the wedding to get to know Douglas," Trip asked. Just be cool, I thought. You are cool, calm, and collected. Cool as a cucumber. You're Coolio. This will all be over in a minute, and you will have gotten away with it once again.

"This is *not* Douglas," I inexplicably blurted out. Note to self: must seriously practice being more cool. "This is Jack. Douglas and I broke up a few days—mere hours, really—before your wedding and I was too embarrassed to tell you, so I made Jack dress up and pretend to be Douglas so that I could keep my dignity intact for your wedding. Which I did! I think. But now, it's all okay, because I got engaged to Jack, not Douglas, and we're really happy and everything's perfect and we're getting married this summer and now that you know we can, like, totally invite you."

I took a deep breath.

"Brooke, you're hilarious," Trip said, laughing so hard I was sure he would bust a gut right there on the sidewalk outside of our apartment building. "I forgot how funny you are."

"That Brooke," Jack said to Trip in his Scottish accent, "she's a real firecracker, isn't she?" I hadn't heard Jack do the accent in so long that I'd forgotten how sexy he sounded when he did it. All I could think was that I loved him even more right at that moment. I was totally pathetic, but he loved me anyway. I wanted to reach over and give him a huge kiss. So I did.

"But that would make a great movie," Trip said, taking out a tiny notepad and jotting something down. "You guys are a great couple." Jack and I smiled back at him. "Enjoy being engaged now. Once you get married, it's totally different."

"Um, okay?" I managed to cough out, and Jack pulled me closer to him, as if trying to prevent me from catching Trip's jaded outlook.

"You know, Ava and I might actually end up moving to New York this summer," Trip said. "That's why we're here this week. We're negotiating a theater deal." Trip went on and on about the deal and the play and the really, really amazing director they had lined up, but I didn't hear a thing. I was still registering the fact that Trip and Ava would be moving back to New York. Just in time for my wedding. "I mean," Trip continued, "Ava really wants to move back to New York. She really is a theater rat, did you know that? That's how she got her start. She's really dying to come back. She hates L.A. All the people out there are so phony."

"I couldn't agree more," Jack said with a full-on Scottish accent. A full on *genuine* Scottish accent.

"When's your big day?"

"For what?" I asked.

"Your wedding, kiddo! I want to make sure we are in town! Although, if we move back to New York, I suppose we'll always be in town!"

"Great," I said, trying to sound as if I really did think that it was great. "What's our date, honey?" I asked Jack, trying to figure out a way to avoid telling Trip our actual date. With Trip and Ava's schedule, if we just didn't tell them the date, I was sure they would be unable to attend.

"I can't remember," Jack replied, obviously playing the same game. See why I'm marrying him?

"Hell, you know what? I don't even care where we are for your big day. Even if we are filming on location in Fiji this summer, we are making it back to New York for your wedding!"

"Jolly good!" Jack said with an English accent. I could tell he was about thirty seconds away from going Down Under.

"Okay, kids, I've gotta go, but I'll have my assistant call you to set up some dinner plans for this Saturday night. Do you like Pastis?" he asked as he hailed a cab.

"Love it," I said, thinking of an excuse to get out of it before the words were fully out of my mouth.

"Just think, if we move to New York, we can go to Pastis every Saturday!" Trip said, opening the door of the cab that had just pulled over. Trip hopped into the taxicab and stuck his hand out the window to wave goodbye. I waved back as Jack slowly turned his head to look at me. Neither one of us said a word as we walked into the mailroom to get our mail. Jack grabbed our dry cleaning from the doorman and the shopping bags from me and I took the mail out of our mailbox. We reached the elevators and smiled at each other.

"So," I asked him as I got into the elevator and pressed the button for our floor, "for our wedding, do you think that your dad would look good in a kilt?"

SCOT ON THE ROCKS

Reader Questions

1. How would you feel if your ex-boyfriend was getting married before you were? How would you feel if your ex was marrying a fabulously famous Hollywood actress? Would you ever attend an ex-boyfriend's wedding? Have you ever Googled an ex-boyfriend? Checked an ex's wedding registry?

2. What is it about Douglas that Brooke loves so much? Why can't she let him go? Have you ever had someone you simply could not get over?

3. Brooke thinks that Trip's family is amazing and Kennedy-esque, despite the fact that they wouldn't help Trip find a job after law school—it was Brooke's family that did that—and are racist. Why does Brooke think they are so great, and at what point does she begin to see things—and the people in her life—for what they really are?

4. How do Brooke and Vanessa's relationships mirror each other? How do Brooke and Vanessa, themselves, mirror each other? In relationships with friends, do you tend to be close with people who are most like you, or most unlike you? In your romantic relationships?

5. Brooke and Jack initially do not get together because they work at the same law firm. Have you ever dated someone at work? Would you ever date someone at work? Even if your company had strict rules against dating coworkers?

6. Brooke encounters Nina, a girl she was unkind to in high school, and Nina tries to sabotage her. Do you believe in karma and that the bad things you do in life come back to haunt you?

7. Jack dons a kilt for Brooke's ex-boyfriend's wedding. What's the craziest thing someone has done for you out of love? What's the craziest thing *you* would do for love?

8. Why do you think Brooke cuts off her hair in the end? What does this symbolize? Have you ever gone through a physical change that manifested how you were feeling on the inside?

9. Do you think that Brooke and Jack ultimately stay together? Why or why not?

10. The novel is told through Brooke's perspective. How do you think it would be different if it was told through Jack's?

A spectacular debut novel by

Poonam Sharma

Indian-American Vina Chopra desperately tries to
balance her dream corporate life, which finances
her blue martinis and Bulgari with the traditional
Indian upbringing that involves dating "nice"—
read: about as exciting as a humidifier—
Indian doctors.

Will Vina become the girl most likely to find
happiness on her own?

Girl Most Likely To

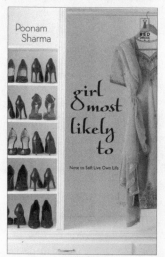

Available wherever
trade paperbacks
are sold.

RED DRESS INK
™

www.RedDressInk.com

RDIPS89550TR

New from the author of
See Jane Date and *The Breakup Club*

Love You to Death
by **Melissa Senate**

On sale January 2007

When did Abby Foote's life become
an episode of *Law & Order?*

On sale wherever
trade paperbacks
are sold.

RED
DRESS
INK ™

www.RedDressInk.com   RDIMS546TR

Award-winning author
MINDY KLASKY
Girl's Guide to Witchcraft

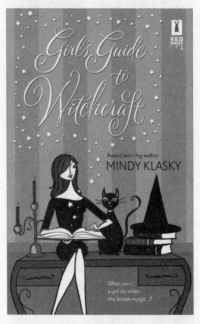

On sale October 2006.

Which is more unlikely? Meeting a single, straight, reasonably attractive, willing-to-commit man? Or discovering a secret cache of magic books?

On sale wherever trade paperbacks are sold.

RED DRESS INK
TM

www.RedDressInk.com

RDIMK607TI

Mystery writer Sophie Katz is back in the
sequel to SEX, MURDER AND A DOUBLE LATTE!

Passion, Betrayal and Killer Highlights

Only this time, she's trying to clear her sister's name
after her brother-in-law is found murdered.

With no help from the San Francisco police department,
who refuse to take Sophie seriously, she finds herself
partnering with sexy P.I. Anatoly Darinsky.

But will Anatoly be able to protect Sophie from her crazy plans
to lure the killer out of hiding? And most importantly, will she be
able to solve the case before her next book-signing tour?

**Available wherever
trade paperbacks
are sold!**

RED DRESS INK ™

www.RedDressInk.com

RDI89552TR

What if you could have it both ways?

New from the author of *Milkrun*
Sarah Mlynowski

Me vs. Me

Gabby Wolf has a tough choice in front of her.
Will she choose married life in Phoenix, or a
career in Manhattan? If only she could have it all.
Maybe her wish is about to come true.

On sale August 2006.

**Available wherever
paperbacks are sold.**

RED DRESS INK ™

www.RedDressInk.com

RDI588TR

On Sale December

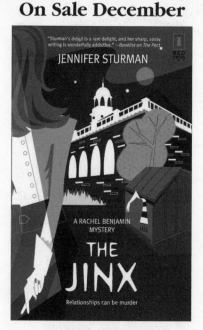

"Sturman's debut is a rare delight, and her sharp, sassy writing is wonderfully addictive." —*Booklist* on *The Pact*

JENNIFER STURMAN

A RACHEL BENJAMIN MYSTERY

THE JINX

Relationships can be murder

THE JINX
by Jennifer Sturman

The much-anticipated sequel to THE PACT!

Rachel Benjamin finally has it all—a great boyfriend and an exciting career. But when trouble strikes and Rachel must take on the role of Miss Marple again, she wonders if she jinxed everything just when she stopped worrying about jinxing things.

Available wherever
trade paperbacks
are sold.

RED
DRESS
INK
™
www.RedDressInk.com

RDIJS540TR

The only thing better than
reading a great book…
is talking about one.

Connect with other readers or speak
with your favorite author online—
the Reader's Ring book club was
created for readers just like you
who are looking for a rich book club
experience and searching for the
next great reading-group book.

Enjoy the exclusive benefits of
the Reader's Ring book club…
and indulge in the exceptional titles
chosen each month that are sure to take
your reading experience to a new level!

Find out more by visiting
www.ReadersRing.com.

RR2007TR